SUPERFICTION,
OR
THE AMERICAN STORY TRANSFORMED

SUPERFICTION,
OR
THE AMERICAN STORY TRANSFORMED

AN ANTHOLOGY

Edited by
JOE DAVID BELLAMY

VINTAGE BOOKS
A Division of Random House, New York

A VINTAGE ORIGINAL, September 1975

Library of Congress Cataloging in Publication Data
Main entry under title:

SuperFiction, or The American story transformed.

Includes bibliographical references.
1. Short stories, American. I. Bellamy, Joe
David. II. Title: The American story transformed.
PZ1.S956 [PS648.S5]   813'.01   75-13368
ISBN 0-394-71523-3

Manufactured in the United States of America

Grateful acknowledgment is made to the following for permission to
reprint previously published stories:

John Batki: "At the National Festival" by John Batki. Copyright ©
1972 by John Batki. Reprinted from *Fiction*, Fall 1972.

Curtis Brown Ltd.: "Saying Goodbye to the President" by Robley
Wilson, Jr., originally published in *Esquire* magazine, February 1974.
Copyright © 1974 by Esquire, Inc.

Delacorte Press/Seymour Lawrence: "Unready to Wear" by Kurt
Vonnegut, Jr. Copyright 1954 by Kurt Vonnegut, Jr. Originally pub-
lished in *Galaxy*. Reprinted from the book *Welcome to the Monkey
House* by Kurt Vonnegut, Jr.

Doubleday & Company, Inc.: "Life Story," copyright © 1968 by John
Barth from the book *Lost in the Funhouse* by John Barth. "The
Loop Garoo Kid" from the book *Yellow Back Radio Broke Down*,
copyright © 1969 by Ishmael Reed.

E.P. Dutton & Co., Inc.: "The Elevator" from *Pricksongs and Des-
cants* by Robert Coover. Copyright © 1969 by Robert Coover. "One's
Ship" from *Phantoms* by Barton Midwood. Copyright © 1966, 1967,
1968, 1969, 1970 by Barton Midwood. A selection adapted from the
novel *Quake* by Rudolph Wurlitzer. Copyright © 1972 by Rudolph
Wurlitzer.

Farrar, Straus & Giroux, Inc.: "Manikin" from *Going Places* by Leonard Michaels. Copyright © 1964, 1966, 1967, 1968, 1969 by Leonard
Michaels. "Sentence" from *City Life* by Donald Barthelme. Copyright
© 1968, 1969, 1970 by Donald Barthelme. "Sentence" originally appeared in *The New Yorker*.

Harper & Row Publishers, Inc.: "Order of Insects" from *In the Heart
of the Heart of the Country* (1968) by William H. Gass. Copyright ©
1961 by William H. Gass.

Alfred A. Knopf, Inc.: "Queen Louisa" (text only) from *The King's
Indian* by John Gardner. Copyright © 1972, 1973, 1974 by John Gardner. "Under the Microscope" (text only), Copyright © 1968 by John

For Connie, *all to herself*

CONTENTS

SUPERFICTION,
OR
THE AMERICAN STORY TRANSFORMED

INTRODUCTION

In the mid-sixties, the rules of the game of American fiction writing changed so quickly that the transition all but cost fiction its life. A number of the most serious American fiction writers—faced with encroachments from other media, a depleted pantheon haunted by dead giants, and bothersome aesthetic prophecies—turned away from so-called realism toward a variety of new modes and attitudes. How are we to understand this sweeping change in the literary climate? A number of explanations have been offered.

Just as photography helped turn painters away from representationalism, one argument goes, so film, TV, and the new journalism conspired to deflect serious fiction writers away from realism. When it comes to representing *things,* the argument goes, one picture *is* worth a thousand words, and one movie may be worth a trillion. Having lost out in the contest to "represent reality," fiction could survive only if it abandoned "reality" altogether and turned instead to the power of words to stimulate the imagination.

Introduction

How else to account for the parade of droll and murderous visions that began to take shape in American fiction of the mid-sixties? Gathering in momentum and frenzied imaginative energy through the seventies, such visions seemed the most conspicuous aspect of a bewildering range of experimentation with the forms of "the short story" which would have stunned early twentieth-century masters of the genre.

A weariness with worn-out fictional conventions was partly responsible, some critics believe; the new writing indicated that fiction was at last catching up with the waves of innovation and consolidation that had already taken place decades before in other, less refractory arts such as painting, music, or film.

But perhaps the most revealing explanation for the recent obsession with forms and visions can be located in the vagaries and intense dislocations of contemporary American experience. As early as 1961, that erstwhile American realist Philip Roth began saying that the toughest problem for the American writer was that the substance of the American experience itself was so abnormally and fantastically strange, it had become an "embarrassment to one's own meager imagination." [1] Suddenly fiction writers were struggling to discover modes equivalent to their emotional and imaginative perception of this strangeness.

This was approximately the point, in other words, at which American experience itself began to seem surreal. The apocalyptical ambience of the sixties was gearing up. What followed—Vietnam, assassinations, the new drug culture, continuing national fragmentation and embarrassment, increasing sense of the loss of a shared reality, real people becoming more and more disposable, social relations becoming more and more businesslike and ritualized and compartmentalized—only accelerated the process. There was less and less need to relate personally to the vast horde of strangers—mass murderers, junkies, hardhats, mad bombers, sadists, perverts, freaks of all kinds—and more and more desire for intimate relations with Walter Cronkite and Jane Fonda, the Beatles and Howard Cosell, Archie Bunker and Iron Butterfly, the Playmate of the Month and the Lord of the Rings—all disembodied personalities reaching fingers of light, shape, print, or sound directly into our brains with new immediacy, yet dispensing with the old social ratios, requiring hardly more than passive, dumb attentiveness from us to mold a relationship.

If reality becomes surrealistic, what must fiction do to be realistic? Critic Robert Scholes predicted a "return to a more verbal kind of fiction . . . , a less realistic and more artistic kind of narrative: more shapely, more evocative; more concerned with ideas and ideals, less concerned with things." And he called this new direction "fabulation." [2]

Whatever one calls it—fabulation, fantasy, or irrealism (John Barth's word for it via Borges)—the fiction of the sixties was suddenly full of worlds where fantasies are allowed to get up and walk around; where little green spacemen may be "real"; where a man on his way home from a quiet visit to the zoo, as in Kurt Vonnegut's "Unready to Wear," [3] accidentally learns how to walk right out of his body, and the discovery changes human life "more than the invention of fire, numbers, the alphabet, agriculture, or the wheel." Or a character may wake up, as in Rudolph Wurlitzer's "Quake," to find himself being abruptly herded into a crumbling football stadium with a mass of naked maniacs to await the end of the world—and it ain't no joke. Though sometimes it might be—as in Robert Coover's "The Elevator," where the narrator-protagonist sifts playfully through the collective fictive detritus covering the important (if widely overlooked) subject of public elevators. Involved in an elaborate fantasy of plunging to his death locked in erotic embrace with the elevator operator, Coover's hero still exercises the artistic freedom to step neatly out of his fantasized structure at the last instant and take the stairs, allowing the elevator to whiz down the shaft and crash without him. In this kind of fiction, the laws of nature are sometimes quietly suspended, as in Ursule Molinaro's "Chiaroscuro," where a third eye erupts in the middle of a woman's forehead as the most startling symptom of the awakening of hideous insights about her life that she cannot face. In all these cases, in exchange for a sense of prosaic reality we get a dreamlike world with big horrors and big jokes—but generally full of surprises.

What was developing during the sixties was a growing awareness, among new journalists and fiction writers alike, that the old conventions based on the probabilities of the experiential world, which had supposedly guaranteed "objectivity," weren't adequate to new experience, on the one hand; and that, on the other, they were faulty—since even a modest understanding of the way language works led to the realization that selection, arrangement, and attitudinal investment affect every "realistic" account. The new fiction was thus the expression of radical new doubts about the nature of "reality" and the validity of the fiction-making process in relation to "reality."

Origins and Antecedents

In attempting to make sense of American fiction of the last decade, our understanding is decidedly enhanced if we adopt the view that the history of fiction from Defoe and Richardson to the present embodies a series of advances toward greater and greater inwardness and individuation, or at least a series of different but effectively more intense ventures in that direction: forays inward. Forays *inward* over the course of nearly three centuries, I would argue, led logically to the

genesis of the mental processes that account for the evolution of the dominant inward-turning modes of the
present: fantasy/fabulation/irrealism, neo-gothic, myth/
parable, metafiction, and parody/put-on—the varieties
of superfiction.

In speaking of the "new concept of inwardness" that
characterized the rise of the novel, critic and novelist
Leslie Fiedler described that revolution as one marked
by "the invention of a new kind of self, a new level of
mind; for what has been happening since the eighteenth
century seems more like the development of a new organ
than the mere finding of a new way to describe old experience." [4] Careful study of the origins of prose fiction
in the eighteenth century reveals the important historical connection between the birth of the genre and a
unique set of economic, political, social, and philosophical features—industrial capitalism, Puritanism
and, especially, the emergence of individualism—an ide-
ology primarily based *not* on the tradition of the past
but on the autonomy and ascendancy of the individual
within society. Literary scholar Ian Watt has shown what
an unprecedented leap Samuel Richardson's narrative
mode represented, for example, with its interest in the
"minute-by-minute content of consciousness," and how
it reflected a much larger change in outlook, "the transition from the objective, social and public orientation of
the classical world to the subjective, individualist and
private orientation of the life and literature of the last
two hundred years." [5]

Implicit in Leslie Fiedler's discussion of the novel
throughout his monumental study *Love and Death in
the American Novel* is his belief that the history of
American fiction continues the snowballing effect of individuation and inwardness that began with Richardson: ". . . for the novel must continue to carry the torch
to the back of the cave . . . or surrender its birthright, its
essential function." [6] The hallmarks of the new age of

the novel were mass production and lonely consumption, a process that still goes on.

In the early twentieth century, when modernist writers, from Virginia Woolf to William Faulkner, revamped the idea of "character" and "retreated" into consciousness, traditional critics bemoaned the loss of authorial authority and the absence of "memorable" characters. "There is something burglarious about these silent entries into a private and alien consciousness," [7] Mary McCarthy complained. Erich Auerbach, W. J. Harvey, and others seemed inclined to dismiss the whole modern tradition as closet drama. The crucial insight that many such readers overlooked was that emphasis on consciousness—a significant turn toward greater inwardness—was an abandonment not of character but of the idea of self *as other*. Instead of *looking at* the characters in a piece of fiction, the twentieth-century reader was *feeling through* them. Even though the effect of this change was a diminution of the reader's ability to "remember" these bodies as "characters," he was still quite capable of experiencing a novel or a story vividly and memorably. It was really merely the external and social aspects of character that were falling away as common social meanings became so dubious for some writers that only an affirmation of inner meanings seemed possible.

To put it another way, in traditional fiction, we meet "characters" who are looking out—at society, manners, plots; in the early-twentieth-century novel of consciousness or modernist short fiction, we are *inside* a character (or characters) looking out. In the world of the contemporary superfictionist, we are most frequently inside a character (or characters) looking *in*—or these inner phantasms are projected outward, and in a sometimes frightening, sometimes comical reversal, the outside "reality" begins to look more and more like a mirror of the inner landscape—there is so little difference between the two.

Introduction

"Through a dream landscape . . . a girl flees in terror and [is] alone amid crumbling castles, antique dungeons, and ghosts. . . . She nearly escapes her terrible persecutors, who seek her out of lust and greed, but is caught; escapes again and is caught; escapes once more and is caught . . . ; finally [she may break] free altogether and . . . [be] married to the virtuous lover who has all along worked . . . to save her." [8] This is the classic gothic plot as it comes down to us from the eighteenth century.

At the center of the story is the "virgin" in flight, the Persecuted Maiden who, under one name or another, has been fleeing violation ever since Pamela took off at a frantic clip through Richardson's novel, and even before. But one significant difference between the Richardsonian and early gothic treatments of the pursuit of the Maiden was that in the former, virtue was invariably triumphant, while in the latter the emphasis was upon portraying the powers of darkness. Incest was often the underlying sin, the archetypal root of the gothic tradition, a breach of the primal taboo, and frequently involved some offense committed against the father.[9]

Neo-gothic modes in contemporary American fiction offer bizarre variants and interpolations on this basic prototype. In Joyce Carol Oates's "By the River," for example, a "sinful" young woman is shockingly punished by her deranged father. In John Hawkes's "The Universal Fears," the sinful "daughters" unexpectedly assault and inflict incredible physical damage, near castration, upon the "father." The "maiden in flight" in Leonard Michaels' "Manikin" is dated, cornered, and raped by the dark, brooding stranger and later hangs herself in guilt and humiliation. In Thomas Pynchon's "In Which Esther Gets a Nose Job," the maiden, frightfully, though symbolically, molested by the aggressive seducer, returns to the scene of the crime enthusiastically to act out her literal "fall from virtue"—thus "fleeing" into the very arms of the villain.

The neo-gothic aspects of the new fiction—its extreme, obsessive, sometimes arbitrary or perverse violence; its macabre, grotesque, or terrifying events—exemplify what Herman Kahn would call "Late Sensate" art, the art of a culture in a state of decline.[10] The simplest explanation for neo-gothic is that it reflects the present violence of American life. This mood or mode is not, after all, limited to fiction. We have Roman Polanski and Sam Peckinpah and Ken Russell knocking them dead in the movie theaters, and what used to be called teeny-boppers dancing kinky dances to Alice Cooper's necrophiliacal rock operas. If nothing else, the neo-gothic phenomenon in fiction is an escalation brought about to attract audiences jaded by the routine of real horror on the evening news.

Whether or not we accept Kahn's pessimistic attitude toward it, this inward-turning, which makes manifest the hyper-violence of dreams, has been around in one form or another in American fiction for a long time. It may be less an expression of cultural degeneration than of a logical progression in the American imaginative tradition. To borrow again from Leslie Fiedler's *Love and Death in the American Novel*, "Our fiction is essentially and at its best nonrealistic, even anti-realistic . . . , not merely in flight from the physical data of the actual world, in search of a (sexless and dim) Ideal; from Charles Brockden Brown to William Faulkner or Eudora Welty, Paul Bowles and John Hawkes, it is, bewilderingly and embarrassingly, a gothic fiction, nonrealistic and negative, sadist and melodramatic."[11] Other critics, among them Richard Chase and Irving Malin, have, of course, pointed out that the gothic and the romance—as opposed to the realistic novel—are the most characteristic works of the American imagination.

Introduction

One could argue that American experience has always seemed violent, surreal, gothic. And possibly we have always been degenerating! In any case, current neo-gothic, with its predilection for the ferocity of dreams, is a natural bedfellow of irrealist impulses and interiority. Whatever the influence of contemporary culture and the literary tradition upon neo-gothicism, one must always bear in mind that nightmares antedate and are the true prototype of all gothic forms.

Myth/Parable

Myth is a way of making up or organizing the world that antedates philosophy or the realistic novel, and therefore a logical resource to explore in a period of acute introspection, aggravated sensibilities, historical awareness, and formal experimentation. Deeply rooted in inner consciousness, myths, according to Jungian definition, are still a primary means by which archetypes, essentially unconscious forms, become articulate to the conscious mind—a complex version of the idea that the truth of the world is buried within. A parable, of course, is usually a simple story illustrating a moral or religious lesson, and it may contain mythical or archetypal elements.

Experiments with myth and parable in American fiction of the sixties and seventies reflect many of the same attitudes, premises, and disillusionments as the other forms we have discussed: loss of faith in mimetic methods, turning inward, the search for deeper meanings, the projection of fantasy creatures ("characters") into the "outside" world as a way of dramatizing experience. In addition, the use of character as archetype holds out the promise of finding universality in seeming particularity—a unitive strategy in the face of cultural dissolution.

A rich example of recent experimentation with

Introduction

myth and parable, John Gardner's "Queen Louisa" incorporates many of the most characteristic aspects of superfiction: the fairy-tale form, in which the heroine may change from an "enormous toad to a magnificently beautiful redheaded woman with a pale, freckled nose"; the use of deliberately anti-illusionist devices in the midst of the tallest of tales; and the droll tone of the put-on. But even more crucial to an understanding of this story is the historical echo of the chivalric love tradition and the didactic use of the parable of the rosebush at the end of the story. Here we have, in an ancient and venerable setting, a battle of ideas made tangible: a classic battle between good and evil. The forces of evil do exist in the world, Gardner seems to be saying, but just as the rosebush blooms more brightly with each swing of the witch's ax against it, so the forces of evil in real life may be thwarted and *are* by the end of the story. Queen Louisa, the good queen, is victorious. Gardner cleverly saves himself, however, from an ending too simplistically affirmative—and makes a shrewd metaphysical observation at the same time—by commenting that, well, maybe the rosebush *was* cut down after all, since the queen is insane and "can never know anything for sure, and perhaps the whole story was taking place in a hotel in Philadelphia."

William Gass's "Order of Insects," on the other hand, is clearly intended as an answer to Kafka's "Metamorphosis." In contrast to the anguish and bitter ignominy of Gregor Samsa's life as a gigantic cockroach, Gass's heroine (who identifies with an insect even if she does not literally become one) is so awed by the absurd discovery of beauty in the grace and order of insects that it seems to her to epitomize the orderliness of a universe that all living things share. This is a story heavy with wonder and meditation and, once again, simple, but not simple-minded, affirmation.

The growing use of myth and parable in fiction can

be seen as part of the wave of reaction in American culture to the apparent failure of objective science to solve human problems and improve the human condition. It represents a yearning for ritualistic satisfactions and a search for a new kind of ordering principle—a viable American mythology. Also, perhaps, it is an expression of nostalgia for a literature of charismatic wisdom and authority, for tribal solidarity, for the fabled restorative magic of the oracle.

Of course, many writers of the modernist era, including Eliot, Joyce, Kazantzakis, Yeats, and Pound had been preoccupied with myth too. The theories of Freud, Jung, Frazer, and others provided a natural impetus. What is new is the sudden spate of fictionists (Updike, Barth, Gardner, Katz) inviting their readers to interpret "the way we live now" in the light of traditional sources of archetypal patterns. John Updike in *The Centaur* can thus present a modern situation, for instance, and refer the reader to a familiar (or not so familiar) analogy, hoping, with luck, to revitalize the old mythological resonance on the one hand and capture some of the mystical reverberations for his modern situation on the other.

Like Barton Midwood in "One's Ship," the writer can satirize an archetypal human situation—in this case, the mating ritual as seen from a quirky masculine viewpoint—by placing his generalized characters in a timeless primeval setting. Or, like Robley Wilson, Jr., in "Saying Good-bye to the President," he can take a crack at trying to discover or create new mythical material especially significant for our time and place—through, for instance, a dramatization of the ancient theme of "the fall of the king." By concentrating on our recent national trauma of leadership, this peculiarly powerful little fiction suggests both the eagerness and the pathos with which the United States followed the downfall of Richard Nixon. (It was written, incidentally, prior to the impeachment hearings and resignation.) A variation of this sort of experimentation has been attempted by writers (e.g., Steve Katz in "Mythology: Plastic Man") who believe that new sources of myths may be unearthed from pop culture: sports, songs, comic books, and so on. According to Leslie Fiedler, this is just the place to look for them. It is high time for writers to "cancel out those long overdue accounts to Greece and Rome." [12]

Metafiction/Parody/Put-on

Fiction in which the conventions or techniques of the story itself became the subject matter has become a commonplace of recent practice—an inward turning toward pure theory. Among the many motivations for this sort of self-conscious but sometimes entertaining game-playing have been an impulse toward joking and parody, now that the rules of the game are so clearly understood and mastered; a yen for "new" subject matter free of clichés and old bugaboos; and sometimes simply a voguish parading of intellect brought about by the historical fact that most writers these days hang out in universities where they are apt to pick up critical baggage, perspective, and sophistication that eventually finds its way into their work in one way or another.

In a willful mass revolt against the Jamesian prescription of author self-effacement, many current practitioners call for the "truth of the page" and set out to write deliberately anti-illusionist fiction, to defy all the verities and still try to keep the old ball rolling. One way to subvert a willing suspension of disbelief is to call attention to the conventions of the fiction one is in the process of creating, or to comment on or parody the form —as, for example, Ishmael Reed and Judith Rascoe attempt with the Western in "The Loop Garoo Kid" and "A Lot of Cowboys." Sometimes this sort of parody has even taken potshots at the literary culture itself, as in

Introduction

John Updike's "Under the Microscope" or in John Batki's "At the National Festival." The joy of invention apparent in this work may seem to be its greatest virtue. The serious effect of such horseplay, however, is to undergird the rightness of the individual and idiosyncratic vision of experience as against the implicit attitude of much conventional fiction that reality is a thing, essence, landscape we can all agree upon and wish fervently for art to imitate.

The most important impetus for this sort of fiction has been the expression of anxiety over the epistemological validity of the fiction-making process, plus an intensified concern with the forms, ideas, and language that might revitalize it.

It was more than sheer frivolity, for instance, that motivated John Barth in "Life-Story" to attempt to write a story against apparently impossible odds by deliberately setting up nearly insurmountable technical obstacles to his own success; and more than defiant virtuosity that motivated Donald Barthelme in a story like "Sentence" to attempt to do the same by cramming a whole story into one sentence and then omitting the period. While Barth's "Life-Story" is a self-conscious satiric "story" about the process of writing a self-conscious satiric story, it is, more importantly, a sophisticated essay on the state of the art. The ironic clincher in "Life-Story" is that, despite Barth's narrator's cantankerous will to make his creation unlike any story ever written, it does meet many of the standard definitions of what a conventional story should do: that is, something happens; the protagonist's experience in the story leads to a basic change in his viewpoint, etc.—but, paradoxically, while conforming with superficial accuracy to these definitions, "Life-Story" mocks them mercilessly.

What Barthelme gives us, in a sentence . . . about itself . . . is, in fact, a study of the peculiar nature of sentences that concretizes William Gass's dictum that

Introduction

there "are no events but words in fiction." [13] Or, as
Barthelme's sentence itself reminds us toward the end:
"the sentence itself is a man-made object."

Through the use of similar techniques, Gilbert Sorrentino's love story, "The Moon in Its Flight," offers an
answer to the question "How do you write a love story
in an age when all love stories have become sentimental?" Turning on a risky theme—youth, alas, cannot be
recaptured; lost love, lost opportunities are forever lost
—the story is saved from sentimentality by an impatient
narrator who keeps distracting the reader with re-
minders that this is only a story and yet enticing the
reader *by* his disclaimers into believing it to be an intimate autobiographical confession.

In Ronald Sukenick's story "What's Your Story,"
the narrator says: "I sit at my desk, making this up. . . ."
His use of "strike" makes the reader conscious of his ongoing revisions. A parody of Mafia and espionage
"thrillers" is in progress, but the unifying focus is upon
the writer sitting at his desk and his *relationship* with
his desk and his imagination—and other desks he has
written on, views out his window from these various
desks, or pictures on various walls near these various
desks. If Joan comes into his room while he is writing, she goes into the story. Since a story is a man-made
object, Sukenick, Barth, Barthelme, and Sorrentino seem
to be saying, you can put anything in or leave anything
out (for example, note the comical way Sukenick puts *in*
Ruby Geranium's tie).

Why should writers insist on emphasizing in their
stories: "This is just a story. These are just words. This
is all made up"? "Adequate adjustment to the present
can be achieved only through ever-fresh perception of
it," Sukenick would say. [14] These fictions all dramatize
the sweeping perception that art and language help
create reality rather than serving as inert vehicles
through which a self-evidently recognizable external re-

ality is made manifest—a major ideological split between the new fiction and the old. Language, these writers are saying, *helps to constitute our reality*. Imagination (making things up) is a major form of perception, not a mere literary luxury but an absolutely necessary means of getting from one moment to the next. Fiction-making is seen, therefore, not only as a way of making up the world but also as an indispensable way of making sense of it.

What, then, is the upshot of these developments?

The world, both of ideas and of facts, has changed drastically; and the artistic ethos must be expected to change with it. Readers have sometimes been troubled by the newest fictions in which conflicts are not conventionally resolved, and expectations are not conventionally satisfied. Precisely because many of these stories speak for a new order of existence, and a new perception of that existence, they offer new and special difficulties as well as heightened pleasures. However, if one reads the history of prose fiction as, among other things, a history of increasingly bold and complicated forays inward, toward a confrontation with human consciousness and unconsciousness, then, whatever its changes, new American superfiction carries on the same tradition with impressive fidelity to this original and ancient impulse.

Joe David Bellamy

Canton, New York
January, 1975

NOTES

[1] Philip Roth, "Writing American Fiction," *Commentary* 31 (March, 1961), p. 224.

[2] Robert Scholes, *The Fabulators* (New York: Oxford, 1967), p. 12.

[3] Aesthetic change is seldom perfectly monolithic. Though Vonnegut's "Unready to Wear" did not receive wide circulation or serious attention until the publication of his retrospective collection *Welcome to the Monkey House* in 1968, the story was originally published by *Galaxy Science Fiction* in 1953! (For more detailed comment on the special vagaries of Vonnegut's career, see *The Vonnegut Statement* by Klinkowitz and Somer.) In a similar case, William Gass's story "Order of Insects," though it appeared originally in 1961 in *The Minnesota Review,* did not see wider circulation until the appearance of his collection *In the Heart of the Heart of the Country and Other Stories* in 1968. That events seemed to come to a head in the mid-sixties does not, of course, argue against the likelihood of such isolated, slightly earlier examples in similar modes.

Notes

[4] Leslie Fiedler, *Love and Death in the American Novel* (Cleveland and New York: World Publishing Company, 1962), p. xxviii.

[5] Ian Watt, *The Rise of the Novel* (Berkeley: University of California Press, 1962), p. 176.

[6] Fiedler, p. 42.

[7] Mary McCarthy, "Characters in Fiction," in *Critical Approaches to Fiction,* ed. Kumar and McKean (New York: McGraw-Hill, 1968), pp. 87–88.

[8] Fiedler, p. 107.

[9] Fiedler, pp. 108–109.

[10] Herman Kahn and Anthony J. Wiener, *The Year 2000* (New York: MacMillan, 1967), pp. 40–41.

[11] Fiedler, p. xxiv.

[12] In a lecture.

[13] William H. Gass, *Fiction and the Figures of Life* (New York: Knopf, 1970), p. 30.

[14] Ronald Sukenick, *Wallace Stevens: Musing the Obscure* (New York: New York University Press, 1967), p. 3.

FANTASY
FABULATION
IRREALISM

UNREADY TO WEAR

Kurt Vonnegut, Jr.

I don't suppose the oldsters, those of us who weren't born into it, will ever feel quite at home being amphibious—amphibious in the new sense of the word. I still catch myself feeling blue about things that don't matter any more.

I can't help worrying about my business, for instance—or what used to be my business. After all, I spent thirty years building the thing up from scratch, and now the equipment is rusting and getting clogged with dirt. But even though I know it's silly of me to care what happens to the business, I borrow a body from a storage center every so often, and go around the old hometown, and clean and oil as much of the equipment as I can.

Of course, all in the world the equipment was good for was making money, and Lord knows there's plenty of that lying around. Not as much as there used to be, because there at first some people got frisky and threw it all around, and the wind blew it every which way. And a lot of go-getters gathered up piles of the stuff and hid it

23

somewhere. I hate to admit it, but I gathered up close to a half million myself and stuck it away. I used to get it out and count it sometimes, but that was years ago. Right now I'd be hard put to say where it is.

But the worrying I do about my old business is bush league stuff compared to the worrying my wife, Madge, does about our hold house. That thing is what she herself put in thirty years on while I was building the business. Then no sooner had we gotten nerve enough to build and decorate the place than everybody we cared anything about got amphibious. Madge borrows a body once a month and dusts the place, though the only thing a house is good for now is keeping termites and mice from getting pneumonia.

Whenever it's my turn to get into a body and work as an attendant at the local storage center, I realize all over again how much tougher it is for women to get used to being amphibious.

Madge borrows bodies a lot oftener than I do, and that's true of women in general. We have to keep three times as many women's bodies in stock as men's bodies, in order to meet the demand. Every so often, it seems as though a woman just *has* to have a body, and doll it up in clothes, and look at herself in a mirror. And Madge, God bless her, I don't think she'll be satisfied until she's tried on every body in every storage center on Earth.

It's been a fine thing for Madge, though. I never kid her about it, because it's done so much for her personality. Her old body, to tell you the plain blunt truth, wasn't anything to get excited about, and having to haul the thing around made her gloomy a lot of the times in the old days. She couldn't help it, poor soul, any more than anybody else could help what sort of body they'd been born with, and I loved her in spite of it.

Well, after we'd learned to be amphibious, and after we'd built the storage centers and laid in body supplies and opened them to the public, Madge went hog wild. She borrowed a platinum blonde body that had been donated by a burlesque queen, and I didn't think we'd ever get her out of it. As I say, it did wonders for her self-confidence.

I'm like most men and don't care particularly what body I get. Just the strong, good-looking, healthy bodies were put in storage, so one is as good as the next one. Sometimes, when Madge and I take bodies out together for old times' sake, I let her pick out one for me to match whatever she's got on. It's a funny thing how she always picks a blond, tall one for me.

My old body, which she claims she loved for a third of a century, had black hair, and was short and paunchy, too, there toward the last. I'm human and I couldn't help being hurt when they scrapped it after I'd left it, instead of putting it in storage. It was a good, homey, comfortable body; nothing fast and flashy, but reliable. But there isn't much call for that kind of body at the centers, I guess. I never ask for one, at any rate.

The worst experience I ever had with a body was when I was flimflammed into taking out the one that had belonged to Dr. Ellis Konigswasser. It belongs to the Amphibious Pioneers' Society and only gets taken out once a year for the big Pioneers' Day Parade, on the anniversary of Konigswasser's discovery. Everybody said it was a great honor for me to be picked to get into Konigswasser's body and lead the parade.

Like a plain damn fool, I believed them.

They'll have a tough time getting me into that thing again—ever. Taking that wreck out certainly made it plain why Konigswasser discovered how people could do without their bodies. That old one of his practically *drives* you out. Ulcers, headaches, arthritis, fallen arches —a nose like a pruning hook, piggy little eyes, and a complexion like a used steamer trunk. He was and still

25

is the sweetest person you'd ever want to know, but, back when he was stuck with that body, nobody got close enough to find out.

We tried to get Konigswasser back into his old body to lead us when we first started having the Pioneers' Day Parades, but he wouldn't have anything to do with it, so we always have to flatter some poor boob into taking on the job. Konigswasser marches, all right, but as a six-foot cowboy who can bend beer cans double between his thumb and middle finger.

Konigswasser is just like a kid with that body. He never gets tired of bending beer cans with it, and we all have to stand around in our bodies after the parade, and watch as though we were very impressed.

I don't suppose he could bend very much of anything back in the old days.

Nobody mentions it to him, since he's the grand old man of the Amphibious Age, but he plays hell with the bodies. Almost every time he takes one out, he busts it, showing off. Then somebody has to get into a surgeon's body and sew it up again.

I don't mean to be disrespectful of Konigswasser. As a matter of fact, it's a respectful thing to say that somebody is childish in certain ways, because it's people like that who seem to get all the big ideas.

There is a picture of him in the old days down at the Historical Society, and you can see from that that he never did grow up as far as keeping up his appearance went—doing what little he could with the rattle-trap body Nature had issued him.

His hair was down below his collar, he wore his pants so low that his heels wore through the legs above the cuffs, and the lining of his coat hung down in festoons all around the bottom. And he'd forget meals, and go out into the cold or wet without enough clothes on, and he would never notice sickness until it almost killed him. He was what we used to call absent-minded. Looking back now, of course, we say he was starting to be amphibious.

Konigswasser was a mathematician, and he did all his living with his mind. The body he had to haul around with that wonderful mind was about as much use to him as a flatcar of scrap iron. Whenever he got sick and *had* to pay some attention to his body, he'd rant somewhat like this:

"The mind is the only thing about human beings that's worth anything. Why does it have to be tied to a bag of skin, blood, hair, meat, bones, and tubes? No wonder people can't get anything done, stuck for life with a parasite that has to be stuffed with food and protected from weather and germs all the time. And the fool thing wears out anyway—no matter how much you stuff and protect it!

"Who," he wanted to know, "really wants one of the things? What's so wonderful about protoplasm that we've got to carry so damned many pounds of it with us wherever we go?

"Trouble with the world," said Konigswasser, "isn't too many people—it's too many bodies."

When his teeth went bad on him, and he had to have them all out, and he couldn't get a set of dentures that were at all comfortable, he wrote in his diary, "If living matter was able to evolve enough to get out of the ocean, which was really quite a pleasant place to live, it certainly ought to be able to take another step and get out of bodies, which are pure nuisances when you stop to think about them."

He wasn't a prude about bodies, understand, and he wasn't jealous of people who had better ones than he did. He just thought bodies were a lot more trouble than they were worth.

He didn't have great hopes that people would really evolve out of their bodies in his time. He just wished they would. Thinking hard about it, he walked through a park in his shirtsleeves and stopped off at the zoo to watch the lions being fed. Then, when the rainstorm turned to sleet, he headed back home and was interested to see firemen on the edge of a lagoon, where they were using a pulmotor on a drowned man.

Witnesses said the old man had walked right into the water and had kept going without changing his expression until he'd disappeared. Konigswasser got a look at the victim's face and said he'd never seen a better reason for suicide. He started for home again and was almost there before he realized that that was his own body lying back there.

He went back to reoccupy the body just as the firemen got it breathing again, and he walked it home, more as a favor to the city than anything else. He walked it into his front closet, got out of it again, and left it there.

He took it out only when he wanted to do some writing or turn the pages of a book, or when he had to feed it so it would have enough energy to do the few odd jobs he gave it. The rest of the time, it sat motionless in the closet, looking dazed and using almost no energy. Konigswasser told me the other day that he used to run the thing for about a dollar a week, just taking it out when he really needed it.

But the best part was that Konigswasser didn't have to sleep any more, just because *it* had to sleep; or be afraid any more, just because *it* thought it might get hurt; or go looking for things *it* seemed to think it had to have. And, when *it* didn't feel well, Konigswasser kept out of it until it felt better, and he didn't have to spend a fortune keeping the thing comfortable.

When he got his body out of the closet to write, he did a book on how to get out of one's own body, which was rejected without comment by twenty-three publishers. The twenty-fourth sold two million copies, and the book changed human life more than the invention of fire, numbers, the alphabet, agriculture, or the wheel. When somebody told Konigswasser that, he snorted that they were damning his book with faint praise. I'd say he had a point there.

By following the instructions in Konigswasser's book for about two years, almost anybody could get out of his body whenever he wanted to. The first step was to understand what a parasite and dictator the body was most of the time, then to separate what the body wanted or didn't want from what you yourself—your psyche— wanted or didn't want. Then, by concentrating on what you wanted, and ignoring as much as possible what the body wanted beyond plain maintenance, you made your psyche demand its right and become self-sufficient.

That's what Konigswasser had done without realizing it, until he and his body had parted company in the park, with his psyche going to watch the lions eat, and with his body wandering out of control into the lagoon.

The final trick of separation, once your psyche grew independent enough, was to start your body walking in some direction and suddenly take your psyche off in another direction. You couldn't do it standing still, for some reason—you had to walk.

At first, Madge's and my psyches were clumsy at getting along outside our bodies, like the first sea animals that got stranded on land millions of years ago, and who could just waddle and squirm and gasp in the mud. But we became better at it with time, because the psyche can naturally adapt so much faster than the body.

Madge and I had good reason for wanting to get out. Everybody who was crazy enough to try to get out at the first had good reasons. Madge's body was sick and wasn't going to last a lot longer. With her going in a little while, I couldn't work up enthusiasm for sticking around much longer myself. So we studied Konigswasser's book and tried to get Madge out of her body before it died. I went along with her, to keep either one of us from getting lonely. And we just barely made it—six weeks before her body went all to pieces.

That's why we get to march every year in the Pioneers' Day Parade. Not everybody does—only the first five thousand of us who turned amphibious. We were guinea pigs, without much to lose one way or another, and we were the ones who proved to the rest how pleasant and safe it was—a heck of a lot safer than taking chances in a body year in and year out.

Sooner or later, almost everybody had a good reason for giving it a try. There got to be millions and finally more than a billion of us—invisible, insubstantial, indestructible, and, by golly, true to ourselves, no trouble to anybody, and not afraid of anything.

When we're not in bodies, the Amphibious Pioneers can meet on the head of a pin. When we get into bodies for the Pioneers' Day Parade, we take up over fifty thousand square feet, have to gobble more than three tons of food to get enough energy to march; and lots of us catch colds or worse, and get sore because somebody's body accidentally steps on the heel of somebody else's body, and get jealous because some bodies get to lead and others have to stay in ranks, and—oh, hell, I don't know what all.

I'm not crazy about the parade. With all of us there, close together in bodies—well, it brings out the worst in us, no matter how good our psyches are. Last year, for instance, Pioneers' Day was a scorcher. People couldn't help being out of sorts, stuck in sweltering, thirsty bodies for hours.

Well, one thing led to another, and the Parade Marshal offered to beat the daylights out of my body with his body, if my body got out of step again. Naturally, being Parade Marshal, he had the best body that year, except for Konigswasser's cowboy, but I told him to soak his fat head, anyway. He swung, and I ditched my body right there, and didn't even stick around long enough to find out if he connected. He had to haul my body back to the storage center himself.

I stopped being mad at him the minute I got out of the body. I understood, you see. Nobody but a saint could be really sympathetic or intelligent for more than a few minutes at a time in a body—or happy, either, except in short spurts. I haven't met an amphibian yet who wasn't easy to get along with, and cheerful and interesting—as long as he was outside a body. And I haven't met one yet who didn't turn a little sour when he got into one.

The minute you get in, chemistry takes over—glands making you excitable or ready to fight or hungry or mad or affectionate, or—well, you never know *what's* going to happen next.

That's why I can't get sore at the enemy, the people who are against the amphibians. They never get out of their bodies and won't try to learn. They don't want anybody else to do it, either, and they'd like to make the amphibians get back into bodies and stay in them.

After the tussle I had with the Parade Marshal, Madge got wind of it and left *her* body right in the middle of the Ladies' Auxiliary. And the two of us, feeling full of devilment after getting shed of the bodies and the parade, went over to have a look at the enemy.

I'm never keen on going over to look at them. Madge likes to see what the women are wearing. Stuck with their bodies all the time, the enemy women change their clothes and hair and cosmetic styles a lot oftener than we do on the women's bodies in the storage centers.

I don't get much of a kick out of the fashions, and almost everything else you see and hear in enemy territory would bore a plaster statue into moving away.

Usually, the enemy is talking about old-style reproduction, which is the clumsiest, most comical, most inconvenient thing anyone could imagine, compared with what the amphibians have in that line. If they aren't talking about that, then they're talking about food, the gobs of chemicals they have to stuff into their bodies. Or they'll talk about fear, which we used to call politics—job politics, social politics, government politics.

The enemy hates that, having us able to peek in on them any time we want to, while they can't ever see us unless we get into bodies. They seem to be scared to death of us, though being scared of amphibians makes as much sense as being scared of the sunrise. They could have the whole world, except the storage centers, for all the amphibians care. But they bunch together as though we were going to come whooping out of the sky and do something terrible to them at any moment.

They've got contraptions all over the place that are supposed to detect amphibians. The gadgets aren't worth a nickel, but they seem to make the enemy feel good—like they were lined up against great forces, but keeping their nerve and doing important, clever things about it. Know-how—all the time they're patting each other about how much know-how they've got, and about how we haven't got anything by comparison. If know-how means weapons, they're dead right.

I guess there is a war on between them and us. But we never do anything about holding up our side of the war, except to keep our parade sites and our storage centers secret, and to get out of bodies every time there's an air raid, or the enemy fires a rocket, or something.

That just makes the enemy madder, because the raids and rockets and all cost plenty, and blowing up things nobody needs anyway is a poor return on the taxpayer's money. We always know what they're going to do next, and when and where, so there isn't any trick to keeping out of their way.

But they are pretty smart, considering they've got bodies to look after besides doing their thinking, so I always try to be cautious when I got over to watch them. That's why I wanted to clear out when Madge and I saw a storage center in the middle of one of their fields. We hadn't talked to anybody lately about what the enemy was up to, and the center looked awfully suspicious.

Madge was optimistic, the way she's been ever since she borrowed that burlesque queen's body, and she said the storage center was a sure sign that the enemy had seen the light, that they were getting ready to become amphibious themselves.

Well, it looked like it. There was a brand-new center, stocked with bodies and open for business, as innocent as you please. We circled it several times, and Madge's circles got smaller and smaller, as she tried to get a close look at what they had in the way of ladies' ready-to-wear.

"Let's beat it," I said.

"I'm just looking," said Madge. "No harm in looking."

Then she saw what was in the main display case, and she forgot where she was or where she'd come from.

The most striking woman's body I'd ever seen was in the case—six feet tall and built like a goddess. But that wasn't the payoff. The body had copper-colored skin, chartreuse hair and fingernails, and a gold lamé evening gown. Beside that body was the body of a blond, male giant in a pale blue field marshal's uniform, piped in scarlet and spangled with medals.

I think the enemy must have swiped the bodies in a raid on one of our outlying storage centers, and padded and dyed them, and dressed them up.

"Madge, come back!" I said.

The copper-colored woman with the chartreuse hair moved. A siren screamed and soldiers rushed from hiding places to grab the body Madge was in.

33

The center was a trap for amphibians!

The body Madge hadn't been able to resist had its ankles tied together, so Madge couldn't take the few steps she had to take if she was going to get out of it again.

The soldiers carted her off triumphantly as a prisoner of war. I got into the only body available, the fancy field marshal, to try to help her. It was a hopeless situation, because the field marshal was bait, too, with its ankles tied. The soldiers dragged me after Madge.

The cocky young major in charge of the soldiers did a jig along the shoulder of the road, he was so proud. He was the first man ever to capture an amphibian, which was really something from the enemy's point of view. They'd been at war with us for years, and spent God knows how many billions of dollars, but catching us was the first thing that made any amphibians pay much attention to them.

When we got to the town, people were leaning out of windows and waving their flags, and cheering the soldiers, and hissing Madge and me. Here were all the people who didn't want to be amphibious, who thought it was terrible for anybody to be amphibious—people of all colors, shapes, sizes, and nationalities, joined together to fight the amphibians.

It turned out that Madge and I were going to have a big trial. After being tied up every which way in jail all night, we were taken to a courtroom, where television cameras stared at us.

Madge and I were worn to frazzles, because neither one of us had been cooped up in a body that long since I don't know when. Just when we needed to think more than we ever had, in jail before the trial, the bodies developed hunger pains and we couldn't get them comfortable on the cots, no matter how we tried; and, of course, the bodies just had to have their eight hours sleep.

Unready to Wear

The charge against us was a capital offense on the books of the enemy—*desertion*. As far as the enemy was concerned, the amphibians had all turned yellow and run out on their bodies, just when their bodies were needed to do brave and important things for humanity.

We didn't have a hope of being acquitted. The only reason there was a trial at all was that it gave them an opportunity to sound off about why they were so right and we were so wrong. The courtroom was jammed with their big brass, all looking angry and brave and noble.

"Mr. Amphibian," said the prosecutor, "you are old enough, aren't you, to remember when all men had to face up to life in their bodies, and work and fight for what they believed in?"

"I remember when the bodies were always getting into fights, and nobody seemed to know why, or how to stop it," I said politely. "The only thing everybody seemed to believe in was that they didn't like to fight."

"What would you say of a soldier who ran away in the face of fire?" he wanted to know.

"I'd say he was scared silly."

"He was helping to lose the battle, wasn't he?"

"Oh, sure." There wasn't any argument on that one.

"Isn't that what the amphibians have done—run out on the human race in the face of the battle of life?"

"Most of us are still alive, if that's what you mean," I said.

It was true. We hadn't licked death, and weren't sure we wanted to, but we'd certainly lengthened life something amazing, compared to the span you could expect in a body.

"You ran out on your responsibilities!" he said.

"Like you'd run out of a burning building, sir," I said.

"Leaving everyone else to struggle on alone!"

"They can all get out the same door that we got out

35

Kurt Vonnegut, Jr.

of. You can all get out any time you want to. All you do is figure out what you want and what your body wants, and concentrate on—"

The judge banged his gavel until I thought he'd split it. Here they'd burned every copy of Konigswasser's book they could find, and there I was giving a course in how to get out of a body, over a whole television network.

"If you amphibians had your way," said the prosecutor, "every body would run out on his responsibilities, and let life and progress as we know them disappear completely."

"Why, sure," I agreed. "That's the point."

"Men would no longer work for what they believe in?" he challenged.

"I had a friend back in the old days who drilled holes in little square thingmajigs for seventeen years in a factory, and he never did get a very clear idea of what they were for. Another one I knew grew raisins for a glassblowing company, and the raisins weren't for anybody to eat, and he never did find out why the company bought them. Things like that make me sick—now that I'm in a body, of course—and what I used to do for a living makes me even sicker."

"Then you despise human beings and everything they do," he said.

"I like them fine—better than I ever did before. I just think it's a dirty shame what they have to do to take care of their bodies. You ought to get amphibious and see how happy people can be when they don't have to worry about where their body's next meal is coming from, or how to keep it from freezing in the wintertime, or what's going to happen to them when their body wears out."

"And that, sir, means the end of ambition, the end of greatness!"

"Oh, I don't know what about that," I said. "We've

36

got some pretty great people on our side. They'd be great in *or* out of bodies. It's the end of fear is what it is." I looked right into the lens of the nearest television camera. "And *that's* the most wonderful thing that ever happened to people."

Down came the judge's gavel again, and the brass started to shout me down. The television men turned off their cameras, and all the spectators, except for the biggest brass, were cleared out. I knew I'd really said something. All anybody would be getting on his television set now was organ music.

When the confusion died down, the judge said the trial was over, and that Madge and I were guilty of desertion.

Nothing I could do could get us in any worse, so I talked back.

"Now I understand you poor fish," I said. "You couldn't get along without fear. That's the only skill you've got—how to scare yourselves and other people into doing things. That's the only fun you've got, watching people jump for fear of what you'll do to their bodies or take away from their bodies."

Madge got in her two cents' worth. "The only way you can get any response from anybody is to scare them."

"Contempt of court!" said the judge.

"The only way you can scare people is if you can keep them in their bodies," I told him.

The soldiers grabbed Madge and me and started to drag us out of the courtroom.

"This means war!" I yelled.

Everything stopped right there and the place got very quiet.

"We're already at war," said a general uneasily.

"Well, *we're* not," I answered, "but we will be, if you don't untie Madge and me this instant." I was fierce and impressive in that field marshal's body.

"You haven't any weapons," said the judge, "no know-how. Outside of bodies, amphibians are nothing."

"If you don't cut us loose by the time I count ten," I told him, "the amphibians will occupy the bodies of the whole kit and caboodle of you and march you right off the nearest cliff. The place is surrounded." That was hogwash, of course. Only one person can occupy a body at a time, but the enemy couldn't be sure of that. "One! Two! Three!"

The general swallowed, turned white, and waved his hand vaguely.

"Cut them loose," he said weakly.

The soldiers, terrified, too, were glad to do it. Madge and I were freed.

I took a couple of steps, headed my spirit in another direction, and that beautiful field marshal, medals and all, went crashing down the staircase like a grandfather clock.

I realized that Madge wasn't with me. She was still in that copper-colored body with the chartreuse hair and fingernails.

"What's more," I heard her saying, "in payment for all the trouble you've caused us, this body is to be addressed to me at New York, delivered in good condition no later than next Monday."

"Yes, ma'am," said the judge.

When we got home, the Pioneers' Day Parade was just breaking up at the local storage center, and the Parade Marshal got out of his body and apologized to me for acting the way he did.

"Heck, Herb," I said, "you don't need to apologize. You weren't yourself. You were parading around in a body."

That's the best part of being amphibious, next to not being afraid—people forgive you for whatever fool thing you might have done in a body.

Oh, there are drawbacks, I guess, the way there are drawbacks to everything. We still have to work off and on, maintaining the storage centers and getting food to keep the community bodies going. But that's a small drawback, and all the big drawbacks I ever heard of aren't real ones, just old-fashioned thinking by people who can't stop worrying about things they used to worry about before they turned amphibious.

As I say, the oldsters will probably never get really used to it. Every so often, I catch myself getting gloomy over what happened to the pay-toilet business it took me thirty years to build.

But the youngsters don't have any hangovers like that from the past. They don't even worry much about something happening to the storage centers, the way us oldsters do.

So I guess maybe that'll be the next step in evolution—to break clean like those first amphibians who crawled out of the mud into the sunshine, and who never did go back to the sea.

THE ELEVATOR

Robert Coover

1

Every morning without exception and without so much as reflecting upon it, Martin takes the self-service elevator to the fourteenth floor, where he works. He will do so today. When he first arrives, however, he finds the lobby empty, the old building still possessed of its feinting shadows and silences, desolate though mutely expectant, and he wonders if today it might not turn out differently.

It is 7:30 A.M.: Martin is early and therefore has the elevator entirely to himself. He steps inside: this tight cell! he thinks with a kind of unsettling shock, and confronts the panel of numbered buttons. One to fourteen, plus "B" for basement. Impulsively, he presses the "B"—seven years and yet to visit the basement! He snorts at his timidity.

After a silent moment, the doors rumble shut. All

night alert waiting for this moment! The elevator sinks slowly into the earth. The stale gloomy odors of the old building having aroused in him an unreasonable sense of dread and loss, Martin imagines suddenly he is descending into hell. *Tra la perduta gente,* yes! A mild shudder shakes him. Yet, Martin decides firmly, would that it were so. The old carrier halts with a quiver. The automatic doors yawn open. Nothing, only a basement. It is empty and nearly dark. It is silent and meaningless.

Martin smiles inwardly at himself, presses the number "14." "Come on, old Charon," he declaims broadly, "Hell's the other way!"

2

Martin waited miserably for the stench of intestinal gas to reach his nostrils. Always the same. He supposed it was Carruther, but he could never prove it. Not so much as a telltale squeak. But it was Carruther who always led them, and though the other faces changed, Carruther was always among them.

They were seven in the elevator: six men and the young girl who operated it. The girl did not participate. She was surely offended, but she never gave a hint of it. She possessed a surface detachment that not even Carruther's crude proposals could penetrate. Much less did she involve herself in the coarse interplay of men. Yet certainly, Martin supposed, they were a torment to her.

And, yes, he was right—there it was, faint at first, almost sweet, then slowly thickening, sickening, crowding up on him—

"Hey! Who fahred thet shot!" cried Carruther, starting it.

"Mart fahred-it!" came the inexorable reply. And then the crush of loud laughter.

"*What!* Is that Martin fartin' again?" bellowed another, as their toothy thicklipped howling congealed around him.

"Aw *please,* Mart! *don't fart!*" cried yet another. It would go on until they left the elevator. The elevator was small: their laughter packed it, jammed at the walls. "Have a heart, Mart! don't *part* that fart!"

It's not me, *it's not me,* Martin insisted. But only to himself. It was no use. It was fate. Fate and Carruther. (More laughter, more brute jabs.) A couple of times he had protested. "Aw, Marty, you're just modest!" Carruther had thundered. Booming voice, big man. Martin hated him.

One by one, the other men filed out of the elevator at different floors, holding their noses. "Old farty Marty!" they would shout to anyone they met on their way out, and it always got a laugh, up and down the floor. The air cleared slightly each time the door opened.

In the end, Martin was always left alone with the girl who operated the elevator. His floor, the fourteenth, was the top one. When it all began, long ago, he had attempted apologetic glances toward the girl on exiting, but she had always turned her shoulder to him. Maybe she thought he was making a play for her. Finally he was forced to adopt the custom of simply ducking out as quickly as possible. She would in any case assume his guilt.

Of course, there was an answer to Carruther. Yes, Martin knew it, had rehearsed it countless times. The only way to meet that man was on his home ground. And he'd do it, too. When the time came.

The Elevator

3

Martin is alone on the elevator with the operator, a young girl. She is neither slender nor plump, but fills charmingly her orchid-colored uniform. Martin greets her in his usual friendly manner and she returns his greeting with a smile. Their eyes meet momentarily. Hers are brown.

When Martin enters the elevator, there are actually several other people crowded in, but as the elevator climbs through the musky old building, the others, singly or in groups, step out. Finally, Martin is left alone with the girl who operates the elevator. She grasps the lever, leans against it, and the cage sighs upward. He speaks to her, makes a lighthearted joke about elevators. She laughs and

Alone on the elevator with the girl, Martin thinks: if this elevator should crash, I would sacrifice my life to save her. Her back is straight and subtle. Her orchid uniform skirt is tight, tucks tautly under her blossoming hips, describes a kind of cavity there. Perhaps it is night. Her calves are muscular and strong. She grasps the lever.

The girl and Martin are alone on the elevator, which is rising. He concentrates on her round hips until she is forced to turn and look at him. His gaze coolly courses her belly, her pinched and belted waist, past her taut breasts, meets her excited stare. She breathes deeply, her lips parted. They embrace. Her breasts plunge softly against him. Her mouth is sweet. Martin has forgotten whether the elevator is climbing or not.

4

Perhaps Martin will meet Death on the elevator. Yes, going out for lunch one afternoon. Or to the drugstore for cigarettes. He will press the button in the hall on the fourteenth floor, the doors will open, a dark smile will beckon. The shaft is deep. It is dark and silent. Martin will recognize Death by His silence. He will not protest.

He *will* protest! oh God! no matter what the
  the sense of emptiness underneath breath lurching
  out
The shaft is long and narrow. The shaft is dark.
He will not protest.

5

Martin, as always and without so much as reflecting upon it, takes the self-service elevator to the fourteenth floor, where he works. He is early, but only by a few minutes. Five others join him, greetings are exchanged. Though tempted, he is not able to risk the "B," but presses the "14" instead. Seven years!

As the automatic doors press together and the elevator begins its slow complaining ascent, Martin muses absently on the categories. This small room, so commonplace and so compressed, he observes with a certain melancholic satisfaction, this elevator contains them all: space, time, cause, motion, magnitude, class. Left to our own devices, we would probably discover them. The other passengers chatter with self-righteous smiles (after all, they are on time) about the weather, the elections, the work that awaits them today. They stand, apparently motionless, yet moving. Motion: perhaps that's all there is to it after all. Motion and the medium. Energy and weighted particles. Force and matter. The image grips him purely. Ascent and the passive reorganization of atoms.

At the seventh floor, the elevator stops and a woman departs it. Only a trace of her perfume remains. Martin alone remarks—to himself, of course—her absence, as the climb begins again. Reduced by one. But the totality of the universe is suffused: each man contains all of it, loss is inconceivable. Yet, if that is so—and a tremor shudders coolly through Martin's body—then the totality is as nothing. Martin gazes around at his four remaining fellow passengers, a flush of compassion washing in behind the tremor. One must always be alert to the possibility of action, he reminds himself. But none apparently need him. If he could do the work for them today, give them the grace of a day's contemplation . . .

The elevator halts, suspended and vibrant, at the tenth floor. Two men leave. Two more intermediate stops, and Martin is alone. He has seen them safely through. Although caged as ever in his inexorable melancholy, Martin nonetheless smiles as he steps out of the self-service elevator on the fourteenth floor. "I am pleased to participate," he announces in full voice. But, as the elevator doors close behind him and he hears the voided descent, he wonders: Wherein now is the elevator's totality?

6

The cable snaps at the thirteenth floor. There is a moment's deadly motionlessness—then a sudden breathless plunge! The girl, terrified, turns to Martin. They are alone. Though inside his heart is bursting its chambers in terror, he remains outwardly composed. "I think it is safer lying on your back," he says. He squats to the floor, but the girl remains transfixed with shock. Her thighs are round and sleek under the orchid skirt, and in the shadowed— "Come," he says. "You may lie on me. My body will absorb part of the impact." Her hair caresses his cheek, her buttocks press like a sponge into his groin. In love, moved by his sacrifice, she weeps. To calm her, he clasps her heaving abdomen, strokes her soothingly. The elevator whistles as it drops.

7

Martin worked late in the office, clearing up the things that needed to be done before the next day, routine matters, yet part of the uninterrupted necessity that governed his daily life. Not a large office, Martin's, though he needed no larger, essentially neat except for the modest clutter on top of his desk. The room was equipped only with that desk and a couple of chairs, bookcases lining one wall, calendar posted on another. The overhead lamp was off, the only light in the office being provided by the fluorescent lamp on Martin's desk.

Martin signed one last form, sighed, smiled. He retrieved a cigarette, half-burned but still lit, from the ashtray, drew heavily on it, then, as he exhaled with another prolonged sigh, doubled the butt firmly in the black bowl of the ashtray. Still extinguishing it, twisting it among the heap of crumpled filters in the ashtray, he glanced idly at his watch. He was astonished to discover that the watch said twelve-thirty—and had stopped! Already after midnight!

He jumped up, rolled down his sleeves, buttoned them, whipped his suit jacket off the back of his chair, shoved his arms into it. Bad enough twelve-thirty—but my God! how much *later* was it? The jacket still only three-quarters of the way up his back, tie askew, he hastily stacked the loose papers on his desk and switched off the lamp. He stumbled through the dark room out into the hallway, lit by one dull yellow bulb, pulled his office door to behind him. The thick solid catch knocked hollowly in the vacant corridor.

He buttoned his shirt collar, straightened his tie and the collar of his jacket, which was doubled under on his right shoulder, as he hurried down the passageway past the other closed office doors of the fourteenth floor to the self-service elevator, his heels hammering away the stillness on the marble floor. He trembled, inexplicably. The profound silence of the old building disturbed him. Relax, he urged himself; we'll know what time it is soon enough. He pushed the button for the elevator, but nothing happened. Don't tell me I have to walk down! he muttered bitterly to himself. He poked the button again, harder, and this time he heard below a solemn rumble, a muffled thump, and an indistinct grinding plaint that grieved progressively nearer. It stopped and the doors of the elevator opened to receive him. Entering, Martin felt a sudden need to glance back over his shoulder, but he suppressed it.

Once inside, he punched the number "1" button on the self-service panel. The doors closed, but the elevator, instead of descending, continued to climb. Goddamn this old wreck! Martin swore irritably, and he jiggled the "1" button over and over. Just this night! The elevator stopped, the doors opened, Martin stepped out. Later, he wondered why he had done so. The doors slid shut behind him, he heard the elevator descend, its amused rumble fading distantly. Although here it was utterly dark, shapes seemed to form. Though he could see nothing distinctly, he was fully aware that he was not alone. His hand fumbled on the wall for the elevator button. Cold wind gnawed at his ankles, the back of his neck. Fool! wretched fool! he wept, there *is* no fifteenth floor! Pressed himself against the wall, couldn't find the button, couldn't even find the elevator door, and even the very wall was only

8

Carruther's big voice boomed in the small cage.

"Mart fahred-it!" came the certain reply. The five men laughed. Martin flushed. The girl feigned indifference. The fetor of fart vapours reeked in the tight elevator.

"Martin, damn it, cut the fartin'!"

Martin fixed his cool gaze on them. "Carruther fucks his mother," he said firmly. Carruther hit him full in the face, his glasses splintered and fell, Martin staggered back against the wall. He waited for the second blow, but it didn't come. Someone elbowed him, and he slipped to the floor. He knelt there, weeping softly, searched with his hands for his glasses. Martin tasted the blood from his nose, trickling into his mouth. He couldn't find the glasses, couldn't even see.

"Look out, baby!" Carruther thundered. "Farty Marty's jist tryin' to git a free peek up at your pretty drawers!" Crash of laughter. Martin felt the girl shrink from him.

9

Her soft belly presses like a sponge into his groin. No, safer on your back, love, he thinks, but pushes the thought away. She weeps in terror, presses her hot wet mouth against his. To calm her, he clasps her soft buttocks, strokes them soothingly. So sudden is the plunge, they seem suspended in air. She has removed her skirt. How will it feel? he wonders.

10

Martin, without so much as reflecting on it, automatically takes the self-service elevator to the fourteenth floor, where he works. The systematizing, that's what's wrong, he concludes, that's what cracks them up. He is late, but only by a few minutes. Seven others join him, anxious, sweating. They glance nervously at their watches. None of them presses the "B" button. Civilities are hurriedly interchanged.

Their foolish anxiety seeps out like a bad spirit, enters Martin. He finds himself looking often at his watch, grows impatient with the elevator. Take it easy, he cautions himself. Their blank faces oppress him. Bleak. Haunted. Tyrannized by their own arbitrary regimentation of time. Torture self-imposed, yet in all probability inescapable. The elevator halts jerkily at the third floor, quivering their sallow face-flesh. They frown. No one has pushed the three. A woman enters. They all nod, harrumph, make jittery little hand motions to incite the doors to close. They are all more or less aware of the woman (she has delayed them, damn her!), but only Martin truly remarks—to himself—her whole presence, as the elevator resumes its upward struggle. The accretion of tragedy. It goes on, ever giving birth to itself. Up and down, up and down. Where will it end? he wonders. Her perfume floats gloomily in the stale air. These deformed browbeaten mind-animals. Suffering and insufferable. Up and down. He closes his eyes. One by one, they leave him.

He arrives, alone, at the fourteenth floor. He steps

Robert Coover

out of the old elevator, stares back into its spent emptiness. There, only there, is peace, he concludes wearily. The elevator doors press shut.

11

Here on this elevator, my elevator, created by me, moved by me, doomed by me, I, Martin, proclaim my omnipotence! In the end, doom touches all! MY doom! I impose it! TREMBLE!

12

The elevator shrieks insanely as it drops. Their naked bellies slap together, hands grasp, her vaginal mouth closes spongelike on his rigid organ. Their lips lock, tongues knot. The bodies: how will they find them? Inwardly, he laughs. He thrusts up off the plummeting floor. Her eyes are brown and, with tears, love him.

13

But—ah!—the doomed, old man, the DOOMED! What are they to us, to ME? ALL! We, I love! Let their flesh sag and dewlaps tremble, let their odors offend, let their cruelty mutilate, their stupidity enchain—but let them laugh, father! FOREVER! let them cry!

The Elevator

14

but hey! theres this guy see he gets on the goddamn elevator and its famous how hes got him a doodang about five feet long Im not kiddin you none five feet and he gets on the—yeah! can you imagine a bastard like that boardin a friggin pubic I mean public elevator? hoohah! no I dont know his name Mert I think or Mort but the crux is he is possessed of this motherin digit biggern ole Rahab see—do with it? I dont know I think he wraps it around his leg or carries it over his shoulder or somethin jeezuss! what a problem! why I bet hes *killt* more poor bawdies than I ever dipped my poor worm in! once he was even a—listen! Carruther tells this as the goddamn truth I mean he *respects* that bastard—he was even one a them jackoff gods I forget how you call them over there with them Eyetalians after the big war see them dumb types when they seen him furl out this here five foot hose of his one day—he was just tryin to get the goddamn knots out Carruther says —why they thought he musta been a goddamn jackoff god or somethin and wanted to like employ him or whatever you do with a god and well Mort he figgered it to be a not so miserable occupation dont you know better anyhow than oildrillin with it in Arabia or stoppin holes in Dutch dikes like hes been doin so the bastard he stays on there a time and them little quiff there in that Eyetalian place they grease him up with hogfat and olive oil and all workin together like vested virgins they pull him off out there in the fields and spray the crops and well Mort he says *he* says its the closest hes ever got to the real mccoy jeezuss! hes worth a thousand laughs! and they bring him all the old aunts and grannies and he splits them open a kinda stupendous euthanasia for the old ladies and he blesses all their friggin

procreations with a swat of his doodang and even does
a little welldiggin on the side but he gets in trouble with
the Roman churchers on accounta not bein circumcised
and they wanta whack it off but Mort says no and they
cant get close to him with so prodigious a batterin ram
as hes got so they work a few miracles on him and
wrinkle up old pud with holy water and heat up his
semen so it burns up the fields and even one day ig-
nites a goddamn volcano and *jeezuss!* he wastes no time
throwin that thing over his shoulder and hightailin it
outa there I can tell you! but now like Im sayin them
pastoral days is dead and gone and hes goin up and
down in elevators like the rest of us and so here he is
boardin the damn cage and theys a bunch of us bastards clownin around with the little piece who operates
that deathtrap kinda brushin her swell butt like a occasional accident and sweet jeezus her gettin fidgety and
hot and half fightin us off and half pullin us on and
playin with that lever *zoom!* wingin up through that
scraper and just then ole Carruther jeezuss he really
breaks you up sometimes that crazy bastard he hefts up
her little purple skirt and whaddaya know! the little
quiff aint wearin no skivvies! its somethin *beautiful*
man I mean a sweet cleft peach right outa some foreign
orchard and poor ole Mort he is kinda part gigglin and
part hurtin and for a minute the rest of us dont see the
pointa the whole agitation but then that there incredible thing suddenly pops up quivery right under his chin
like a friggin eye of god for crissake and then theres
this big wild rip and man! it rears up and splits outa
there like a goddamn redwood topplin *gawdamighty!*
and knocks old Carruther *kapow!* right to the deck! his
best buddy and that poor little cunt she takes one glim
of that impossible rod wheelin around in there and
whammin the walls and she faints dead away and
jeeezusss! she tumbles right on that elevator lever and
man! I thought for a minute we was *all* dead

The Elevator

15

They plunge, their damp bodies fused, pounding furiously, in terror, in joy, the impact is

I, Martin, proclaim against all dooms the indestructible seed

Martin does not take the self-service elevator to the fourteenth floor, as is his custom, but, reflecting upon it for once and out of a strange premonition, determines instead to walk the fourteen flights. Halfway up, he hears the elevator hurtle by him and then the splintering crash from below. He hesitates, poised on the stair. Inscrutable is the word he finally settles upon. He pronounces it aloud, smiles faintly, sadly, somewhat wearily, then continues his tedious climb, pausing from time to time to stare back down the stairs behind him.

QUAKE

Rudolph Wurlitzer

... It was hot. I crawled towards the western part of the circle, at a right angle from the guard. Then I turned and made my way along the edge of the rope towards him. When I reached him I threw him the watch and everything in my pockets and then put my hand over the line. He slipped the watch over his wrist and gestured at me with the rifle. He was about eighteen and his eyes were glazed and his mouth slack.

"No difference," he said.

"I'll probably be able to stand up and walk right over you in a few minutes," I said.

"No difference," he repeated. He held his rifle on me and his hands were steady. I crawled around the inside of the circle. There were dull explosions in the distance and the sudden whine of a chainsaw in back of the colonial house. I stopped half way around, up on the northwest section. I sat crosslegged and swayed back and forth while a large red wagon with automobile tires was slowly pulled towards the circle by four shirtless men. Bodies were piled on the wagon and when one fell off the men stopped to put it back on. Another fell off and they left it where it fell. They took a long time going around a deep crevice and coming back across the parking space in front of the Texaco station. They stopped a few feet in front of the circle. They were young and muscular as if they all belonged to the same college fraternity or water polo team. They lifted the bodies off the wagon and dropped them over the rope. There were sixteen bodies and they were all shot through the back of the head. I walked to the center of the circle. The man with the handlebar mustache was cutting his wrists with a large piece of glass. He was cutting very slowly and the blood oozed along his wrist and dripped slowly onto the pile of glass and pebbles in front of him. I sat down facing him, my back to the dead men.

"They really fucked it up this time," he whispered. "Never mind Alabama or Alaska. I want a sweet sound. Listen, this was no accident. Lucy says this, Lucy says that. You can take it from this piece of poor white trash. It has all come down. Are you listening? You have some titles I don't know about, you say them. Un Poco Loco. You know that one? Say me down. Oooooooooo, now. That's right. Ease on out of there. Oooooooooo . . ."

He lay back on the grass, keeping his arms to his side. He murmured and laughed to himself. He didn't make very much noise. Blood was all over the grass now and spreading out around him. They had finished piling up the bodies and had pulled the wagon away. It had gotten stuck in a deep split in the road and they had just walked away. A pistol shot cracked behind me. The guard in front of us stood up and looked around but he didn't seem overly anxious. He sat down against the overturned station wagon and checked the breech in his rifle. I couldn't look at what was happening next to me. He wasn't doing anything that I had to pay attention to but the blood was beginning to freak me. I had to move a few feet away. The move brought me closer to Helena. I had forgotten about her, even to the point of not seeing her. She was still breathing, her leg bent up underneath her and her arms folded over her eyes. I needed her to be awake. I needed her to be afraid so that I could reassure her. I slapped her face and she moaned but she didn't wake up. I didn't know how to intrude on her more than that. A voice screamed from inside the ruins of the colonial house.

To my left, from the east, on the road where the red wagon had been abandoned, appeared a loose line of men and women. They were guarded by five men with fatigue hats and they walked slowly towards us. I concentrated on the pile of pebbles and glass in front of me. I needed to string a yellow rope inside the first one. I needed to remember my passport picture. The man with the handlebar mustache was dead. Helena lay on her side looking at me, although there was no focus to her gaze. The line of prisoners had passed the red wagon. There were women with the men and a few small children. Their clothes were torn and several of them were naked. They stopped outside the circle. A white haired man in a red bathrobe and heavy thonged sandals stepped up to one of the guards.

"I'll ask you one more time," he said loudly. "What is the meaning of this? You have exposed my wife and children to unspeakable horrors and all this while we are faced with a terrible tragedy. Have you people gone mad?"

The guard looked past him without expression. The man stepped closer to him and yelled:

"Answer me, you cretin. We still have rights. This is still a democracy. I'll prosecute your ass out of this entire state. I demand to know your name."

"Arthur," the guard replied quietly. Then he hit him on the side of the head with the butt of his rifle.

Quake

The man pitched forward across the yellow rope. A guard lifted his feet up and dumped him inside the circle. I recognized Orville. He was walking up to the circle dragging his shotgun by the barrel. He seemed distraught. He walked up to the circle and addressed the prisoners.

"All right," he said. He was unable to look at them directly. "Give me your attention now. You people are being held in custody until this day gets sorted out. Don't complain and for god's sake don't try to run away. For various reasons you are all under arrest. You will be informed of your rights later. But for now you have no rights until the city is under control. Now remove your clothes and step inside the yellow rope there."

An old woman sank to the ground. Several men stood with their arms folded, refusing to remove their clothes.

"I won't tolerate this," Orville screamed. He lifted up his shotgun. "Anyone not undressed in two minutes will be shot. Now please, do as I say."

They undressed. The women held their hands over their pubic areas. The men were less shy but felt compelled to make jokes about their flabby stomachs and pale complexions. I lay back and shut my eyes. I could hear them crowding into the center of the circle, trying to avoid the bodies piled near the rope. They milled about looking for a place to sit. I felt far away, closer to the dead body next to me, and unable to say anything or even look at them. A child cried and others joined in. Their mothers tried to hush them but gave up as the crying grew louder. There was a tap on my shoulder.

"Do you know what's happening in here?" a man's voice asked. "Why have we been singled out rather than others? You've been here for a while. You saw us come in, didn't you?"

"I saw you," I said.

I heard him settle down beside me. "How come you

57

don't open your eyes? Are you OK? What're you, trau-
matized?"

"I'm resting," I said. "It's been a hard day."

"Jesus Christ," he said. "I just asked. Listen, there
are more of us than there are of them and we could
maybe overrun them or something."

I didn't answer.

"Did you hear what I said?" he asked. "Huh?"

"I heard you," I said.

"Then why don't you respond? What are you,
wounded? If you're wounded just say so. That's all. But
we got to pull together, do you know what I mean?
Huh? I *said* do you know what I mean?"

"Fuck off," I said.

"Whew," he said. "They really got to you, didn't
they? You won't make it, mister. I'll tell you that. And I
don't give a shit either."

He waited for a moment and then he moved away.
I could hear shouts and the grinding of a large machine.
Get me outside, I thought. Just let me stand outside and
guard these people. I'll shoot their limbs off one by one
if they make a false move. I'll hunt around and find
more victims to put inside the circle. I'll wear a fatigue
cap and swear allegiance to a fucking softball team. . . .
I wanted to join up, that was all. The crowd had settled down and the children had stopped crying. I could
even hear a bird chirping somewhere on the grass. There
was a tap on the back of my head.

"They want you to take off your clothes." It was a
girl's voice. I opened my eyes. She had long blond hair
and a smooth oval face, the kind you see in hair spray
or toothpaste ads. Her nipples brushed against my chest.
I put one hand on her thigh and sat up.

"How long have you been here?" she asked. She sat
back and put her arms around her legs.

I didn't reply.

"I think they'll let us go, don't you?" she asked. "As

soon as there are no more aftershocks they'll let us go."

I stood up and took off my clothes. The girl looked me over.

"Do I suit you?"

"Oh sure," she said. "Why not?"

The guard gestured at me with his rifle to come over. I walked to the edge of the circle.

"Get that broad undressed," he said. He pointed to Helena.

"She's unconscious," I said. "Her leg is broken and she's probably fucked up in the head."

"It doesn't matter. Get her bare assed."

"Who are you guys, anyway?" I asked.

"We're a national outfit. We've been training for years for something like this."

"Yeah, but who are you?"

"Neighborhood people. We're sanctioned. You don't have to worry about it. The ALPCS."

He turned away. Another guard was walking clockwise around the circle, his rifle on his shoulder. I walked back to Helena. The girl with the blond hair remained in the same position. She watched me, her mouth slightly open. I bent over Helena, removing her sequined dancing slippers. Helena's eyes were open, but she was staring off to the side at the pile of dead bodies. She didn't move when I touched her.

"I have to take off your clothes," I said. "They want us bare assed. It makes us more submissive."

I unzipped her orange leotards. A bone had punctured her skin above her knee cap and I couldn't slide her leotards down more than a foot. She wasn't wearing panties and her pubic hair had been shaved. There was a soft roll of fat around her stomach.

"Is she your wife?" the girl asked.

"She was trapped in a building. We got out together."

"She doesn't look too bad for someone her age," the girl said.

"She used to be an actress."

"Oh wow," the girl said. "I think I've seen her. There was one with Natalie Wood she was in. And then she played this neurotic nurse who was trying to marry this doctor and when the leading lady ran off with him she jumped in front of a subway. Only she lived."

I leaned against Helena's leg while trying to remove her white sweater. She screamed. I tried to comfort her but she had passed out. A few people looked over at us.

"I need your help," I said. The girl crawled over and together we removed Helena's sweater. She wore no bra and there were scars around the bottom of her breast where she might have been operated on.

"Did you fuck her?" the girl asked.

"I didn't have time," I said.

"Would you make it with her if you could? I mean, say there was this little cabin right now on the beach and no one else was around. Would you get it on with her?"

"Yeah, sure," I said. Helena's face was misshapen from pain. She looked grotesque.

"I'd do it," the girl said very quickly. "I'd make it with both of you. At the same time. And I'd take speed while I did it and then I'd come back for more. What d'you think of that?"

"I think that's fantastic."

She was leaning back against the man with the handlebar mustache. Part of her ass was resting in his dark blood. His arms were flung out to the side and his head was snapped back on the grass so that it seemed he was staring open mouthed at the blue sky. She was crying quietly, her hands playing with a piece of glass.

"I'm freaking out," she said. "I'm scared shitless if you want to know and I want to fuck someone so bad it's driving me crazy. I'm seventeen and I've made it enough to know what it does to me. I want to get out of all this.

Quake

I don't want to know about any of it. I don't know how to deal with it. I was at my girl friend's house and something fell on her head and killed her. I think it was a bookcase. I ran outside and fell in with two weird guys. They were running off to blow up some TV station or something. They got killed. That's how come I'm here."

I touched her hand but she shrank back.

"Don't touch me," she snarled. "I don't want anyone touching me."

I stood up and walked counter-clockwise around the inside of the circle. As I passed the guard walking the opposite way we nodded to each other. Perhaps in some way I was guarding him as well. I stepped on glass and the bottom of my foot bled. The pain helped me concentrate on each step. I walked around the pile of bodies. An old man lay spread-eagled over the pile and a toeless foot stuck straight up between the stiff legs of three women. The line of smoke from the Hollywood Hills had thickened and spread to the east. To the south a machine gun opened up and then abruptly stopped. I took a leap over the rope. The guard paused and smiled at me.

"Some mess, ain't it?"

"It is." He had long curly brown hair and wore blue overalls and army combat boots. He had squashed up his new fatigue hat, turning the brim up at the sides to make it look old and weathered.

"You from around here?" he asked.

"I was staying at a motel on Santa Monica. They grabbed me coming out of a building. Me and some others were trying to rescue people stuck in there."

"That might be," he said seriously. "Of course we've had some godawful problems with hard hat rescue workers. They killed more than thirty of us when we moved into this area. One of them lobbed a grenade into one of our trucks. No need for that. We could have worked it out."

"Most of these people were rousted out of their homes and just marched over here and put through a bad scene."

"Yeah, it was hard for me too. I woke up on the eighth floor and the whole goddamn building was coming down underneath me. I stood in the middle of the floor and went down with it. I just kept light-stepping it all the way down. I had to pay attention, you know what I mean?"

He walked on. I passed him again but he didn't nod. The girl had begun to walk clockwise around the circle, twenty or thirty feet behind the other guard. I was walking against them, face to face. If we had shifted our positions and moved a little differently we might have imitated the orbits of the sun and moon. A small boy stood in the middle of the circle, spinning as fast as he could until he dropped. Two other children imitated him, whirling and holding their arms straight out. "Unnhhh . . . Unnnhhh . . ." The sounds came from my stomach. I stretched and moved my neck around. The girl passed me, swinging her arms easily and smiling. An old man wobbled towards the line. He had a round pot belly and flabby testicles that hung down in loose sacs. There was a stiff curious tilt to his bald head. He made his way up to the rope and grabbed it with one hand. With the other he waved us on.

"Soooooeeeee," he cried. "Round em up. Round em up."

He walked beside me, talking to himself and slapping his hands together. When the girl passed us he moved away and began a smaller circle further in towards the center. He walked around the man with the handlebar mustache and Helena and the two bound bodies. I was getting tired. The walk wasn't working. The old man's legs suddenly buckled and he fell, landing near Helena. The guard stopped walking and lit a cigarette. The girl changed her direction and fell in alongside me.

"This is terrific walking around like this," she said. "It does a funny thing to me. All the guards look at me wanting to jump me and you make dirty signs at me. I don't mind."

I changed my direction but she turned as well so I turned back again. I tried to growl but what came out was a low moan.

"Are you all right?" she asked.

"Get ready," I said.

She reached out with her fingers and grasped my wrist. Our fingers locked and she skipped to synchronize her steps with mine.

"You think I'm young, don't you?" she asked.

"No."

"I am. I'm just young enough to be totally wiped out and just old enough to be hysterical. But the fact that I can say that is far out, don't you think? Get ready for what?"

"Get ready to die."

It sounded completely false. I didn't know what that meant with her and neither, of course, did she. I said it again but I felt nothing. We walked in silence. She withdrew her hand from mine and after a few steps reached back again. With my other hand I let the rope run through my fingers.

"That's your trip," she said. "I'm not going to get into that one."

"Everything's going to work out," I said. "Don't worry about it."

We walked back to the center of the circle and sat down. She told me about her brother who had two fingers cut off with an axe and went to college in Oregon where he was engaged to a girl from Ohio. Her mother and father lived in Santa Barbara and ran a surfboard and skin diving business. Her great aunt had killed a prowler with a shot gun. She was afraid of heights but grooved on organic food and rock festivals. I started to tell her that I had been pointing for a disaster like this for a long time and that I recognized a lot of what was around me, but I stopped and let out a long sigh: "Waaaaaa . . ." I started to shake and she stood up and walked over to the rope. Orville was walking up the road. He stopped at the overturned station wagon and waved at the other girls to come over. The girl returned and put her hand in mine and asked me some questions:

"Do you go to the movies?"

"Yes."

"Do you listen to music?"

"On the radio."

"Do you have friends?"

"In passing."

"Do you have a girl friend or a wife?"

"No."

"Have you had one lately?"

"About six months ago I stayed with a woman for a while."

"Did you like it?"

"Yes and no."

"What do you do all day?"

"Wait mostly."

"For what?"

"I don't know."

We walked over to the edge of the circle. Orville paced from the overturned station wagon to the rope. The guards had taken up positions around us. Finally Orville stopped and addressed us:

"We've found it necessary to move you to another place. There will be other groups joining you. We're going to walk down this street and get on the Freeway. We're going to take it very slowly. If we don't make the Freeway we'll do it some other way. We have three miles to walk. It will be all right if you wear your shoes but that's all."

After a few whispered words with the guards, he walked back down the road. Everyone stood up and sorted through the shoes after they were thrown over the rope. The shoes made people shrink inside themselves, as if they had been made even more naked and exposed. A fat blond woman with curlers in her hair sat down and cried. Then she beat her fists on the grass. Her husband tried to bend down and put his arms around her but she shrugged him off. "It's your fault," she screamed. "You and your weird friends." He walked off to the other side of the circle. The guards smoked and ate candy bars and checked their rifles. I found my sandals and put them on. The girl linked her arm through mine. She was wearing sandals.

"What about that woman who broke her leg?" she asked.

Helena lay on her back. Her eyes were closed.

"She'll get left behind," the girl said.

"She can't walk. It's probably better to leave her. She'll never make it otherwise."

"They'll kill her." The girl withdrew her arm and walked away. She stood next to the rope with her back to me. Helena had opened her eyes. I walked over to her and kneeled down. Her lips moved but I couldn't hear. I pressed closer.

"Water," she whispered.

"We don't have any," I said.

"I have to take a leak."

Urine squirted out of her and dribbled down her leg.

"Get me moved," she said. "I can feel the car around me. I can feel the wreck. Who's coming to get me? My leg is hurting like crazy. Don't panic. I'm all right. I'm going to get away after this."

Her words ran together and then they stopped. She

closed her eyes. I walked to the edge of the circle and motioned to a guard.

"There's a lady over there who can't make it," I said. "Her leg is broken."

"Leave her," the guard said. "We'll find something to do with her."

They took down the rope and we stood patiently, waiting for a direction. A guard shouted for attention:

"All right now. I want a line. Two by two. I don't care who you pair up with but do it fast. Keep it close and don't get any ideas about going for a stroll. We got about three miles and we're going to do it as fast as we can. All right, form up."

The girl took my hand and we moved into the middle of the line. Then we all marched away. We passed the overturned station wagon and turned down a small side street. The middle of the street was torn and ripped apart and we kept to lawns as much as possible. Most of the houses were down but a few stood completely untouched. We saw no one. It was very quiet walking down the side street. A middle-aged couple whispered angrily to each other in front of us. They were suntanned and lean and walked very easily. He wanted to make a run for it but she was for staying in the line. She told him that he should try it alone, that it would be a relief to be away from him. He slapped her, not missing a step, and she turned her head away, sobbing and calling him an indulgent mother fucker. He told her that she was rotten spoiled and that she had no identity of her own and that she had bored the shit out of him for the past five years. She told him that was all right with her because she had been balling Bert for the last two years. They walked on in sullen silence. We passed two men standing in front of the ruins of a large shopping center. They wore pistols and fatigue hats and were eating apples. One of them called out to the guard leading us·

Quake

"They're drifting in from the east now. They crossed over La Brea and are dug in near Sierra Bonita. Watch out for helicopters. They got a few of their own. God knows who's supplying them. It might be that group from up in the valley. Congressman-what's-his-face?"

They threw a few apples to the guards as we passed. An old couple in front weaved in and out of the line. A guard poked them with the butt of his rifle and they stumbled and fell. They lay in each other's arms, the old man cradling his wife's head.

"You want money?" he screamed. "You pay the fucking gas bill. We got nothing. Nothing. Why us? I ain't been two blocks either way from my house in ten years. I didn't know those people. They just come in and set up their radios. You want to shoot us, go ahead. I ask you. Do me a favor. Right between the eyes."

We walked on, leaving them behind. . . .

We turned a corner and walked past small factories and warehouses. Two blocks ahead of us a group of men in fatigue hats sat near the remains of a red brick high school. A small concrete stadium stood to the right of the high school. There was a long shiver through the line and then a soft whimpering sigh. We were prodded through a gate and onto a football field. The afternoon sun was beginning to slide towards the smoke filled horizon and hazy shadows streaked across the field. Perhaps it was Saturday. I remembered it was fall. More than fifty naked men and women sat on the field. Some were wounded and dying. A deep crevice ran in a jagged line across the center of the field. The stands faced us on the west, with smoke rising up behind them. The seats were thirty rows deep and sections had fallen in at both ends but the center sections were still intact. Guards sat and slept in the stands and stood in groups around the south end of the field. The goal posts on the south side were still standing. I sat down on the forty-five yard line and faced them. I only existed. And yet I still had the evening and night and what lay beyond to get through. My eyes recorded what was in front of me but only as a reflex, a habit that no longer mattered. A few men and women wandered among the prisoners, looking for relatives or someone they recognized. But there were no recognitions, no news, no information. I had lost sight of the girl. I walked towards the eastern side of the field, looking for her. I stepped over the sideline but was waved back by a guard. We had been restricted to the field. I walked along the northern side of the crevice. It was two feet across at its widest and seemed to have no bottom. The girl was not around. I walked towards the middle of the field looking for a place where I could jump across. A few bodies had fallen into the crevice or lay at the edge. Most of them were dead although a few hung about as if wanting to make the plunge. The crevice narrowed and I stepped across. A hand reached up for me but I danced away like a broken field runner. Then my ankle gave out and I tripped. I lay on my stomach, barely able to breathe. Two men lay beside me, their eyes open, their cheeks pressed to the grass. We looked at each other.

"I thought you was O. J. Simpson," said one of the faces. It was a thin face with loose upper dentures and black swollen eyes. "Comin on down, then swivel hipping side steps and falling for extra yardage. You're a player, all right. I'll bet you could make it to the crack if you was to give it half a try."

"What about Jim Brown?" the other face said. Blood trickled out the side of his mouth and his long blond hair was matted with dirt and oil. "Jim Brown was a tank. He'd drag two people with him up to that crack. He didn't bother jiving and juking with the hips. He just rolled. Three steps would get him into that crack."

"That dates you," said the other. "They got new

Quake

kinds of runners now. It's a new day now. Them that do 9.3 in the hundred and like to weigh over two twenty. These boys are the New Breed, you know what I mean. Corn fed and they got good medical care and nothing to overcome. Everyone's an All-American now. Hell, hundreds of em could make it into that crack and drag their tacklers along with em."

The man with the loose upper dentures squinted at me. "You trying to make it into the crack or are you running away from the crack?"

"I don't belong to any team," I said.

"A lot of people have slipped into that crack." He rolled over on his back. "I'm coming away from it myself. First two hours I was here you couldn't keep me away from it. I was very close to dropping in."

I stood up and stepped over him. He grabbed my ankle and gave it a twist and I kicked him in the face. We struggled silently and then I managed to slip away. I limped towards the goal posts, resting on the ten yard line. . . .

Three men sat with their backs to me, facing the crevice. They were talking slowly, with great effort.

"Tell you one thing more . . . this ain't just an earthquake. . . . More is at stake here. Whole state like this. Mobs. Looting. Maybe the whole country. They've set off the worst. Inhuman things. . . ."

"I don't want to be around. I'll tell you that. I ain't scared of dying now. I knew this would happen. Never did anything. Never prepared. Never could think about it."

"When I find the son-of-a-bitch that's responsible for marching me off like a convict, I'll kill him . . . I'll . . . have . . . his . . . ass. I'm no threat. . . . I was standing on my lawn watching the fire across the street. I'm gonna do more than press charges. . . ."

"They got no call . . . to hold us. . . . They haven't said what we done. Go on up and ask one of those guys with a ribbon in his hat. . . . Both my legs are broke. . . ."

"They don't listen."

I crawled past them. Some of the guards had started a fire on the western side of the field and were cooking steaks and lambchops. I crawled past the thirty and up to the thirty-five yard line. Prisoners were walking numbly towards the food, standing near the sidelines and staring at the smoking meat. The girl sat near the crevice. She was slowly bowing her head over and over again, as if she was throwing up. She looked at me without recognition.

"I met some nice people," she said.

She looked past me and smiled. I sat with her and together we stared into the crevice.

"What do you think is down there?" she asked.

"Nothing," I said.

"Oh, I think there's a lot down there. I think there's more than you know down there."

"No one knows," I said. "Why should you know? You don't have to know. You don't even have to know what's going to happen."

"I have to know," she said.

A man crawled towards the crevice. He was old and fat and his belly hung underneath him like a balloon full of water. When he reached the edge of the crevice he stopped, folding his hands underneath his head and shutting his eyes.

"Are you going to crawl in?" the girl asked.

The man didn't answer. He opened his eyes and looked sadly at her as she crawled up to the edge. I grabbed her ankle but she shrugged me off. She sat on the edge and swung her legs over. I sat beside her, swinging my own legs over but grabbing on to the grass.

"What if we're pushed from behind?" she said. "They've been pushing people in, you know. I dare you not to look back."

Quake

I didn't look back. She looked back and then giggled.

"I don't think it's so deep," she said. "Not more than a mile."

"Why don't you shut up?" said the man across the crevice.

"I'm sorry," the girl said. "I really think I'm sorry. Are you going to jump in?"

He looked at us and dangled his short legs over the edge.

"I might take a jump or I might not," he said. "I'm not even sure I'm thinking about it."

"I think you ought to jump," I said. "You're just jerking yourself off like this."

"Yeah," he said. "I don't know whether I'm a jumper or not. Ask me two days ago and I'm not a jumper. I got to think on it now."

He looked off towards the sidelines, banging his heels against the side of the crevice. The guards held the steaks and lambchops in their hands and ripped the meat apart with their teeth. Occasionally one of the guards would throw a bone to the prisoners and they would dive and fight for it. The field was becoming agitated. There was more noise and movement among the prisoners and the guards had begun to drink heavily. Three men and a woman left the sidelines and walked to the crevice. The woman and two of the men sat down on the side I was sitting on. They sat far apart, their legs over the edge and their eyes staring off across the field. The other man jumped over the crevice, jumped back again and then hopped over to the far side. He sat down, with his legs over the edge. I recognized him as the man with the black cowboy boots who had spent some time walking beside the girl. He waved at her and she smiled at him.

"I don't need that meat," he said. "It's weird how they're getting hungry over there. Couldn't eat right now. Nossir. I'd throw it all up." He spoke more to himself than to her and it was hard to hear his voice. The girl swayed forward and then sideways and ran her tongue over her lips.

"Well I'm hungry," the fat man said. "I don't remember the last time I ate. I don't remember anything. I can barely remember what kind of a job I had, who my wife was, what sports my kids played, where the fuck I even used to live. You're goddamn right I'm hungry. They should throw us something. That's what this country is all about, putting stuff into you. They deny you that and you know the worst has happened. There's food lying all over the streets. We could have one of the great meals of all time."

One of the other men began to cry. Finally he stood up and walked away, towards the goal posts. The shadows had reached the other side of the field and the sun was hidden behind clouds of smoke. There were screams and shouts as the guards tossed more bones and scraps of meat onto the field.

"I'm from West Virginia," the fat man said. His eyes were locked onto the cooking meat. "They've got beer over there now. And potato chips. I don't believe this. It's a regular cook out. We got about ten seconds left and they're barbecuing the shit out of everything. I can't stand it. I'm from Wheeling, near the Ohio line."

He stood up and walked towards the sidelines. The man with the black cowboy boots lowered himself into the crevice and disappeared. The fat man walked back and forth from the forty-five to the thirty yard line. Once he fell forward in a scramble for a bone but he was too slow. All of the guards were gathered on the side of the field now except for three men with red and green ribbons on their fatigue hats who sat in the stands. The fat man stepped across the line and grabbed a lambchop from the improvised grill. He ran back into the center of the field, stuffing it into his mouth with both hands.

Two more men rushed the grill and grabbed steaks. The crowd suddenly spilled across the line. A guard shot a man through the head with his pistol. The girl and I stood up and tried to run towards the goal posts. People fell near us. She stumbled and fell and I knelt by her as a black ran by with a gun, firing into the stands. There were answering shots and he was hit in the stomach and head. He fell backwards, landing in the girl's lap. She rocked him back and forth.

"You're dying," she said to him. "I can tell because all the blood is pouring out of you and I don't know how to turn off the faucet."

I placed him on the ground.

"I've met some very nice people today," she said. "And others not so nice."

A few of the prisoners had made their way to the stands and managed to find weapons. Two men were shot very quickly in front of us. Three prisoners forgot about the crevice and fell in as they ran across the field. A man and a woman crawled by.

"We have nothing to lose," said the man.

"Lie here," the woman said. "Pretend we're dead."

"We're already dead," the man said. He raised her up and together they staggered across the field, flailing their arms and shouting. A woman slid across the grass and touched the girl's hand. She shrank back but the woman reached out again for her and the girl held her hand. The woman was bleeding badly from the shoulder and neck.

"Take my ring," the woman said to the girl. She tried to pull a diamond ring off her finger but she wasn't strong enough. The girl pulled it off for her and slipped it over her own finger.

"Tell Harry Stralinger that I didn't make it," the woman said. "He lives on 302 Cuesta Way. Tell him that he can go to all the Holiday Inns he wants to and that I would have gone to Acapulco with him, only not on that weekend that Robert was around. He wouldn't have survived against Robert."

She died on the grass in front of us. I raised my hand to stop the girl from standing up and a bullet went through my palm. The girl smiled.

"You won't be able to wave to me now," she said. "You'll have to use your other hand. But maybe you're left handed anyway."

She walked towards the center of the field. I sat up and watched her cross the forty yard line. A bullet smacked into her shoulder and she spun and fell. I crawled forward and lay down beside her. She groaned but kept her eyes closed.

"I'm always pulling bodies off you," I said.

"You can shoot me," she said. "That's what you've wanted to do all along."

"We'll be all right if we don't move," I said.

"I'm not moving. You're the one who's moving. You don't have to keep following me around."

I tried to stop her wound but there was nothing around that would serve as a bandage.

"I can't get my eyes open," she said. "Say something to me. How do I know you haven't crawled off?"

"It's a relief to know I'm not as bad off as you," I said.

"Say something else," she said.

I opened up my mouth. "Ooooooooooooooo," came out.

"Oh no," she said. I could barely hear her. "No, don't do that. You're putting me on. That's like the night. Be something else."

I couldn't speak. The pain in my hand was causing me to forget where I was.

"I know. I know," she said. "But hold me anyway."

I rolled over on her, covering her with my stomach, my arms and legs. My limp cock was pressed between her thighs, my bloody hand reached down to her waist. I held her and the blood gurgled up between her clenched teeth. There were pistol shots on the far side of the field as guards walked among the wounded and shot them through the head. I held her tighter, afraid that she would cry out. I even thought of strangling her, except that she was still whispering to me, pleading to be held, to be pressed into the earth. . . .

CHIAROSCURO:
a treatment of
light & shade

Ursule Molinaro

for Rudi

She first noticed the bump on Sunday morning. Her first Sunday in the art critic's elaborate downtown apartment. 3 days after she'd moved in with him.

On a Thursday, when she always did things; when things always seemed to happen in her life. When she'd finally let the art critic convince her to move out of her parents' house & in with him. After convincing her that living with one's parents was living with one's past, when one was past 20.

She'd been brushing her teeth when something made her look up. & she saw it in the still unfamiliar elaborate bathroom mirror: a pale oblong swelling in the middle of her forehead. Slightly above the eyebrows.

It made her think of the young horns of deer. Which she'd watched rub their lowered heads against the pine trunks on her grandparents' country place, during vacations.

For whom her grandfather used to put out glittering bricks of red salt.

Chiaroscuro: a treatment of light & shade

The bump wasn't red. & it wasn't shaped like a sprouting deer horn. More like a small-bird's egg, laid horizontally between   slightly above   her eyebrows.

It didn't hurt when she touched it. Nor when she rubbed it, after it began to itch.

She decided to cover it with bangs, to hide it from the art critic. Who would be easier to deceive than her parents.

From whom she'd tried to hide years of bruised vacation knees & school-winter earaches. & post-pubescent monthly migraines. Until a forgetful limp or pang of pain betrayed her to their two-fold vigilance.

Her mother had been a registered nurse before she'd married. & was forever on the lookout for symptoms, to justify using her dormant skills. Stripping off her numerous rings to plunge into avid first-aid, with the same joyful anticipation with which she plunged into the bra boxes during a sale at Saks.

& her father enjoyed diagnosing whatever malfunction his daughter's forgetful body had betrayed, in a way he could not afford to diagnose his patients' afflictions: as self-inflicted. The body's translation of a self-dissatisfied   usually idle   mind. That felt bored. With being healthily anonymous. & tried to cop out. From an art class   gym   a math exam. & was punishing itself for being bored/lazy. For not being more popular/beautiful. Etc.

Amply illustrated with examples from Greek mythology.

Before he'd administer a usually unpleasant medication. A usually intentionally unpleasant medication, intended to discourage his daughter from self-inflicted cop-out relapses. Encouraging her usually to try to hide future symptoms better longer.

. . . She was practiced at the art of deception: she hummed, separating front strands of wetted hair.

Which was shoulder-long & very thick. Crunchily satisfying to cut into.

Her parents had always insisted that she comb it straight back   away from her face   out of her eyes. Which were a deep-set deep brown. & very small. & gave the   false   impression of nearsightedness.

The art critic's elaborate bathroom mirror fleetingly reflected the carefully forgotten face of a boy who'd called her 'Pig Eyes' during an art class, in high school.

She blanketed it with a strand of wetted hair still to be cut. & wondered what the art critic would think of her bangs.

& quickly put her hand over the bump. & turned rashly at the sight of his Sagittarian centaur face smiling over the top of her head in the mirror. & wondered resentfully how he'd managed to come in when she was positive she'd locked the door. If he had perhaps some kind of PlayBuggs' gadget that opened bachelor bathroom doors from the outside after they'd been locked from the inside, permitting him to walk in on his lady visitors.

& wondered if the art critic had convinced   how many   other girls to move in with him before he convinced her. If he had perhaps failed to convince all the other girls before convincing her . . .

But the door had stayed locked. & no one had come in. She was safely alone. & hallucinating, in the elaborate bathroom mirror.

Feeling giddy with filial disobedience: she thought. Still . . . at her age . . .

The art critic would like her bangs: she assured her giddily fringed new face. Like her better with bangs, after she told him that her parents considered a hair-hidden forehead an advertisement for loose morals. The shingle of freelance prostitutes & pimps. He'd think perhaps rightly so   that living with him was beginning to free her.

Chiaroscuro: a treatment of light & shade

She'd mime the instant Sunday breakfast drama for him which her disobedient bangs would have provoked at home. If she were still living at home: she thought.

She had a vision of her mother's ring-stripped hands reaching across the Sunday breakfast table. Across 4 carefully separated stacks of Sunday papers:

The stack which had been read by her father, but not yet by her mother. The stack which had been read by her mother, but not yet by her father. The stack which had not yet been read by either. & the stack which had been read by both. On top of which sat her mother's fat black & white cat. Formally erect, on top of the breakfast table.

Across all of which her mother's reaching ring-stripped hands were brushing the bangs to either side of her forehead. With proprietary disregard for her over 20, almost 21-year-old daughter's bodily privacy & right to self-determination.

Her mother's eager outcry, as her brushing hands found & exposed the bump.

Her avid question: Where she'd been? What kind of place had she moved into, down town, to be coming home with a bedbug bite that size?

& her father's gently joyful contra-diagnosis: That the swelling was too big for a bedbug. A spider-bite, more likely. Perhaps a poisonous spider. The classical Erinys. Which their daughter had gone way out of her way to attract to the center of her forehead. Because she felt guilty because she had left home. To punish herself for feeling guilty because she'd left home. Everything every imaginable human relationship & subsequent emotion had been covered by the Greeks in their mythology . . .

Her mother's and father's combined Sunday thumbs & index fingers, feeling her re-exposed forehead above below around the bump. Pressing down on it . . .

She would go to see them as soon as the bump

79

cleared up: she thought. Pressing half-dry bangs into place. Evaluating their side-effect in the art critic's still more elaborate hand mirror. Of 18th century silver.

In which she didn't look as huge & homely as she usually looked to herself. In the familiar   strictly functional   bathroom mirror at home. In her parents' house.

Which was perhaps the effect of the bangs.

Unless the art critic's mirrors were elaborately flattering. Intentionally so, like most of the things he said & did; & owned. To boost his   & his visitors'   morning ego.

She didn't remember feeling so good since before she'd started school. When she'd tried to go on a vinegar and mustard diet, in first grade, after somebody told her that the Chinese fed vinegar and mustard to their dogs, to keep them tiny.

The art critic was standing on his head, in his living room, his heels propped against the wall between the 2 elaborately draped windows. Clad in the custom-knitted purple-&-black-striped jump suit in which he stood on his head every morning, before breakfast, to keep his hair from falling out.

Any further . . . : she thought. Smiling to herself as she tiptoed past his inverted blood-rushed centaur face. To the window to his left. & slipped behind the floor-long drapes. & looked down into the sunny Sunday street.

At a small blue truck that had been parked down there the morning before. & the morning before that. Friday morning. Her first morning in the apartment. When she'd first seen the pouchy little grey-haired man play the fiddle, in his truck, on a folding chair, beside the steering wheel.

When she'd first read the window sign on the third

floor, directly across from her, that WANTED LAP-SEAM FOLDERS, male or female.

While she waited for the art critic to finish standing on his head. For his long well-groomed hands   with a well-defined half-moon at the base of each long well-groomed fingernail   to reach through the slightly parted drapes & draw her back into the living room.

& notice her bangs.

On which he complimented her   on her new liberated self   when he noticed them when they sat down for breakfast at the oval Biedermeier living room table. & laughed heartily, when she mimed her parents' unanimous disapproval for him.

Which prompted a discourse on the fashion-swayed concepts of beauty & ugliness. On which he elaborated all through breakfast.

On the sophisticated beauty of a certain kind of ugliness   a sensuous kind of ugliness   in art as well as in life. That was *not* subject to fashion.

By which he did not mean the ugliness of chicken-chinned chicks. & chicken-legged old ladies with a youthful cackle. Whose ugliness was not subject to fashion either. Who were   incidentally   often surprisingly promiscuous. Often found surprisingly good-looking partners to be promiscuous with. In whose good-looking faces they stared as though they were mirrors.

Who were   incidentally   quite often surprisingly good lays. Which their often good-looking partners were often not.

The frigid ugliness of certain beautiful people. Male as well as female. Who had stifled what sensuality they might have had to begin life with, for fear of ruffling their beauty.

The warm-glowing beauty of sensuality.

Which it took an older person to appreciate. An

81

older man to bring out, in a young girl. To surface her
dormant desirability. To have the patience it took to
peel away the layers of self-critical impression-making.
Making her feel more desirable, & less unique . .

& quite impatient. Waiting for him to finish eating
his second soft-boiled egg.

Looking at him across the oval table she had the
strange impression that she was looking at another face,
behind his 40-some-year-old centaur face. With longer,
less firm cheeks. & a higher forehead. At a loose-lipped
mouth, puckering toward the spoon in a liver-spotted
hand. Which trembled slightly, spilling a drool of yolk.

Which flooded her heart with an astonished tenderness.

For the fear, in the other   older   face behind
his face. A fear of loneliness. Of shabbily aging   alone
in the elaborate apartment. With no young girl to
convince of her dormant desirability.

She wanted to hold his face. To hold her face close
to his, like a mirror of youth. To shield it   with her
new liberated face   from the fearfully aging one behind it.

To make love to him. Again. On the elaborate living room carpet. On which they'd made love the morning before. & the morning before that; Friday morning;
her first morning in his apartment. After breakfast, when
he preferred to make love.

Which was another reason why he had wanted her
to move in with him. To be able to make love to her in
the morning, after breakfast.

Before he disappeared behind the closed door of his
Second-Empire bedroom, for the remainder of the day,
until dinner time, to continue writing 'Portraits of
Anonymous Geniuses.' On which he'd been writing for

several years. When he wasn't writing art criticisms. In his Second-Empire bed.

He had finished eating the second soft-boiled egg. & smiled at her across the oval table. & walked around it. & stood behind her chair. & drew the collar of her sweater away from her neck, in the front. & smiled down into the opening. Complimenting her on her no-longer-dormant sensuality, when her nipples stood up, in anticipation of his touch. & kissed her on her bangs. & pulled her head backward, by her thick shoulder-long hair.   Which was her best feature. & a sure measure of a woman's sensuality-potential.   & tilted her chair way back. Bending over her to kiss her upturned face. Smiling down at her.

& abruptly let go of the chair. Jolting her forward, against the table. & clamped one of his long well-groomed hands over the middle of her forehead. Bluntly; one long well-groomed half-mooned fingernail digging into the skin beside the bump.

Which must have shown through her bangs. When the bangs fell backward, when he tilted her chair.

She glanced up at his bluntly clamping hand. Sideways. Into his set disgusted face. & into the set disgusted fearfully aging other face that was still behind it. With hard staring eyes.

She pried his hand loose from the bump. & replaced it with one of her own. & wriggled out from between her chair & the table. & walked out of the living room, as casually as she could, with one hand on her forehead.

& locked herself into the bathroom, to look at the bump.

& gasped, when a large luminously blue eye opened   in the elaborate mirror   in the middle of her forehead. Slightly above the eyebrows. Where the bump had been. & tenderly smiled at her.

It was the most beautiful eye she'd ever seen: she

thought. Smiling back at it. Making it close & open. Close and open. & blink. & wink. Her heart drowning in a second flood of astonished tenderness.

For her parents. Still sitting at their Sunday breakfast table. Without her. Peering out from behind Sunday-paper screens to exchange misgivings about her moving out. & in with the art critic.

In whose elaborately lonely down town apartment she could not stay, now.

Nor could she move back in with her parents.

Who would continue to breakfast without her & dine without her. & to diagnose self-inflicted afflictions. & to go shopping for bras. & pretend that everything they did was essential. That life   at least their 2 paper-screened Sunday lives   had a purpose.

Which her absence made easier to believe. Relieving their make-belief of the witness. & judge. Of the childishly judging third person that turned a couple into a crowd.

A lonely crowd of 3. Cheating on solitude by living alone together.

Each assuring the other 2   often with irritated intensity   of his/her/their indispensability.

Convincing themselves   & each other   & hopefully a number of extraneous others   that they had fulfilled/or were fulfilling their purpose in life. By marrying/or making love. & procreating. & pursuing/or studying for a career.

& by worrying about each other. & an occasional extraneous other. Which they called: loving. Each other & the occasional extraneous others. But not themselves. Which they called: narcissism; selfishness.

Calculating the worry-coefficient of each about the other & occasional others. In order to determine whether the other & others worried sufficiently in return.

Reassuring themselves and each other   often

Chiaroscuro: a treatment of light & shade

with intense irritation; an occasional hiccough or pride
that they had done/or were doing their best.

Which was considerably better than the best of
most others. & not so easy as it might look   to certain
envious others   considering most others' chronic lack
of cooperation.

Playing for themselves & each other   & for the
greatest possible number of others   roles which they
expected most others to expect them to play. Which they
expected the greatest possible number of others to
applaud.

For which they rehearsed in front of kaleidoscopic
paper-mirrors:

The registered mother . . . the loving nurse . . . the
wedded siren.

The cunningly mythological doctor-husband-father.
Who told bed-time stories about the emulatable Ulysses
. . . that ingenious survivalist whose legendary mind
outfoxed all matter . . .

To the lonely only pig-eyed daughter. Who saw better than she looked. Had inherited her father's legendary intelligence rather than her mother's legendary
beauty.

Who re-invented   or added to   pubescently
stupid high school jokes for which her legendarily inherited colossal intelligence felt nothing but contempt.

Like: You are well come . . .

Everybody was feeling Mary, so Mary left, so they
jumped for Joy . . .

The Purple Torrent, by Hyman Schlitz; a book-of-
the-month selection . . .

2 nuns in a European railroad carriage. Seated
across from a man who is traveling with a kitten. Which
is strictly forbidden, on European railroads. Who is
therefore   traveling with the kitten inside his pants.

Which still   or again   have buttons rather

than a zipper.   The kitten is getting restless &
reaches out through the man's fly, trying to escape. & one
nun says to the other: 'Sister, aren't you glad we took
the veil before those things grew claws'. . .

With which to purchase pig-eye indulgences from
normal-size classmates who looked better than they saw.
For whom she felt nothing but contempt.

Who contracted a severe hatred for the ingeniously
surviving Ulysses   whom Circe should have turned
into the pig he was, rather than his pig-companions
during a bedtime-story blinding of the Cyclops.

A hatred she later extended to James Joyce. In spite
of his eye trouble. When she started reading Joyce, during her first year at Columbia.

After having extended it   much much earlier;
still in grade school   to her colossally intelligent pig-
eyed self.

At which the beautiful eye smiled luminous tender-
blue forgiveness. For her colossally presumptuous intelligence.

Before it shed one limpid-blue tear.

Apprehending the 2 band-aids which she was going
to put over it. Crosswise, over its closing lid. Before she
combed the bangs over it.

Before she ventured out of the bathroom.

& tiptoed through the living room. Past the half-
turned back of the art critic. Who had sunk into her
chair, at the oval Biedermeier table. & was holding both
hands over his face; both elbows in her dirty breakfast
plate.

Before she opened & closed the door of his apartment.

Before her father's legendarily cunning hands performed their first plastic surgery. In his empty Sunday-
evening office. With the once-registered assistance of her
mother.

Chiaroscuro: a treatment of light & shade

Which left only a 1¼-inch-long scar in the middle of her forehead. Slightly above   between   the eyebrows. Like a thin, barely perceptible frown.

She hardly had any recollection of the long bus ride up town. Except for a balding man with long flabby cheeks & a hearing aid. Who'd sat yawning in the back. Whose yawns had sounded like the roars of a beast in a zoo.

NEO-GOTHIC

BY THE RIVER

Joyce Carol Oates

Helen thought: "Am I in love again, some new kind of love? Is that why I'm here?"

She was sitting in the waiting room of the Yellow Bus Lines station; she knew the big old room with its dirty tile floor and its solitary telephone booth in the corner and its candy machine and cigarette machine and popcorn machine by heart. Everything was familiar, though she had been gone for five months, even the old woman with the dyed red hair who sold tickets and had been selling them there, behind that counter, for as long as Helen could remember. Years ago, before Helen's marriage, she and her girl friends would be driven into town by someone's father and after they tired of walking around town they would stroll over to the bus station to watch the buses unload. They were anxious to see who was getting off, but few of the passengers who got off stayed in Oriskany—they were just passing through, stopping for a rest and a drink, and their faces seemed to say that they didn't think much of the town. Nor did they seem to think much of the girls from the country who stood around in their colorful dresses and smiled shyly at strangers, not knowing any better: they were taught to be kind to people, to smile first, you never knew who it might be. So now Helen was back in Oriskany, but this time she had come in on a bus herself. Had ridden alone, all the way from the city of Derby, all alone, and was waiting for her father to pick her up so she could go back to her old life without any more fuss.

It was hot. Flies crawled languidly around; a woman with a small sickly-faced baby had to keep waving them away. The old woman selling tickets looked at Helen as if her eyes were drawn irresistibly that way, as if she knew every nasty rumor and wanted to let Helen know that she knew. Helen's forehead broke out in perspiration and she stood, abruptly, wanting to dislodge that old woman's stare. She went over to the candy machine but did not look at the candy bars; she looked at herself in the mirror. Her own reflection always made her feel better. Whatever went on inside her head—and right now she felt nervous about something—had nothing to do with the way she looked, her smooth gentle skin and the faint freckles on her forehead and nose and the cool, innocent green of her eyes; she was just a girl from the country and anyone in town would know that, even if they didn't know her personally, one of those easy, friendly girls who hummed to themselves and seemed always to be glancing up as if expecting something pleasant, some deliberate surprise. Her light brown hair curled back lazily toward her ears, cut short now because it was the style; in high school she had worn it long. She watched her eyes in the mirror. No alarm there, really. She would be back home in an hour or so. Not her husband's home, of course, but her parents' home. And her face in the mirror was the face she had always seen—twenty-two she was now, and to her that seemed very old, but she looked no different from the way she had looked on her wedding day five years ago.

But it was stupid to try to link together those two Helens, she thought. She went back to the row of seats and sat heavily. If the old woman was still watching, she did not care. A sailor in a soiled white uniform sat nearby, smoking, watching her but not with too much interest; he had other girls to recall. Helen opened her purse and looked inside at nothing and closed it again. The man she had been living with in the city for five months had told her it was stupid—no, he had not used that word; he said something fancy like "immature"—to confuse herself with the child she had been, married woman as she was now, and a mother, an adulterous married woman. . . . And the word *adulterous* made her lips turn up in a slow bemused smile, the first flash of incredulous pride one might feel when told at last the disease that is going to be fatal. For there were so many diseases and only one way out of the world, only one death and so many ways to get to it. They were like doors, Helen thought dreamily. You walked down a hallway like those in movies, in huge wealthy homes, crystal chandeliers and marble floors and . . . great sweepings lawns . . . and doors all along those hallways; if you picked the wrong door you had to go through it. She was dreamy, drowsy. When thought became too much for her —when he had pestered her so much about marrying him, divorcing her husband and marrying him, always him!—she had felt so sleepy she could not listen. If she was not interested in a word her mind wouldn't hear it but made it blurred and strange, like words half heard in dreams or through some thick substance. You didn't have to hear a word if you didn't want to.

So she had telephoned her father the night before and told him the 3:15 bus and now it was 3:30; where was he? Over the telephone he had sounded slow and solemn, it could have been a stranger's voice. Helen had never liked telephones because you could not see smiles or gestures and talking like that made her tired. Listening to her father, she had felt for the first time since she had run away and left them all behind—husband, baby girl, family, in-laws, the minister, the dreary sun-bleached look of the land—that she had perhaps died and only imagined she was running away. Nobody here trusted the city; it was too big. Helen had wanted to go there all her life, not being afraid of anything, and so she had gone, and was coming back; but it was an odd feeling, this dreamy ghostliness, as if she were really dead and coming back in a form that only looked like herself. . . . She was bored, thinking of this, and crossed her bare legs. The sailor crushed out a cigarette in the dirty tin ashtray and their eyes met. Helen felt a little smile tug at her lips. That was the trouble, she knew men too well. She knew their eyes and their gestures—like the sailor rubbing thoughtfully at his chin now, as if he hadn't shaved well enough but really liked to feel his own skin. She knew them too well and had never figured out why: her sister, four years older, wasn't like that. But to Helen the same man one hundred times or one hundred men, different men, seemed the same. It was wrong, of course, because she had been taught it and believed what she had been taught; but she could not understand the difference. The sailor watched her but she looked away, half closing her eyes. She had no time for him. Her father should be here now, he would be here in a few minutes, so there was no time; she would be home in an hour. When she thought of her father, the ugly bus station with its odor of tobacco and spilled soft drinks seemed to fade away—she remembered his voice the night before, how gentle and soft she had felt listening to that voice, giving in to the protection he represented. She had endured his rough hands, as a child, because she knew they protected her, and all her life they had protected her. There had always been trouble, sometimes the kind you laughed about later and sometimes not; that was one of the reasons she had married John, and before John there had been others—just boys who didn't count, who had no jobs and thought mainly about their cars. Once, when she was fifteen, she had called her father from a roadhouse sixty miles away; she and her best friend Annie had gotten mixed up with some men they had met at a picnic. That had been frightening, Helen thought, but now she could have handled them. She gave everyone too much, that was her trouble. Her father had said that. Even her mother. Lent money to girls at the telephone company where she'd worked; lent her girl friends clothes; would run outside when some man drove up and blew his horn, not bothering to get out and knock at the door the way he should. She liked to make other people happy, what was wrong with that? Was she too lazy to care? Her head had begun to ache.

Always her thoughts ran one way, fast and innocent, but her body did other things. It got warm, nervous, it could not relax. Was she afraid of what her father's face would tell her? She pushed that idea away, it was nonsense. If she had to think of something, let it be of that muddy spring day when her family had first moved to this part of the country, into an old farmhouse her father had bought at a "bargain." At that time the road out in front of the house had been no more than a single dirt lane . . . now it was wider, covered with blacktop that smelled ugly and made your eyes shimmer and water with confusion in the summer. Yes, that big old house. Nothing about it would have changed. She did not think of her own house, her husband's house, because it mixed her up too much right now. Maybe she would go back and maybe not. She did not think of him—if she wanted to go back she would, he would take her in. When she tried to think of what had brought her back, it was never her husband—so much younger, quicker, happier than the man she had just left—and not the little girl, either, but something to do with her family's house and that misty, warm day seventeen years ago when they had first moved in. So one morning when that man left for work her thoughts had turned back to home and she had sat at the breakfast table for an hour or so, not clearing off the dishes, looking at the coffee left in his cup as if it were a forlorn reminder of him—a man she was even then beginning to forget. She knew then that she did not belong there in the city. It wasn't that she had stopped loving this man —she never stopped loving anyone who needed her, and he had needed her more than anyone—it was something else, something she did not understand. Not her husband, not her baby, not even the look of the river way off down the hill, through the trees that got so solemn and intricate with their bare branches in winter. Those things she loved, she hadn't stopped loving them because she had had to love this new man more . . . but something else made her get up and run into the next room and look through the bureau drawers and the closet, as if looking for something. That evening, when he returned, she explained to him that she was going back. He was over forty, she wasn't sure how much, and it had always been his hesitant, apologetic manner that made her love him, the odor of failure about him that mixed with the odor of the drinking he could not stop, even though he had "cut down" now with her help. Why were so many men afraid, why did they think so much? He did something that had to do with keeping books, was that nervous work? He was an attractive man but that wasn't what Helen had seen in him. It was his staring at her when they had first met, and the way he had run his hand through his thinning hair, telling her in that gesture that he wanted her and wanted to be young enough to tell her so. That had been five months ago.

By the River

The months all rushed to Helen's mind in the memory she had of his keen intelligent baffled eyes, and the tears she had had to see in them when she went out to call her father. . . .

Now, back in Oriskany, she would think of him no more.

A few minutes later her father came. Was that really him? she thought. Her heart beat furiously. If blood drained out of her face she would look mottled and sick, as if she had a rash . . . how she hated that! Though he had seen her at once, though the bus station was nearly empty, her father hesitated until she stood and ran to him. "Pa," she said, "I'm so glad to see you." It might have been years ago and he was just going to drive back home now, finished with his business in town, and Helen fourteen or fifteen, waiting to go back with him.

"I'll get your suitcase," he said. The sailor was reading a magazine, no longer interested. Helen watched her father nervously. What was wrong? He stooped, taking hold of the suitcase handle, but he did not straighten fast enough. Just a heartbeat too slow. Why was that? Helen took a tissue already stained with lipstick and dabbed it on her forehead.

On the way home he drove oddly, as if the steering wheel, heated by the sun, were too painful for him to hold. "No more trouble with the car, huh?" Helen said.

"It's all right," he said. They were nearly out of town already. Helen saw few people she knew. "Why are you looking around?" her father said. His voice was pleasant and his eyes fastened seriously upon the road, as if he did not dare look elsewhere.

"Oh, just looking," Helen said. "How is Davey?"

Waiting for her father to answer—he always took his time—Helen arranged her skirt nervously beneath her. Davey was her sister's baby, could he be sick? She had forgotten to ask about him the night before. "Nothing's wrong with Davey, is there, Pa?" she said.

"No, nothing."

"I though Ma might come, maybe," Helen said.

"No."

"Didn't she want to? Mad at me, huh?"

In the past her mother's dissatisfaction with her had always ranged Helen and her father together; Helen could tell by a glance of her father's when this was so. But he did not look away from the road. They were passing the new high school, the consolidated high school Helen had attended for a year. No one had known what "consolidated" meant or was interested in knowing. Helen frowned at the dark brick and there came to her mind, out of nowhere, the word *adulterous*, for it too had been a word she had not understood for years. A word out of the Bible. It was like a mosquito bothering her at night, or a stain on her dress—the kind she would have to hide without seeming to, letting her hand fall over it accidentally. For some reason the peculiar smell of the old car, the rattling sunshades above the windshield, the same old khaki blanket they used for a seat cover did not comfort her and let her mind get drowsy, to push that word away.

She was not sleepy, but she said she was.

"Yes, honey. Why don't you lay back and try to sleep, then," her father said.

He glanced toward her. She felt relieved at once, made simple and safe. She slid over and leaned her head against her father's shoulder. "Bus ride was long, I hate bus rides," she said. "I used to like them."

"You can sleep till we get home."

"Is Ma mad?"

"No."

His shoulder wasn't as comfortable as it should have been. But she closed her eyes, trying to force sleep. She remembered that April day they had come here—their moving to the house that was new to them, a house of their own they would have to share with no one else, but a house it turned out had things wrong with it, secret things, that had made Helen's father furious. She could not remember the city and the house they had lived in there, but she had been old enough to sense the simplicity of the country and the eagerness of her parents, and then the angry perplexity that had followed. The family was big—six children then, before Arthur died at ten—and half an hour after they had moved in, the house was crowded and shabby. And she remembered being frightened at something and her father picking her up right in the middle of moving, and not asking her why she cried—her mother had always asked her that, as if there were a reason—but rocked her and comforted her with his rough hands. And she could remember how the house had looked so well: the ballooning curtains in the windows, the first things her mother had put up. The gusty spring air, already too warm, smelling of good earth and the Eden River not too far behind them, and leaves, sunlight, wind; and the sagging porch piled with cartons and bundles and pieces of furniture from the old house. The grandparents—her mother's parents—had died in that old dark house in the city, and Helen did not remember them at all except as her father summoned them back, recalling with hatred his wife's father—some little confused argument they had had years ago that he should have won. That old man had died and the house had gone to the bank, somewhere mysterious, and her father had brought them all out here to the country. A new world, a new life. A farm. And four boys to help, and the promise of such good soil. . . .

Her father turned the wheel sharply. "Rabbit run acrost," he said. He had this strange air of apology for whatever he did, even if it was something gentle; he hated to kill animals, even weasels and hawks. Helen wanted to cover his right hand with hers, that thickened, dirt-creased hand that could never be made clean. But she said, stirring a little as if he had awakened her, "Then why didn't Ma want to come?"

They were taking a long, slow curve. Helen knew without looking up which curve this was, between two wheat fields that belonged to one of the old, old families, those prosperous men who drove broken-down pickup trucks and dressed no better than their own hired hands, but who had money, much money, not just in one bank but in many. "Yes, they're money people," Helen remembered her father saying, years ago, passing someone's pasture. Those ugly red cows meant nothing to Helen, but they meant something to her father. And so after her father had said that—they had been out for a drive after church—her mother got sharp and impatient and the ride was ruined. That was years ago. Helen's father had been a young man then, with a raw, waiting, untested look, with muscular arms and shoulders that needed only to be directed to their work. "They're money people," he had said, and that had ruined the ride, as if by magic. It had been as if the air itself had changed, the direction of the wind changing and easing to them from the river that was often stagnant in August and September, and not from the green land. With an effort Helen remembered that she had been thinking about her mother. Why did her mind push her into the past so often these days?—she only twenty-two (that was not old, not really) and going to begin a new life. Once she got home and took a bath and washed out the things in the suitcase, and got some rest, and took a walk down by the river as she had as a child, skipping stones across it, and sat around the round kitchen table with the old oilcloth cover to listen to their advice ("You got to grow up, now. You ain't fifteen any more"—that had been her mother, last time), then she would decide what to do. Make her decision about her husband and the baby and there would be nothing left to think about.

"Why didn't Ma come?"

"I didn't want her to," he said.

Helen swallowed, without meaning to. His shoulder was thin and hard against the side of her face. Were those same muscles still there, or had they become worn away like the soil that was sucked down into the river every year, stolen from them, so that the farm Helen's father had bought turned out to be a kind of joke on him? Or were they a different kind of muscle, hard and compressed like steel, drawn into themselves from years of resisting violence?

"How come?" Helen said.

He did not answer. She shut her eyes tight and distracting, eerie images came to her, stars exploding and shadowy figures like those in movies—she had gone to the movies all the time in the city, often taking in the first show at eleven in the morning, not because she was lonely or had nothing to do but because she liked movies. Five-twenty and he would come up the stairs, grimacing a little with the strange inexplicable pain in his chest: and there Helen would be, back from downtown, dressed up and her hair shining and her face ripe and fresh as a child's, not because she was proud of the look in his eyes but because she knew she could make that pain of his abate for a while. And so why had she left him, when he had needed her more than anyone? "Pa, is something wrong?" she said, as if the recollection of that other man's invisible pain were in some way connected with her father.

He reached down vaguely and touched her hand. She was surprised at this. The movie images vanished— those beautiful people she had wanted to believe in, as she had wanted to believe in God, and the saints in their movie-world heaven—and she opened her eyes. The sun was bright. It had been too bright all summer. Helen's mind felt sharp and nervous, as if pricked by tiny needles, but when she tried to think of what they could be no explanation came to her. She would be home soon, she would be able to rest. Tomorrow she could get in touch with John. Things could begin where they had left off—John had always loved her so much, and he had always understood her, had known what she was like. "Ma isn't sick, is she?" Helen said suddenly. "No," said her father. He released her fingers to take hold of the steering wheel again. Another curve. Off to the side, if she bothered to look, the river had swung toward them —low at this time of year, covered in places with a fine brown-green layer of scum. She did not bother to look.

"We moved out here seventeen years ago," her father said. He cleared his throat; the gesture of a man unaccustomed to speech. "You don't remember that."

"Yes, I do," Helen said. "I remember that."

"You don't, you were just a baby."

"Pa, I remember it. I remember you carrying the big rug into the house, you and Eddie. And I started to cry and you picked me up. I was such a big baby, always crying. . . . And Ma came out and chased me inside so I wouldn't bother you."

"You don't remember that," her father said. He was driving jerkily, pressing down on the gas pedal and then letting it up, as if new thoughts continually struck him. What was wrong with him? Helen had an idea she didn't like: he was older now, he was going to become an old man.

If she had been afraid of the dark, upstairs in that big old farmhouse in the room she shared with her sister, all she had had to do was to think of him. He had a way of sitting at the supper table that was so still, so silent, you knew nothing could budge him. Nothing could frighten him. So, as a child, and even now that she was grown up, it helped her to think of her father's face—those pale surprised green eyes that could be simple or cunning, depending upon the light, and the lines working themselves in deeper every year around his mouth, and the hard angle of his jaw going back to the ear, burned by the sun and then tanned by it, turned into leather, then going pale again in the winter. The sun could not burn its color deep enough into that skin that was almost as fair as Helen's. At Sunday school she and the other children had been told to think of Christ when they were afraid, but the Christ she saw on the little Bible bookmark cards and calendars was no one to protect you. That was a man who would be your cousin, maybe, some cousin you liked but saw rarely, but He looked so given over to thinking and trusting that He could not be of much help; not like her father. When he and the boys came in from the fields with the sweat drenching their clothes and their faces looking as if they were dissolving with heat, you could still see the solid flesh beneath, the skeleton that hung onto its muscles and would never get old, never die. The boys —her brothers, all older—had liked her well enough, Helen being the baby, and her sister had watched her most of the time, and her mother had liked her too—or did her mother like anyone, having been brought up by German-speaking parents who had had no time to teach her love? But it had always been her father she had run to. She had started knowing men by knowing him. She could read things in his face that taught her about the faces of other men, the slowness or quickness of their thoughts, if they were beginning to be impatient, or were pleased and didn't want to show it yet. Was it for this she had come home?—And the thought surprised her so that she sat up, because she did not understand. Was it for this she had come home? "Pa," she said, "like I told you on the telephone, I don't know why I did it. I don't know why I went. That's all right, isn't it? I mean, I'm sorry for it, isn't that enough? Did you talk to John?"

"John? Why John?"

"What?"

"You haven't asked about him until now, so why now?"

"What do you mean? He's my husband, isn't he? Did you talk to him?"

"He came over to the house almost every night for two weeks. Three weeks," he said. Helen could not understand the queer chatty tone of his voice. "Then off and on, all the time. No, I didn't tell him you were coming."

"But why not?" Helen laughed nervously. "Don't you like him?"

"You know I like him. You know that. But if I told him he'd of gone down to get you, not me."

"Not if I said it was you I wanted. . . ."

"I didn't want him to know. Your mother doesn't know either."

"What? You mean you didn't tell her?" Helen looked at the side of his face. It was rigid and bloodless behind the tan, as if something inside were shrinking away and leaving just his voice. "You mean you didn't even tell Ma? She doesn't know I'm coming?"

"No."

The nervous prickling in her brain returned suddenly. Helen rubbed her forehead. "Pa," she said gently, "why didn't you tell anybody? You're ashamed of me, huh?"

He drove on slowly. They were following the bends of the river, that wide shallow meandering river the boys said wasn't worth fishing in any longer. One of its tributaries branched out suddenly—Mud Creek, it was called, all mud and bullfrogs and dragonflies and weeds —and they drove over it on a rickety wooden bridge that thumped beneath them. "Pa," Helen said carefully, "you said you weren't mad, on the phone. And I wrote you that letter explaining. I wanted to write some more, but you know . . . I don't write much, never even wrote to Annie when she moved away. I never forgot about you or anything, or Ma. . . . I thought about the baby, too, and John, but John could always take care of himself. He's smart. He really is. I was in the store with him one time and he was arguing with some salesmen and got the best of them; he never learned all that from his father. The whole family is smart, though, aren't they?"

"The Hendrikses? Sure. You don't get money without brains."

"Yes, and they got money too, John never had to worry. In a house like his parents' house nothing gets lost or broken. You know? It isn't like it was at ours, when we were all kids. That's part of it—when John's father built us our house I was real pleased and real happy, but then something of them came in with it too. Everything is s'post to be clean and put in its place, and after you have a baby you get so tired. . . . But his mother was always real nice to me. I don't complain about them. I like them all real well."

"Money people always act nice," her father said. "Why shouldn't they?"

"Oh, Pa!" Helen said, tapping at his arm. "What do you mean by that? You always been nicer than anybody I know, that's the truth. Real nice. A lot of them with those big farms, like John's father, and that tractor store they got—they complain a lot. They do. You just don't hear about it. And when that baby got polio, over in the Rapids—that real big farm, you know what I mean?—the McGuires. How do you think they felt? They got troubles just like everybody else."

Then her father did a strange thing: here they were, seven or eight miles from home, no house near, and he stopped the car. "Want to rest for a minute," he said. Yet he kept staring out the windshield as if he were still driving.

"What's wrong?"

"Sun on the hood of the car. . . ."

Helen tugged at the collar of her dress, pulling it away from her damp neck. When had the heat ever bothered her father before? She remembered going out to the farthest field with water for him, before he had given up that part of the farm. And he would take the jug from her and lift it to his lips and it would seem to Helen, the sweet child Helen standing in the dusty corn, that the water flowed into her magnificent father and enlivened him as if it were secret blood of her own she have given him. And his chest would swell, his reddened arms eager with muscle emerging out from his rolled-up sleeves, and his eyes now wiped of sweat and exhaustion. . . . The vision pleased and confused her, for what had it to do with the man now beside her? She stared at him and saw that his nose was queerly white and that there were many tiny red veins about it, hardly more than pen lines; and his hair was thinning and jagged, growing back stiffly from his forehead as if he had brushed it back impatiently with his hand once too often. When Eddie, the oldest boy, moved away now and lost to them, had pushed their father hard in the chest and knocked him back against the supper table, that same amazed white look had come to his face, starting at his nose.

"I was thinking if, if we got home now, I could help Ma with supper," Helen said. She touched her father's arm as if to wake him. "It's real hot, she'd like some help."

"She doesn't know you're coming."

"But I . . . I could help anyway." She tried to smile, watching his face for a hint of something: many times in the past he had looked stern but could be made to break into a smile, finally, if she teased him long enough. "But didn't Ma hear you talk on the phone? Wasn't she there?"

By the River

"She was there."

"Well, but then. . . ."

"I told her you just talked. Never said nothing about coming home."

The heat had begun to make Helen dizzy. Her father opened the door on his side. "Let's get out for a minute, go down by the river," he said. Helen slid across and got out. The ground felt uncertain beneath her feet. Her father was walking and saying something and she had to run to catch up with him. He said: "We moved out here seventeen years ago. There were six of you then, but you don't remember. Then the boy died. And you don't remember your mother's parents and their house, that goddamn stinking house, and how I did all the work for him in his store. You remember the store down front? The dirty sawdust floor and the old women coming in for sausage, enough to make you want to puke, and pigs' feet and brains out of cows or guts or what the hell they were that people ate in that neighborhood. I could puke for all my life and not get clean of it. You just got born then. And we were dirt to your mother's people, just dirt. I was dirt. And when they died somebody else got the house, it was all owned by somebody else, and so we said how it was for the best and we'd come out here and start all over. You don't remember it or know nothing about us."

"What's wrong, Pa?" Helen said. She took his arm as they descended the weedy bank. "You talk so funny, did you get something to drink before you came to the bus station? You never said these things before. I thought it wasn't just meat, but a grocery store, like the one in. . . ."

"And we came out here," he said loudly, interrupting her, "and bought that son of a bitch of a house with the roof half rotted through and the well all shot to hell . . . and those bastards never looked at us, never believed we were real people. The Hendrikses too. They were like all of them. They looked through me in town, do you know that? Like you look through a window. They didn't see me. It was because hillbilly families were in that house, came and went, pulled out in the middle of the night owing everybody money; they all thought we were like that. I said, we were poor but we weren't hillbillies. I said, do I talk like a hillbilly? We come from the city. But nobody gave a damn. You could go up to them and shout in their faces and they wouldn't hear you, not even when they started losing money themselves. I prayed to God during them bad times that they'd all lose what they had, every bastard one of them, that Swede with the fancy cattle most of all! I prayed to God to bring them down to me so they could see me, my children as good as theirs, and me a harder worker than any of them—if you work till you feel like dying you done the best you can do, whatever money you get. I'd of told them that. I wanted to come into their world even if I had to be on the bottom of it, just so long as they gave me a name. . . ."

"Pa, you been drinking," Helen said softly.

"I had it all fixed, what I'd tell them," he said. They were down by the river bank now. Fishermen had cleared a little area and stuck Y-shaped branches into the dried mud, to rest their poles on. Helen's father prodded one of the little sticks with his foot and then did something Helen had never seen anyone do in her life, not even boys—he brought his foot down on it and smashed it.

"You oughtn't of done that," Helen said. "Why'd you do that?"

"And I kept on and on; it was seventeen years. I never talked about it to anyone. Your mother and me never had much to say, you know that. She was like her father. You remember that first day? It was spring, nice and warm, and the wind came along when we were moving the stuff in and was so different from that smell in the city—my God! It was a whole new world here."

"I remember it," Helen said. She was staring out at the shallow muddy river. Across the way birds were sunning themselves stupidly on flat, white rocks covered with dried moss like veils.

"You don't remember nothing!" her father said angrily. "Nothing! You were the only one of them I loved, because you didn't remember. It was all for you. First I did it for me, myself, to show that bastard father of hers that was dead—then those other bastards, those big farms around us—but then for you, for you. You were the baby. I said to God that when you grew up it'd be you in one of them big houses with everything fixed and painted all the time, and new machinery, and driving around in a nice car, not this thing we got. I said I would do that for you or die."

"That's real nice, Pa," Helen said nervously, "but I never . . . I never knew nothing about it, or. . . . I was happy enough any way I was. I liked it at home, I got along with Ma better than anybody did. And I liked John too, I didn't marry him just because you told me to. I mean, you never pushed me around. I wanted to marry him all by myself, because he loved me. I was always happy, Pa. If John didn't have the store coming to him, and that land and all, I'd have married him anyway—You oughtn't to have worked all that hard for me."

In spite of the heat she felt suddenly chilled. On either side of them tall grass shrank back from the cleared, patted area, stiff and dried with August heat. These weeds gathered upon themselves in a brittle tumult back where the vines and foliage of trees began, the weeds dead and whitened and the vines a glossy, rich green, as if sucking life out of the water into which they drooped. All along the river bank trees and bushes leaned out and showed a yard or two of dead, whitish brown where the water line had once been. This river bent so often you could never see far along it. Only a mile or so. Then foliage began, confused and unmoving. What were they doing here, she and her father? A thought came to Helen and frightened her—she was not used to thinking—that they ought not to be here, that this was some other kind of slow, patient world where time didn't care at all for her or her girl's face or her generosity of love, but would push right past her and go on to touch the faces of other people.

"Pa, let's go home. Let's go home," she said.

Her father bent and put his hands into the river. He brought them dripping to his face. "That's dirty there, Pa," she said. A mad dry buzzing started up somewhere—hornets or wasps. Helen looked around but saw nothing.

"God listened and didn't say yes or no," her father said. He was squatting at the river and now looked back at her, his chin creasing. The back of his shirt was wet. "If I could read Him right it was something like this— that I was caught in myself and them money people caught in themselves and God Himself caught in what He was and so couldn't be anything else. Then I never thought about God again."

"I think about God," Helen said. "I do. People should think about God, then they wouldn't have wars and things. . . ."

"No, I never bothered about God again," he said slowly. "If He was up there or not it never had nothing to do with me. A hailstorm that knocked down the wheat, or a drought—what the hell? Whose fault? It wasn't God's no more than mine so I let Him out of it. I knew I was in it all on my own. Then after a while it got better, year by year. We paid off the farm and the new machines. You were in school then, in town. And when we went into the church they said hello to us sometimes, because we outlasted them hillbillies by ten years. And now Mike ain't doing bad on his own place, got a nice car, and me and Bill get enough out of the farm so it ain't too bad, I mean it ain't too bad. But it wasn't money I wanted!"

He was staring at her. She saw something in his face that mixed with the buzzing of the hornets and fascinated her so that she could not move, could not even try to tease him into smiling too. "It wasn't never money I wanted," he said.

"Pa, why don't we go home?"

"I don't know what it was, exactly," he said, still squatting. His hands touched the ground idly. "I tried to think of it, last night when you called and all night long and driving in to town today. I tried to think of it."

"I guess I'm awful tired from that bus. I . . . I don't feel good," Helen said.

"Why did you leave with that man?"

"What? Oh?" she said, touching the tip of one of the weeds, "I met him at John's cousin's place, where they got that real nice tavern and a dance hall. . . ."

"Why did you run away with him?"

"I don't know, I told you in the letter. I wrote it to you, Pa. He acted so nice and liked me so, he still does, he loves me so much. . . . And he was always so sad and tired, he made me think of . . . you, Pa . . . but not really, because he's not strong like you and couldn't ever do work like you. And if he loved me that much I had to go with him."

"Then why did you come back?"

"Come back?" Helen tried to smile out across the water. Sluggish, ugly water, this river that disappointed everyone, so familiar to her that she could not really get used to a house without a river or a creek somewhere behind it, flowing along night and day: perhaps that was what she had missed in the city?

"I came back because . . . because. . . ."

And she shredded the weed in her cold fingers, but no words came to her. She watched the weed-fragments fall. No words came to her, her mind had turned hollow and cold, she had come too far down to this river bank but it was not a mistake any more than the way the river kept moving was a mistake; it just happened.

Her father got slowly to his feet and she saw in his hand a knife she had been seeing all her life. Her eyes seized upon it and her mind tried to remember: where had she seen it last, whose was it, her father's or her brother's? He came to her and touched her shoulder as if waking her, and they looked at each other, Helen so terrified by now that she was no longer afraid but only curious with the mute marblelike curiosity of a child, and her father stern and silent until a rush of hatred transformed his face into a mass of wrinkles, the skin mottled red and white. He did not raise the knife but slammed it into her chest, up to the hilt, so that his whitened fist struck her body and her blood exploded out upon it.

Afterward, he washed the knife in the dirty water and put it away. He squatted and looked out over the river, then his thighs began to ache and he sat on the ground, a few feet from her body. He sat there for hours as if waiting for some idea to come to him. Then the water began to darken, very slowly, and the sky darkened a little while later—as if belonging to another, separate time—and he tried to turn his mind with an effort to the next thing he must do.

THE UNIVERSAL FEARS

John Hawkes

Monday morning, bright as the birds, and there he stood for the first time among the twenty-seven girls who, if he had only known, were already playing the silence game. He looked at them, they looked at him, he never thought of getting a good grip on the pointer laid out lengthwise on that bare desk. Twenty-seven teen-age girls—homeless, bad-off, unloved, semi-literate, and each one of their poor unattractive faces was a condemnation of him, of all such schools for delinquent girls, of the dockyards lying round them like a seacoast of iron cranes, of the sunlight knifing through the grilles on the windows. They weren't faces to make you smile. Their sexual definition was vague and bleak. Hostile. But even then, in their first institutional moment together, he knew he didn't offer them any better from their point of view—only another fat man in the mid-fifties whose maleness meant nothing more than pants and jacket and belted belly and thin hair blacked with a cheap dye and brushed flat to the skull. Nothing in the new teacher to sigh about. So it was tit for tat, for them the desolation of more of the same, for him the deflation of the first glance that destroyed the possibility of finding just one keen lovely face to make the whole dreary thing worthwhile. Or a body promising a good shape to come. Or one set of sensual lips. Or one sign of adult responsiveness in any of those small eyes. But there was nothing, except the thought that perhaps their very sullenness might actually provide the most provocative landscape for the discovery of the special chemistry of pain that belongs to girls. Still he was already sweating in the armpits and going dry in the mouth.

"Right, girls," he said, "let's come to order."

In a shabby display of friendliness, accessibility, confidence, he slid from behind the desk and stood leaning the backs of his upper thighs against the front edge of it. Through the south window came the sounds of whistles and windlasses, from closer came the sounds of unloading coal. It made him think of a prison within a prison. No doubt the docks were considered the most suitable context for a school, so-called, for girls like these. Yes, the smells of brine and tar and buckets of oil that rode faintly in on the knifing light were only complementary to the stench of the room, to the soap, the thick shellac, the breath of the girls, the smell of their hair. It was a man's world for an apparently sexless lot of girls, and there was only one exotic aroma to be caught on that tide: the flowery wash of the sweet bay rum that clung to the thick embarrassed person of their old teacher new on the job.

"Right, girls," he said, returning warm glance for hostile stare, tic-like winks for the smoky and steady appraisal of small eyes, "right now, let's start with a few names. . . ."

And there they sat, unmoving, silent, ranked at three wooden benches of nine girls each, and all of their faces, whether large or small, thin or broad, dark or light, were blank as paper. Apparently they had made a pact before he entered the room to breathe in unison, so that now wherever he looked—first row on the left, first on the right—he was only too aware of the deliberate and ugly harmony of flat chests or full that were rising and falling slowly, casually, but always together.

Challenging the prof? Had they really agreed among themselves to be uncooperative? To give him a few bad minutes on the first day? Poor things, he thought, and crossed his fatty ankles, rested one flat hand on the uphill side of the belly, and then once more he looked them over at random, bearing down on a pair of shoulders like broken sticks, two thin lips bruised from chewing, a head of loose brown hair and another with a thin mane snarled in elastic bands, and some eyes without lashes, the closed books, claw marks evident on a sallow cheek.

"Girl on the end, there," he said all at once, stopping and swinging his attention back to the long black hair, the boy's shirt buttoned to the throat, the slanted eyes that never moved, "what's your name? Or you," he said, nodding at one of the younger ones, "what's yours?" He smiled, he waited, he shifted his glance from girl to girl, he began to make small but comforting gestures with the hand already resting on what he called his middle mound.

And then they attacked. The nearest bench was going over and coming his way like the side of a house undergoing demolition, and then the entire room was erupting not in noise but in the massed and silent motion of girls determined to drive their teacher out of the door, out of the school, and away, away, if they did not destroy him first right there on the floor. They leaped, they swung round the ends, tight-lipped they toppled against each other and rushed at him. He managed to raise his two hands to the defensive position, fingers fanned out in sheer disbelief and terror, but the cry with which he had thought to stop them merely stuck in his throat, while for an instant longer he stood there pushing air with his trembling outthrust hands. The girls tripped, charged from both sides of the room, swarmed over the fallen benches in the middle, dove with undeniable intent to seize and incapacitate his person.

The pointer, yes, the pointer, it flashed to his mind, invisibly it hovered within his reach, burned like a long thin weapon with which he might have struck them, stabbed them, beaten them, fended them off. But of course the pointer was behind him and he dared not turn, dared not drop the guard of his now frenzied hands. In an instant he saw it all—the moving girls between himself and the door, the impenetrable web of iron battened to each one of the dusty windows, and he knew there was no way out, no help. A shoe flew past his ear, a full-fifty tin of cigarettes hit the high ceiling above his head and exploded, rained down on him in his paralysis and the girls in their charge. No pointer, no handy instrument for self-defense, no assistance coming from anywhere.

And then the sound came on, adding to that turbulent pantomime the shrieks of their anger, so that what until this instant had been impending violence brimming in a bowl of unnatural silence, now became imminent brutality in a conventional context of the audionics of wrath. His own cry was stifled, his head was filled with the fury of that small mob.

"Annette . . . !"

"Deborah . . . !"

"Fuck off . . ."

"Now . . . now . . ."

"Kill him . . . !"

Despite their superior numbers they were not able to smother him in the first rush, and despite his own disbelief and fear he did not go down beneath them without a fight. Quite the contrary, because the first to reach him was of medium height, about fourteen, with her ribs showing through her jersey and a cheap bracelet twirling on her ankle. And before she could strike a blow he caught her in the crook of his left arm and locked her against his trembling belly and squeezed the life from her eyes, the breath from her lungs, the hate from her undersized constricted heart. He felt her warmth, her limpness, her terror. Then he relaxed the pressure of his arm and as the slight girl sank to his feet, he drove a doubled fist into the pimpled face of a young thick-lipped assailant whose auburn hair had been milked of its fire in long days and nights of dockyard rain. The nose broke, the mouth dissolved, his fist was ringed with blood and faded hair.

"You fucking old bastard," said a voice off his left shoulder, and then down he went with a knee in his ribs, arms around his neck and belly, a shod foot in the small of his back. For one more moment, while black seas washed over the deck and the clouds burst, the pit yawned, the molten light of the sun drained down as from a pink collapsing sack in the sky, he managed to keep to his all-fours. And it was exactly in this position that he opened his eyes, looked up, but only in time to receive full in the mouth the mighty downward blow of the small sharp fist of the slant-eyed girl whose name he had first requested. The black hair, the boy's gray workshirt buttoned tight around the neck, a look of steady intensity in the brown eyes, and the legs apart, the body bent slightly down, the elbow cocked, and then the aim, the frown, the little fist landing with unexpected force on the loose torn vulnerable mouth—yes, it was the same girl, no doubt of it.

Blood on the floor. Mouth full of broken china. A loud kick driven squarely between the buttocks. And still through the forests of pain he noted the little

John Hawkes

brassy zipper of someone's fly, a sock like striped candy, a flat bare stomach gouged by an old scar, bright red droplets making a random pattern on the open pages of an outmoded Form One Math. He tried to shake a straddling bony tormentor off his bruised back, bore another shock to the head, another punch in the side, and then he went soft, dropped, rolled over, tried to shield his face with his shoulder, cupped both hurt hands over the last of the male features hiding down there between his legs.

They piled on. He saw the sudden blade of a knife. They dragged each other off, they screamed. He groaned. He tried to worm his heavy beaten way toward the door. He tried to defend himself with hip, with elbow. And beneath that struggling mass of girls he began to feel his fat and wounded body slowing down, stopping, becoming only a still wet shadow on the rough and splintered wood of the classroom floor. And now and then through the shrieking he heard the distant voices.

"Cathy . . ."

"Eleanora . . ."

"Get his fucking globes . . ."

"Get the globes . . ."

They pushed, they pulled, they tugged, and then with his eyes squeezed shut he knew suddenly that they were beginning to work together in some terrible accord that depended on childish unspoken intelligence, cruel cooperation. He heard the hissing of the birds, he felt their hands. They turned him over—face up, belly up—and sat on his still-breathing carcass. One of them tore loose his necktie of cream-colored and magenta silk while simultaneously his only white shirt, fabric bleached and weakened by the innumerable Sunday washings he had given it in his small lavatory sink, split in a long clean easy tear from his neck to navel. They flung his already mangled spectacles against the blackboard. They removed one shoe, one sock, and yanked

118

the shabby jacket off his right shoulder and bounced up and down on his sagging knees, dug fingernails into the exposed white bareness of his right breast. Momentarily his left eye came unstuck and through the film of his tears he noted that the ringleader was the girl with the auburn hair and broken nose. She was riding his thighs, her sleeves were rolled, her thick lower lip was caught between her teeth in a parody of schoolgirl concentration, despite her injury and the blood on her face. It occurred to him that her pale hair deserved the sun. But then he felt a jolt in the middle, a jolt at the hips, and of course he had known all along that it was his pants they were after, pants and underpants. Then she had them halfway down, and he smelled her cheap scent, heard their gasping laughter, and felt the point of the clasp knife pierce his groin.

"He's fucking fat, he is . . ."

"The old suck . . ."

In his welter of pain and humiliation he writhed but did not cry out, writhed but made no final effort to heave them off, to stop the knife. What was the use? And wasn't he aware at last that all his poor street girls were actually bent to an operation of love not murder? Mutilated, demeaned, room a shambles and teacher overcome, still he knew in his fluid and sinking consciousness that all his young maenads were trying only to feast on love.

"Off him! Off him!" came the loud and menacing voice from the doorway while he, who no longer wanted saving, commenced a long low moan.

"Get away from him at once, you little bitches . . . !"

There he was, lying precisely as the victim lies, helplessly inseparable from the sprawled and bloodied shape the victim makes in the middle of the avenue at the foot of the trembling omnibus. He was blind. He could not move, could not speak. But in customary fashion he had the distinct impression of his mangled self as noted, say, from the doorway where the director stood. Yes, it was all perfectly clear. He was quite capable of surveying what the director surveyed—the naked foot, the abandoned knife, the blood like a pattern spread beneath the body, the soft dismembered carcass fouling the torn shirt and crumpled pants. The remnants of significant male anatomy were still in hiding, dazed, anesthetized, but the pinched white hairy groin, still bleeding, was calling itself to his passive consciousness while beckoning the director to a long proud glance of disapproval, scorn, distaste.

Gongs rang, the ambulance came and went, he lay alone on the floor. Had the girls fled? Or were they simply backed against those dusty walls with legs crossed and thumbs hooked in leather belts, casually defying the man in the doorway? Or silent, sullen, knowing the worst was yet to come for them, perhaps they were simply trying to right the benches, repair the room. In any case he was too bruised to regret the hands that did not reach for him, the white ambulance that would forever pass him by.

"Sovrowsky, Coletta, Rivers, Fiume," said the director from his point of authority at the door. "Pick him up. Fix his pants. Follow me. You bitches."

In the otherwise empty room off the director's office was an old leather couch, there not merely for the girls' cramps but, more important, for the director's rest, a fact which he knew intuitively and immediately the moment he came awake and felt beneath him the pinched and puffy leather surface of the listing couch. And now the couch was bearing him down the dirty tide and he was conscious enough of adding new blood to fading stains.

Somebody was matter-of-factly brushing the cut above his eye with the flaming tip of a long and treacherous needle. And this same person, he discovered in the next moment, was pouring a hot and humiliating syrup into the wounds in his groin.

"Look at him," murmured the thin young woman, and made another stroke, another daub at the eye, "look at him, he's coming round."

Seeing the old emergency kit opened and breathing off ammonia on the young woman's knees pressed close together, and furthermore, seeing the tape and scissors in the young woman's bony hands and hearing the tape, seeing the long bite of the scissors, it was then that he did indeed come round, as his helpful young colleague had said, and rolled one gelatinous quarter-turn to the edge of the couch and vomited fully and heavily into the sluggish tide down which he still felt himself sailing, awake or not. His vomit missed the thin black-stockinged legs and narrow flat-heeled shoes of the young teacher seated beside him.

"I warned you," the director was saying, "I told you they were dangerous. I told you they beat your predecessor nearly to death. How do you think we had your opening? And now it's not at all clear you can handle the job. You might have been killed. . . ."

"Next time they'll kill him, rightly enough," said the young woman, raising her brows and speaking through the cheap tin nasal funnel of her narrow mouth and laying on another foot-long strip of tape.

Slowly, lying half on his belly, sinking in the vast hurt of his depthless belly, he managed to lift his head and raise his eyes for one long dismal stare at the impassive face of the director.

"I can handle the job," he whispered, just as vomiting started up again from the pit of his life. From somewhere in the depths of the building he heard the rising screams of the girl with the thick lips, auburn hair, and broken nose.

He was most seriously injured, as it turned out, not in the groin or flanks or belly, but in the head. And

John Hawkes

the amateurish and careless ministrations of the cadaverous young female teacher were insufficient, as even the director recognized. So they recovered his cream and magenta tie, which he stuffed into his jacket pocket, helped to replace the missing shoe and sock, draped his shoulders in an old and hairy blanket, and together steadied him down to his own small ancient automobile in which the young female teacher drove him to the hospital. There he submitted himself to something under two hours of waiting and three at least of professional care, noting in the midst of fresh pain and the smells of antiseptic how the young teacher stood by to see the handiwork of her own first aid destroyed, the long strips of tape pulled off brusquely with the help of cotton swabs and a bottle of cold alcohol, and the head rather than chest or groin wrapped in endless footage of soft gauze and new strips of official tape. He felt the muffling of the ears, the thickening sensation of the gauze going round the top of his head and down his swollen cheeks, was aware of the care taken to leave stark minimal openings for the eyes, the nose, the battered mouth.

"Well," muttered the medical student entrusted with this operation of sculpting and binding the head in its helmet and face-mask of white bandages, "somebody did a job on you, all right."

No sooner had he entered the flat than his little dog Murphy, or Murph for short, glanced at the enormous white hive of antiseptic bandages and then scampered behind the conveniently open downstairs door of the china cabinet, making a thin and steady cry of uncommonly high pitch. He had frightened his own poor little dog, he with his great white head, and now he heard Murph clawing at the lower inside rear wall of the china cabinet and, leaning just inside his own doorway, became freshly nauseous, freshly weak.

"Come out, Murph," he tried to say, "it's me." But

122

within its portable padded cell of bandage, his muffled voice was as wordless as Murphy's. From within the cabinet came the slow circular sounds of Murphy's claws, still accompanied by the steady shrill music of the little animal's panic, so that within the yet larger context of his own personal shock, he knew at once that he must devote himself to convincing the little dog that the man inside the bandages was familiar and unchanged. It could take days.

"Murphy," he meant to say, "shut your eyes, smell my hands, trust me, Murph." But even to his own steady ear the appeal sounded only like a faint wind trapped in the mouth of a mute.

It was dusk, his insulated and mummified head was floating, throbbing, while the rest of him, the masses of beaten and lacerated flesh beneath the disheveled clothes, cried out for sleep and small soft hands to press against him and slowly eliminate, by tender touch, these unfamiliar aches, these heavy pains. He wanted to lie forever on his iron bed, to sit swathed and protected in his broken-down padded chair with Murph on his lap. But the night was inimical, approaching, descending, filling space everywhere, and the flat no longer felt his own. The chair would be as hard as the bed, as unfamiliar, and even Murphy's latest hectic guilt-ridden trail of constraint and relief appeared to have been laid down by somebody else's uncontrollable household pet. Why did the window of his flat give onto the same dockyard scene, though further away and at a different angle, as the window of the schoolroom in which he had all but died? Why didn't he switch on a light, prepare his usual tea, put water in Murphy's bowl? A few minutes later, on hands and knees and with his heavy white head ready to sink to the floor, he suddenly realized that injury attacks identity, which was why, he now knew, that assault was a crime.

He did his clean-up job on hands and knees, he

made no further effort to entice his dog from the china cabinet, he found himself wondering why the young teacher had allowed him to climb to the waiting and faintly kennelish-smelling flat alone. When he had dropped the last of poor little bewhiskered Murphy's fallen fruit into a paper sack now puffy with air and unavoidable waste, and in pain and darkness had sealed the sack and disposed of it in the tin pail beneath the sink, he slowly dragged himself to the side of the iron bed and then, more slowly still, hauled himself up and over. Shoes and all. Jacket and torn shirt and pants and all. Nausea and all. And lay on his side. And for the first time allowed the fingers of one hand to settle gently on the bandages that bound his head, and slowly and gently to touch, poke, caress, explore. Then at last, and with the same hand, he groped and drew to his chin the old yellow comforter that still exhaled the delicate scent of his dead mother.

Teacher Assaulted at Training School for Girls

Mr. Walter Jones, newly appointed to the staff of St. Dunster's Training School for Girls, received emergency treatment today at St. Dunster's Hospital for multiple bruises which, as Mr. Jones admitted and Dr. Smyth-Jones, director of the school, confirmed, were inflicted by the young female students in Mr. Jones's first class at the school. Mr. Jones's predecessor, Mr. William Smyth, was so severely injured by these same students November last that he has been forced into early and permanent retirement. Dr. Smyth-Jones expressed regret for both incidents, but indicated that Mr. Jones's place on the staff would be awaiting him upon his full and, it is to be hoped, early recovery. "The public," he commented, "little appreciates the obstacles faced by educators at a school such as St. Dunster's. After all, within the system for the rehabilitation of criminally inclined female minors, St. Dunster's has been singled out to receive only the most intractable of girls. Occasional injury to our staff and to the girls themselves is clearly unavoidable."

With both hands on the wheel and Murph on his lap and a large soft-brimmed felt hat covering a good half of the offending white head, in this condition and full into the sun he slowly and cautiously drove the tortuous cobbled route toward Rose and Thyme, that brutally distended low-pitted slab of tenements into which his father, Old Jack, as he was known by all, had long since cut his filthy niche. The sun on the roof of the small old coffin of a car was warm, the narrow and dusty interior was filled with the hovering aroma of fresh petrol, and Murph, with his nose raised just to the level of the glass on the driver's side, was bobbing and squirming gently to the rhythm first of the footbrake and then the clutch. As for himself, and aside from the welcome heat of the little dog and the ice and glitter of the new day, it gave him special pleasure to be driving cautiously along with a lighted cigarette protruding from the mouth-slit in the bandages and, now and again, his entire head turning to give some timorous old woman the whole shock full in the face. He was only too conscious that he could move, that he could drive the car, that he filled the roaring but slowly moving vehicle with his bulk and age, that Murph's tiny pointed salt-and-pepper ears rose just above the edge of the window, and then was only too conscious, suddenly, of the forgotten girls.

Why, he asked himself, had he forgotten the girls? Why had he forced from his mind so simply, so unintentionally, the very girls whose entry into his life had been so briefly welcome, so briefly violent? Would he give up? Would he see them again? But why had he

applied for that job in the first place? Surely he had not
been going his own way, finally, after what his nimble
old Dad called the juicy rough. All this pain and confusion for easy sex? Not a bit of it.

And then, making a difficult turn and drawing up
behind a narrow flat-bedded lorry loaded down with
stone and chugging, crawling, suddenly he saw it all, saw
himself standing in Old Jack's doorway with Murph
in his arms, saw his nimble Dad spring back, small and
sallow face already contorted into the familiar look of
alarm, and duck and turn, and from somewhere in the
uncharted litter of that filthy room whip out his trench
knife and standing there against the peeling wall with
his knees knocking and weapon high and face contorted
into that expression of fear and grievous pride common
to most of those who lived in the ruin and desolation of
Rose and Thyme. Then he heard the silent voices as the
little old man threw down the trench knife and wiped
his little beak and small square toothless mouth down
the length of his bare arm.

It's you, is it?

Just me, Dad. Come to visit.

*You might know better than to be stalking up here
like some telly monster with that head of yours and that
dead dog in your arms.*

Murph's all right, Jack. Aren't you, Murph?

*It's that school, that fucking school. My own son
beaten near to death by a bunch of girls and written up
in the papers. I read it, the whole sad story. And then
stalking up here like a murderous monster.*

*They're very strong girls. And there were a lot of
them. Twenty-seven actually.*

*Why were you there? Tell me why, eh? Oh, the
Good Samaritan. . . .*

Yes, the Good Samaritan.

Or were you really after a little juicy rough?

*Mere sex? Not a bit of it. Of course I wouldn't rule
out possibilities, but there's more than that.*

Juicy rough. Walter, juicy rough. Don't lie.

*I believe I want to know how those girls exist with-
out romance. Or do they?*

*Use the glove, Walter! Let me give you the old fur
glove. It does a lovely job. You can borrow it. . . .*

"Yes," he heard himself musing aloud from within
the bundle of antiseptic stuffing that was his head, and
pressing first the brake and then the accelerator, "yes, I
want to be at the bottom where those girls are. Without romance."

At a faster pace now and passing the lorry, he
headed the little dark blue car once more in the direction from which he and Murphy had started out in the
first place. Occasionally it was preferable to meet Old
Jack not in the flesh but in the mind, he told himself,
and this very moment was a case in point.

"No," said the young female teacher in the otherwise empty corridor, "it's you! And still in bandages."

"On the stroke of eight," he heard himself saying
through the mouth-slit, which he had enlarged progressively with his fingers. "I'm always punctual."

"But you're not ready to come back. Just look at
you."

"Ready enough. They couldn't keep me away."

"Wait," she said then, her voice jumping at him and
her face full of alarm, "don't go in there . . . !"

"Must," he said, and shook her off, reached out,
opened the door.

The same room. The same grilled and dusty windows. The same machinery in spidery operation in the
vista beyond. Yes, it might have been his first day, his
first morning, except that he recognized them and
picked them out one by one from the silent rows—the

narrow slant-eyed face, the girl with tuberculosis of the
bone, the auburn-haired ringleader who had held the
knife. Yes, all the same, except that the ringleader was
wearing a large piece of sticking plaster across her nose.
Even a name or two came back to him and for an instant
these names evoked the shadowy partial poem of the forgotten rest. But named or unnamed their eyes were on
him, as before, and though they could not know it, he
was smiling in the same old suit and flaming tie and
dusty pointed shoes. Yes, they knew who he was, and
he in turn knew all about their silence game and actually
was counting on the ugliness, the surprise, of the fully
bandaged head to put them off, to serve as a measure of
what they had done and all he had forgiven even before
they had struck, to serve them as the first sign of courage
and trust.

"Now, girls," he said in a voice they could not hear,
"if you'll take out pencils and paper and listen atten-
tively, we'll just begin." Across the room the pointer
was lying on the old familiar desk like a sword in the
light.

MANIKIN

Leonard Michaels

At the university she met a Turk who studied physics and spoke foreigner's English which in every turn expressed the unnatural desire to seize idiom and make it speak just for himself. He worked nights as a waiter, summers on construction gangs, and shot pool and played bridge with fraternity boys in order to make small change, and did whatever else he could to protect and supplement his university scholarship, living a mile from campus in a room without sink or closet or decent heating and stealing most of the food he ate, and when the University Hotel was robbed it was the Turk who had done it, an act of such speed the night porter couldn't say when it happened or who rushed in from the street to bludgeon him so murderously he took it in a personal way. On weekends the Turk tutored mediocrities in mathematics and French. . . .

He picked her up at her dormitory, took her to a movie, and later, in his borrowed Chevrolet, drove her into the countryside and with heavy, crocodilean sentences communicated his agony amid the alien corn. She attended with quick, encouraging little nods and stared as if each word crept past her eyes and she felt power gathering in their difficult motion as he leaned toward her and with lips still laboring words made indelible sense, raping her, forcing her to variations of what she had never heard of though she was a great reader of avant-garde novels and philosophical commentaries on the modern predicament. . . .

In the cracking, desiccated leather of the Chevrolet she was susceptible to a distinction between life and sensibility, and dropped, like Leda by the swan, squirming, arching, so as not to be touched again, inadvertently, as he poked behind the cushions for the ignition key. She discovered it pulling up her pants and, because it required intelligent speech inconsistent with her moaning, couldn't bring it to his attention; nor would she squat, winding about in her privates, though she hated to see him waste time bunched up twisting wires under the dashboard.

Despite her wild compulsion to talk and despite the frightened, ravenous curiosity of her dormitory clique whom she awakened by sobbing over their beds, Melanie wasn't able to say clearly what finished happening half an hour ago. She remembered the Turk suddenly abandoned English and raved at her in furious Turkish, and she told them about that and about the obscene tattoo flashing on his chest when she ripped his shirt open, and that he stopped the car on a country road and there was a tall hedge, maples, sycamores, and a railroad track nearby, and a train was passing, passing, and passing, and beyond it, her moans, and later an animal trotting quickly on the gravel, and then, with no discontinuity, the motor starting its cough and retch and a cigarette waving at her mouth already lighted as if the worst were over and someone had started thinking of her in another way.

Manikin

The lights of the university town appeared and she smoked the cigarette as the car went down among them through empty streets, through the residential area of the ethical, economic community and twisted into the main street passing store after store. She saw an armless, naked manikin and felt like that, or like a thalidomide baby, all torso and short-circuited, and then they were into the streets around campus, narrow and shaky with trees, and neither of them said a word as he shifted gears, speeding and slowing and working the car through a passage irregular and yet steady, and enclosed within a greater passage as tangible as the internal arcs of their skulls. At the dormitory he stopped the car. She got out running.

Quigley, Berkowitz and Sax could tell that Melanie Green had been assaulted with insane and exotic cruelty: there were fingerprints on her cheeks the color of tea stains and her stockings hung about her ankles like Hamlet's when he exposed himself to Ophelia and called her a whore. So they sucked cigarettes and urged her to phone the Dean of Women, the police and the immigration authorities, as if disseminating the story among representatives of order would qualify it toward annihilation or render it accessible to a punitive response consistent with national foreign policy. Though none of them saw positive value in Melanie's experience it was true, nevertheless, in no future conversation would she complain about being nineteen and not yet discovered by the right man, as it happened, to rape with. Given her face and legs, *that* had always seemed sick, irritating crap, and in the pits of their minds where there were neither words nor ideas but only raging morality, they took the Turk as poetic justice, fatal male, and measure for measure. Especially since he lived now in those pits vis-à-vis Melanie's father, a bearded rabbi with tear bags. "What if your father knew?" asked Quigley, making a gesture of anxious speculation, slender hands turned out flat, palms up, like a Balinese dancer. Melanie felt annoyed, but at least Quigley was there, sticking out her hands, and could be relied on always to be symbolic of whatever she imagined the situation required.

She didn't tell the rabbi, the Dean of Women, police, or immigration authorities, and didn't tell Harry Stone, her fiancé, with whom she had never had all-the-way sexual intercourse because he feared it might destroy the rhythm of his graduate work in Classics. But once, during Christmas vacation, she flew East to visit him and while standing on a stairway in Cambridge, after dinner and cognac, he let her masturbate him and then lay in bed beside her, brooding, saying little except, "I feel like Seymour," and she answering, "I'm sorry." Quigley, Berkowitz and Sax called him "Harry the fairy," but never in the presence of Melanie who read them his letters, brilliantly exquisite and full of ruthless wit directed at everything, and the girls screamed and could hardly wait till he got his degree and laid her. "It'll be made of porcelain," said Sax, and Melanie couldn't refute the proposition (though the girls always told her everything they did with their boyfriends and she owed them the masturbation story) because they were too hot for physiology and wouldn't listen to the whole story, wouldn't hear its tone or any of its music. They were critical, sophisticated girls and didn't dig mood, didn't savor things. They were too fast, too eager to get the point.

She didn't tell the rabbi or any other authority about the rape, and wouldn't dream of telling Harry Stone because he tended to become irrationally jealous and like homosexual Othello would assume she had gone out with armies of men aside from the Turk, which wasn't true. The Turk had been a casual decision, the only one of its kind, determined by boredom with classes

Manikin

and dateless weekends, and partly by a long-distance phone call to Harry Stone in the middle of the night when she needed his voice and he expressed irritation at having been disturbed while translating a difficult passage of Thucydides for a footnote in his dissertation. Furthermore the Turk was interesting-looking, black eyes, a perfect white bite of teeth between a biggish nose and a cleft chin, and because he was pathetic in his tortuous English going out with him seemed merely an act of charity indifferently performed and it was confirmed as such when he arrived in the old Chevrolet and suggested a cowboy movie. He held the door open for her which she could never expect Harry to do, and he tried to talk to her. To her, she felt—though it was clear that his effort to talk depended very much on her effort to listen.

She went to parties on the two weekends following the rape and sat in darkened rooms while a hashish pipe went around and said things too deep for syntax and giggled hysterically, and in the intimate delirium of faces and darkness asked how one might get in touch with an abortionist if, per chance, one needed one. She didn't talk about the rape but remembered the Turk had held her chin and she felt guilty but resistless and saw that his eyes didn't focus and that, more than anything, lingered in her nerves, like birds screaming and inconsummate. She asked her clique about the signs of pregnancy, then asked herself if she weren't peeing more than usual. It seemed to spear down very hot and hard and longer than before, but she ascribed it to sphincters loosened upon the violent dissolution of the veil between vaginal post and lintel. When she asked the girls about an abortionist they laughed maniacally at the idea that any of them might know such a person, but, one at a time, appeared in her room to whisper names and telephone numbers and tell her about the different techniques and the anesthetic she might expect if the man were considerate or brave enough to give her one. "They're afraid of the cops," said Sax, a tough number from Chicago who had been knocked up twice in her freshman year. "They want you out of the office as soon as possible."

Harry surprised her by coming to town during his intersession break and she was so glad to see him she trembled. She introduced him to her house mother and her clique and he ate dinner with her in the dormitory the first night. The next day he went to classes with her and that evening they ate in the best restaurant in town, which wasn't nearly as good as some Harry knew in the East but it was pretty good, and they walked in the Midwestern twilight, watching swallows, listening to night hawks whistle, and she felt an accumulation of sympathy in the minutes and the hours which became an urge, a possibility, and then a strong need to tell him, but she chatted mainly about her clique and said, "Quigley has funny nipples and Berkowitz would have a wonderful figure except for her thighs which have no character. I love Sax's figure. It's like a skinny boy's." Harry made an indifferent face and shrugged in his tweeds, but quick frowns twitched after the facts and she went on, encouraged thus, going on, to go on and on. In his hotel room they had necking and writhing, then lay together breathless, tight, indeterminate, until he began talking about his dissertation. "A revolution in scholarship. The vitiation of many traditional assumptions. They say I write uncommonly well." She told him about the rape. He sat up with words about the impossibility of confidence, the betrayal of expectations, the end of things. He was amazed, he said, the world didn't break and the sky fall down. As far as he was concerned the ceremony of innocence was drowned. While he packed she rubbed her knees and stared at him. He noticed her staring and said, "I don't like you."

Wanda Chung was always in flight around corners, down hallways, up stairs, into bathrooms, and never spoke to people unless obliged to do so and then with fleeting, terrified smiles and her eyes somewhere else. She appeared at no teas or dances, received no calls and no boys at the reception desk, and Melanie and her clique gradually came to think of her as the most interesting girl in the dormitory. One afternoon after classes they decided to go to her room and introduce themselves. She wasn't in so they entered the room and while waiting for her casually examined her closet which was packed with dresses and coats carrying the labels of good stores in San Francisco. Under her bed there were boxes of new blouses and sweaters, and they discovered her desk drawers were crammed with candy and empty candy wrappers. They left her room, never returned, and never again made any effort to introduce themselves to her, but Wanda, who for months had harbored a secret yearning to meet Melanie, decided, the day after Harry Stone left town, to go to Melanie's room and present herself: "I am Wanda Chung. I live downstairs. I found this fountain pen. Could it be yours?" She bought a fountain pen and went to Melanie's room and an instant after she knocked at the door she forgot her little speech and her desire to meet Melanie. The door gave way at the vague touch of her knuckles and started opening as if Wanda herself had taken the knob and turned it with the intention of getting into the room and stealing something, which is how she saw it, standing there as the door unbelievably, remorselessly, opened, sucking all motion and feeling out of her limbs and making her more and more thief in the possible eyes of anyone coming along. And then, into her dumb rigidity, swayed naked feet like bell clappers. She saw Melanie Green hanging by the neck, her pelvis twitching. Wanda dashed to the stairs, down to her room, and locked herself inside. She ate candy until she puked in her lap and fell asleep. . . .

When the Turk read about the suicide he said in a slow, sick voice, "She loved me." He got drunk and stumbled through the streets looking for a fight, but bumping strangers and firing clams of spit at their feet wasn't sufficiently provocative, given his debauched and fiercely miserable appearance, to get himself punched or cursed or even shoved a little. He ended the night in a scrubby field tearing at an oak tree with his fingernails, rolling in its roots, hammering grass, cursing the sources of things until, in a shy, gentle way, Melanie drifted up out of the dew. He refused to acknowledge her presence but then couldn't tolerate being looked at in silence and yelled at her in furious Turkish. She came closer. He seized her in his arms and they rolled together in the grass until he found himself screaming through his teeth because, however much of himself he lavished on her, she was dead.

IN WHICH ESTHER GETS A NOSE JOB

Thomas Pynchon

. . . She touched the tip of her new nose delicately, in secret: a mannerism she'd developed just recently. Not so much to point it out to whoever might be watching as to make sure it was still there. The bus came out of the park onto the safe, bright East Side, into the lights of Fifth Avenue. They reminded her to go shopping tomorrow for a dress she'd seen, $39.95 at Lord and Taylor, which he would like.

What a brave girl I am, she trilled to herself, coming through so much night and lawlessness to visit My Lover.

She got off at First Avenue and tap-tapped along the sidewalk, facing uptown and perhaps some dream. Soon she turned right, began to fish in her purse for a key. Found the door, opened, stepped inside. The front rooms were all deserted. Beneath the mirror, two golden imps in a clock danced the same unsyncopated tango they'd always danced. Esther felt home. Behind the operating room (a sentimental glance sideways through the open door toward the table on which her face had been altered) was a small chamber, in it a bed. He lay, head and shoulders circled by the intense halo of a paraboloid reading light. His eyes opened to her, her arms to him.

"You are early," he said.

"I am late," she answered. Already stepping out of her skirt.

1

Schoenmaker, being conservative, referred to his profession as the art of Tagliacozzi. His own methods, while not as primitive as those of the sixteenth-century Italian, were marked by a certain sentimental inertia, so that Schoenmaker was never quite up to date. He went out of his way to cultivate the Tagliacozzi look: showing his eyebrows thin and semicircular; wearing a bushy mustache, pointed beard, sometimes even a skullcap, his old schoolboy yarmulke.

He'd received his impetus—like the racket itself—from the World War. At seventeen, coeval with the century, he raised a mustache (which he never shaved off), falsified his age and name and wallowed off in a fetid troopship to fly, so he thought, high over the ruined châteaux and scarred fields of France, got up like an earless raccoon to scrimmage with the Hun; a brave Icarus.

Well, the kid never did get up in the air, but they made him a greasemonkey which was more than he'd expected anyway. It was enough. He got to know the guts not only of Breguets, Bristol Fighters and JN's, but also of the birdmen who did go up, and whom, of course, he adored. There was always a certain feudal-homosexual element in this division of labor. Schoenmaker felt like a page boy. Since those days as we know

In Which Esther Gets a Nose Job

democracy has made its inroads and those crude flying-machines have evolved into "weapon systems" of a then undreamed-of complexity; so that the maintenance man today has to be as professional-noble as the flight crew he supports.

But then: it was a pure and abstract passion, directed for Schoenmaker, at least, toward the face. His own mustache may have been partly responsible; he was often mistaken for a pilot. On off hours, infrequently, he would sport a silk kerchief (obtained in Paris) at his throat, by way of imitation.

The war being what it was, certain of the faces—craggy or smooth, with slicked-down hair or bald—never came back. To this the young Schoenmaker responded with all adolescent love's flexibility: his free-floating affection sad and thwarted for a time till it managed to attach itself to a new face. But in each case, loss was as unspecified as the proposition "love dies." They flew off and were swallowed in the sky.

Until Evan Godolphin. A liaison officer in his middle thirties, TDY with the Americans for reconnaissance missions over the Argonne plateau, Godolphin carried the natural foppishness of the early aviators to extremes which in the time's hysterical context seemed perfectly normal. Here were no trenches, after all: the air up there was free of any taint of gas or comrades' decay. Combatants on both sides could afford to break champagne glasses in the majestic fireplaces of commandeered country seats; treat their captives with utmost courtesy, adhere to every point of the duello when it came to a dogfight; in short, practice with finicking care the entire rigmarole of nineteenth-century gentlemen at war. Even Godolphin wore a Bond Street-tailored flying suit; would often, dashing clumsily across the scars of their makeshift airfield toward his French Spad, stop to pluck a lone poppy, survivor of strafing by autumn and the Germans (naturally aware of the Flanders Fields poem in Punch, three years ago when there'd still been an idealistic tinge to trench warfare), and insert it into one faultless lapel.

Godolphin became Schoenmaker's hero. Tokens tossed his way—an occasional salute, a "well done" for the preflights which came to be the boy-mechanic's responsibility, a tense smile—were hoarded fervently. Perhaps he saw an end also to this unrequited love; doesn't a latent sense of death always heighten the pleasure of such an "involvement"?

The end came soon enough. One rainy afternoon toward the end of the battle of Meuse-Argonne, Godolphin's crippled plane materialized suddenly out of all that gray, looped feebly, dipped on a wing toward the ground and slid like a kite in an air current toward the runway. It missed the runway by a hundred yards: by the time it impacted corpsmen and stretcher-bearers were already running out toward it. Schoenmaker happened to be nearby and tagged along, having no idea what had happened till he saw the heap of rags and splinters, already soggy in the rain, and from it, limping toward the medics, the worst possible travesty of a human face lolling atop an animate corpse. The top of the nose had been shot away; shrapnel had torn out part of one cheek and shattered half the chin. The eyes, intact, showed nothing.

Schoenmaker must have lost himself. The next he could remember he was back at an aid station, trying to convince the doctors there to take his own cartilage. Godolphin would live, they'd decided. But his face would have to be rebuilt. Life for the young officer would be, otherwise, unthinkable.

Now luckily for some a law of supply and demand had been at work in the field of plastic surgery. Godolphin's case, by 1918, was hardly unique. Methods had been in existence since the fifth century B.C. for rebuilding noses, Thiersch grafts had been around for forty or so years. During the war new techniques were developed by necessity and were practiced by GP's, eye-ear-nose-and-throat men, even a hastily recruited gynecologist or two. The techniques that worked were adopted and passed on quickly to the younger medics. Those that failed produced a generation of freaks and pariahs who along with those who'd received no restorative surgery at all became a secret and horrible postwar fraternity. No good at all in any of the usual rungs of society, where did they go?

. . . Evan Godolphin proved to be one of them. The doctor was young, he had ideas of his own, which the AEF was no place for. His name was Halidom and he favored allografts: the introduction of inert substances into the living face. It was suspected at the time that the only safe transplants to use were cartilage or skin from the patient's own body. Schoenmaker, knowing nothing about medicine, offered his cartilage but the gift was rejected; allografting was plausible and Halidom saw no reason for two men being hospitalized when only one had to be.

Thus Godolphin received a nose bridge of ivory, a cheekbone of silver and a paraffin and celluloid chin. A month later Schoenmaker went to visit him in the hospital—the last time he ever saw Godolphin. The reconstruction had been perfect. He was being sent back to London, in some obscure staff position, and spoke with a grim flippancy.

"Take a long look. It won't be good for more than six months." Schoenmaker stammered: Godolphin continued: "See him, down the way?" Two cots over lay what would have been a similar casualty except that the skin of the face was whole, shiny. But the skull beneath was misshapen. "Foreign-body reaction, they call it. Sometimes infection, inflammation, sometimes only pain. The paraffin, for instance, doesn't hold shape. Before you know it, you're back where you started." He talked like a man under death sentence. "Perhaps I can pawn my cheekbone. It's worth a fortune. Before they melted it down it was one of a set of pastoral figurines, eighteenth century—nymphs, shepherdesses—looted from a château the Hun was using for a CP; Lord knows where they're originally from—"

"Couldn't—" Schoenmaker's throat was dry—"couldn't they fix it, somehow: start over . . ."

"Too rushed. I'm lucky to get what I got. I can't complain. Think of the devils who haven't even six months to bash around in."

"What will you do when—"

"I'm not thinking of that. But it will be a grand six months."

The young mechanic stayed in a kind of emotional limbo for weeks. He worked without the usual slacking off, believing himself no more animate than the spanners and screwdrivers he handled. When there were passes to be had he gave his to someone else. He slept on an average of four hours a night. This mineral period ended by an accidental meeting with a medical officer one evening in the barracks. Schoenmaker put it as primitively as he felt:

"How can I become a doctor."

Of course it was idealistic and uncomplex. He wanted only to do something for men like Godolphin, to help prevent a takeover of the profession by its unnatural and traitorous Halidoms. It took ten years of working at his first specialty—mechanic—as well as navvy in a score of markets and warehouses, bill-collectors, once administrative assistant to a bootlegging syndicate operating out of Decatur, Illinois. These years of labor were interlarded with night courses and occasional day enrollments, though none more than three semesters in a row (after Decatur, when he could afford it); internship; finally, on the eve of the Great Depression, entrance to the medical free-masonry. . . .

In Which Esther Gets a Nose Job

He kept going by hatred for Halidom and perhaps a fading love for Godolphin. These had given rise to what is called a "sense of mission"—something so tenuous it has to be fed more solid fare than either hatred or love. So it came to be sustained, plausibly enough, by a number of bloodless theories about the "idea" of the plastic surgeon. Having heard his vocation on the embattled wind, Schoenmaker's dedication was toward repairing the havoc wrought by agencies outside his own sphere of responsibility. Others—politicians and machines—carried on wars; others—perhaps human machines—condemned his patients to the ravages of acquired syphilis; others—on the highways, in the factories—undid the work of nature with automobiles, milling machines, other instruments of civilian disfigurement. What could he do toward eliminating the causes? They existed, formed a body of things-as-they-are; he came to be afflicted with a conservative laziness. It was social awareness of a sort, but with boundaries and interfaces which made it less than the catholic rage filling him that night in the barracks with the M.O. It was in short a deterioration of purpose; a decay.

2

Esther met him, oddly enough, through Stencil. . . . Esther had been languishing ripe and hot-eyed about the Rusty Spoon, hating her figure-6 nose and proving as well as she could the unhappy undergraduate adage: "All the ugly ones fuck." The thwarted Stencil, casting about for somebody to take it all out on, glommed on to her despair hopefully—a taking which progressed to sad summer afternoons wandering among parched fountains, sunstruck shop fronts and streets bleeding tar, eventually to a father-daughter agreement casual enough to be canceled at any time should either of them desire, no post-mortems necessary. It struck him with a fine irony that the nicest sentimental trinket for her would be an introduction to Schoenmaker; accordingly, in September, the contact was made and Esther without ado went under his knives and kneading fingers.

Collected for her in the anteroom that day were a rogues' gallery of malformed. A bald woman without ears contemplated the gold imp-clock, skin flush and shiny from temples to occiput. Beside her sat a younger girl, whose skull was fissured such that three separate peaks, paraboloid in shape, protruded above the hair, which continued down either side of a densely acned face like a skipper's beard. Across the room, studying a copy of the Reader's Digest, sat an aged gentleman in a moss-green gabardine suit, who possessed three nostrils, no upper lip and an assortment of different-sized teeth which leaned and crowded together like the headstones of a boneyard in tornado country. And off in a corner, looking at nothing, was a sexless being with hereditary syphilis, whose bones had acquired lesions and had partially collapsed so that the gray face's profile was nearly a straight line, the nose hanging down like a loose flap of skin, nearly covering the mouth; the chin depressed at the side by a large sunken crater containing radial skin-wrinkles; the eyes squeezed shut by the same unnatural gravity that flattened the rest of the profile. Esther, who was still at an impressionable age, identified with them all. . . .

This first day Schoenmaker spent in pre-operative reconnaissance of the terrain: photographing Esther's face and nose from various angles, checking for upper respiratory infections, running a Wassermann. Irving and Trench also assisted him in making two duplicate casts or death-masks. They gave her two paper straws to breathe through and in her childish way she thought of soda shops, cherry Cokes, True Confessions.

In Which Esther Gets a Nose Job

Next day she was back at the office. The two casts were there on his desk, side by side. "I'm twins," she giggled. Schoenmaker reached out and snapped the plaster nose from one of the masks.

"Now," he smiled; producing like a magician a lump of modeling clay with which he replaced the broken-off nose. "What sort of nose did you have in mind?"

What else: Irish, she wanted, turned up. Like they all wanted. To none of them did it occur that the retroussé nose too is an aesthetic misfit: a Jew nose in reverse, is all. Few had ever asked for a so-called "perfect" nose, where the roof is straight, the tip untilted and unhooked, the columella (separating the nostrils) meeting the upper lip at 90°. All of which went to support his private thesis that correction—along all dimensions: social, political, emotional—entails retreat to a diametric opposite rather than any reasonable search for a golden mean.

A few artistic finger-flourishes and wrist-twistings.

"Would that be it?" Eyes aglow, she nodded. "It has to harmonize with the rest of your face, you see." It didn't, of course. All that could harmonize with a face, if you were going to be humanistic about it, was obviously what the face was born with.

"But," he'd been able to rationalize years before, "there is harmony and harmony." So, Esther's nose. Identical with an ideal of nasal beauty established by movies, advertisements, magazines illustrations. Cultural harmony, Schoenmaker called it.

"Try next week then." He gave her the time. Esther was thrilled. It was like waiting to be born, and talking over with God, calm and businesslike, exactly how you wanted to enter the world.

Next week she arrived, punctual: guts tight, skin sensitive. "Come." Schoenmaker took her gently by the hand. She felt passive, even (a little?) sexually aroused. She was seated in a dentist's chair, tilted back and prepared by Irving, who hovered about her like a handmaiden.

Esther's face was cleaned in the nasal region with green soap, iodine and alcohol. The hair inside her nostrils was clipped and the vestibules cleaned gently with antiseptics. She was then given Nembutal.

It was expected this would calm her down, but barbituric acid derivatives affect individuals differently. Perhaps her initial sexual arousal contributed; but by the time Esther was taken to the operating room she was near delirium. "Should have used Hyoscin," Trench said. "It gives them amnesia, man."

"Quiet, schlep," said the doctor, scrubbing. Irving set about arranging his armamentarium, while Trench strapped Esther to the operating table. Esther's eyes were wild; she sobbed quietly, obviously beginning to get second thoughts. "Too late now," Trench consoled her, grinning. "Lay quiet, hey."

All three wore surgical masks. The eyes looked suddenly malevolent to Esther. She tossed her head. "Trench, hold her head," came Shoenmaker's muffled voice, "and Irving can be the anaesthetist. You need practice, babe. Go get the Novocain bottle."

Sterile towels were placed under Esther's head and a drop of castor oil in each eye. Her face was again swabbed, this time with Metaphen and alcohol. Gauze packing was then jammed far up her nostrils to keep antiseptics and blood from flowing down her pharynx and throat.

Irving returned with the Novocain, a syringe, and a needle. First she put the anaesthetic into the tip of Esther's nose, one injection on each side. Next she made a number of injections radially around each nostril, to deaden the wings, or alae, her thumb going down on the plunger each time as the needle withdrew. "Switch to the big one," Schoenmaker said quietly. Irving fished a two-inch needle out of the autoclave. This time the needle was pushed, just under the skin, all the way up each side of the nose, from the nostril to where the nose joined forehead.

No one had told Esther that anything about the operation would hurt: But these injections hurt: nothing before in her experience had ever hurt quite so much. All she had free to move for the pain were her hips. Trench held her head and leered appreciatively as she squirmed, constrained, on the table.

Inside the nose again with another burden of anaesthetic, Irving's hypodermic was inserted between the upper and lower cartilage and pushed all the way up to the glabella—the bump between the eyebrows.

A series of internal injections to the septum—the wall of bone and cartilage which separates the two halves of the nose—and anaesthesia was complete. The sexual metaphor in all this wasn't lost on Trench, who kept chanting, "Stick it in . . . pull it out . . . stick it in . . . ooh that was good . . . pull it out . . ." and tittering softly above Esther's eyes. Irving would sigh each time, exasperated. "That boy," you expected her to say.

After a while Schoenmaker started pinching and twisting Esther's nose. "How does it feel? Hurt?" A whispered no: Schoenmaker twisted harder: "Hurt?" No. "Okay. Cover her eyes."

"Maybe she wants to look," Trench said.

"You want to look, Esther? See what we're going to do to you?"

"I don't know." Her voice was weak, teetering between here and hysteria.

"Watch, then," said Schoenmaker. "Get an education. First we'll cut out the hump. Let's see a scalpel."

It was a routine operation; Schoenmaker worked quickly, neither he nor his nurse wasting any motion. Caressing sponge-strokes made it nearly bloodless. Occasionally a trickle would elude him and get halfway to the towels before he caught it.

Schoenmaker first made two incisions, one on either side through the internal lining of the nose, near the septum at the lower border of the side cartilage. He then pushed a pair of long-handled, curved and pointed scissors through the nostril, up past the cartilage to the nasal bone. The scissors had been designed to cut both on opening and closing. Quickly, like a barber finishing up a high-tipping head, he separated the bone from the membrane and skin over it. "Undermining, we call this," he explained. He repeated the scissors work through the other nostril. "You see you have two nasal bones, they're separated by your septum. At the bottom they're each attached to a piece of lateral cartilage. I'm undermining you all the way from this attachment to where the nasal bones join the forehead."

Irving passed him a chisel-like instrument. "MacKenty's elevator, this is." With the elevator he probed around, completing the undermining.

"Now," gently, like a lover, "I'm going to saw off your hump." Esther watched his eyes as best she could, looking for something human there. Never had she felt so helpless. Later she would say, "It was almost a mystic experience. What religion is it—one of the Eastern ones—where the highest condition we can attain is that of an object—a rock. It was like that; I felt myself drifting down, this delicious loss of Estherhood, becoming more and more a blob, with no worries, traumas, nothing: only Being. . . ."

The mask with the clay nose lay on a small table nearby. Referring to it with quick side-glances, Schoenmaker inserted the saw blade through one of the incisions he'd made, and pushed it up to the bony part. Then lined it up with the line of the new nose-roof and carefully began to saw through the nasal bone on that side. "Bone saws easily," he remarked to Esther. "We're all really quite frail." The blade reached soft septum; Schoenmaker withdrew the blade. "Now comes the tricky part. I got to saw off the other side exactly the same. Otherwise your nose will be lopsided." He inserted the saw in the same way on the other side, studied the mask for what seemed to Esther a quarter of an hour; made several minute adjustments. Then finally sawed off the bone there in a straight line.

"Your hump is now two loose pieces of bone, attached only to the septum. We have to cut that through, flush with the other two cuts." This he did with an angle-bladed pull-knife, cutting down swiftly, completing the phase with some graceful sponge-flourishing.

"And now the hump floats inside the nose." He pulled back one nostril with a retractor, inserted a pair of forceps and fished around for the hump. "Take that back," he smiled. "It doesn't want to come just yet." With scissors he snipped the hump loose from the lateral cartilage which had been holding it; then, with the bone-forceps, removed a dark-colored lump of gristle, which he waved triumphantly before Esther. "Twenty-two years of social unhappiness, nicht wahr? End of act one. We'll put it in formaldehyde, you can keep it for a souvenir if you wish." As he talked he smoothed the edges of the cuts with a small rasp file.

So much for the hump. But where the hump had been was now a flat area. The bridge of the nose had been too wide to begin with, and now had to be narrowed.

Again he undermined the nasal bones, this time around to where they met the cheekbones, and beyond. As he removed the scissors he inserted a right-angled saw in its place. "Your nasal bones are anchored firmly, you see; at the side to the cheekbone, at the top to the forehead. We must fracture them, so we can move your nose around. Just like that lump of clay."

He sawed through the nasal bones on each side,

separating them from the cheekbones. He then took a chisel and inserted it through one nostril, pushing it as high as he could, until it touched bone.

"Let me know if you feel anything." He gave the chisel a few light taps with a mallet; stopped, puzzled, and then began to hammer harder. "It's a rough mother," he said, dropping his jocular tone. Tap, tap, tap. "Come on, you bastard." The chisel point edged its way, millimeter by millimeter, between Esther's eyebrows. "Scheisse!" With a loud snap, her nose was broken free of the forehead. By pushing in from either side with his thumbs, Schoenmaker completed the fracture.

"See? It's all wobbly now. That's act two. Now ve shorten das septum, ja."

With a scalpel he made an incision around the septum, between it and its two adjoining lateral cartilages. He then cut down around the front of the septum to the "spine," located just inside the nostrils at the back.

"Which should give you a free-floating septum. We use scissors to finish the job." With dissecting scissors he undermined the septum along its side and up over the bone as far as the glabella, at the top of the nose.

He passed a scalpel next into one of the incisions just inside the nostril and out the other, and worked the cutting edge around until the septum was separated at the bottom. Then elevated one nostril with a retractor, reached in with Allis clamps and pulled out part of the loose septum. A quick transfer of calipers from mask to exposed septum; then with a pair of straight scissors Schoenmaker snipped off a triangular wedge of septum. "Now to put everything in place."

Keeping one eye on the mask, he brought together the nasal bones. This narrowed the bridge and eliminated the flat part where the hump had been cut off. He took some time making sure the two halves were lined up dead-center. The bones made a curious crackling sound as he moved them. "For your turned-up nose, we make two sutures."

The "seam" was between the recently-cut edge of the septum and the columella. With needle and needle-holder, two silk stitches were taken obliquely, through the entire widths of columella and septum.

The operation had taken, in all, less than an hour. They cleaned Esther up, removed the plain gauze packing and replaced it with sulfa ointment and more gauze. A strip of adhesive tape went on over her nostrils, another over the bridge of the new nose. On top of this went a Stent mold, a tin guard, and more adhesive plaster. Rubber tubes were put in each nostril so she could breathe.

Two days later the packing was removed. The adhesive plaster came off after five days. The sutures came out after seven. The uptilted end product looked ridiculous but Schoenmaker assured her it would come down a little after a few months. It did.

3

That would have been all: except for Esther. Possibly her old hump-nosed habits had continued on by virtue of momentum. But never before had she been so passive with any male. Passivity having only one meaning for her, she left the hospital Schoenmaker had sent her to after a day and a night, and roamed the East Side in fugue, scaring people with her white beak and a certain shock about the eyes. She was sexually turned on, was all: as if Schoenmaker had located and flipped a secret switch or clitoris somewhere inside her nasal cavity. A cavity is a cavity, after all: Trench's gift for metaphor might have been contagious.

Returning the following week to have the stitches

removed, she crossed and uncrossed her legs, batted eye-
lashes, talked soft: everything crude she knew. Schoenmaker had spotted her at the outset as an easy make.

"Come back tomorrow," he told her. Irving was off.
Esther arrived the next day garbed underneath as lacily
and with as many fetishes as she could afford. There
might even have been a dab of Shalimar on the gauze
in the center of her face.

In the back room: "How do you feel."

She laughed, too loud. "It hurts. But."

"Yes, but. There are ways to forget the pain."

She seemed unable to get rid of a silly, half-apolo-
getic smile. It stretched her face, adding to the pain in
her nose.

"Do you know what we're going to do? No, what I
am going to do to you? Of course."

She let him undress her. He commented only on a
black garter belt.

"Oh. Oh God." An attack of conscience: Slab had
given it to her. With love, presumably.

"Stop. Stop the peep-show routine. You're not a virgin."

Another self-deprecating laugh. "That's just it. Another boy. Gave it to me. Boy that I loved."

She's in shock, he thought, vaguely surprised.

"Come. We'll make believe it's your operation. You
enjoyed your operation, didn't you."

Through a crack in the curtains opposite Trench
looked on.

"Lie on the bed. That will be our operating table.
You are to get an intermuscular injection."

"No," she cried.

"You have worked on many ways of saying no. No
meaning yes. That no I don't like. Say it differently."

"No," with a little moan.

"Different. Again."

"No," this time a smile, eyelids at half-mast.

In Which Esther Gets a Nose Job

"Again."

"No."

"You're getting better." Unknotting his tie, trousers in a puddle about his feet, Schoenmaker serenaded her.

> Have I told you, fella
> She's got the sweetest columella
> And a septum that's swept 'em all on their ass;
> Each casual chondrectomy
> Meant only a big fat check to me
> Till I sawed this osteoclastible lass:

[Refrain]:

> Till you've cut into Esther
> You've cut nothing at all;
> She's one of the best, Thir,
> To her nose I'm in thrall.

> She never acts nasty
> But lies still as a rock;
> She loves my rhinoplasty
> But the others are schlock.

> Esther is passive,
> Her aplomb is massive,
> How could any poor ass've
> Ever passed her by?

> And let me to you say
> She puts Ireland to shame;
> For her nose is retroussé
> And Esther's her name. . . .

For the last eight bars she chanted "No" on one and three. . . .

MYTH
PARABLE

QUEEN LOUISA

John Gardner

1

Mad Queen Louisa awakened feeling worried and irritable. That was by no means unusual for her. It had been happening since she was a little girl, or, as she sometimes clearly remembered, a lizard. She fanned herself with the fingers of one hand, anxiously searching, as she always did for the first few minutes, for the deeply buried secret of her soul's unrest. She was not afraid of rape or poverty or death. She'd established these facts beyond a shadow of a doubt many years ago—she'd long since forgotten precisely how, but one cannot keep plowing the same old ground. As for lesser fears, suffice it to say that she'd read all the books in the royal palace —not only those in Slavonic and Latin, but those in German and French as well, and one in English, sometimes reading in her character as queen, sometimes as a huge and sleepy-eyed toad in spectacles—and she'd sys-

John Gardner

tematically crossed off all possible causes of distress from anorexy to zygomatic fever. Despite that, she always woke up worried and irritable. Her solution, which was simple and brilliantly effective, once she was awake to remember it, was to find little nothings to attach her deep, vague worry to. The lady-in-waiting seemed peaked, out of sorts; some trouble with her husband? Or the castle's north wall had moss on it. Do moss roots run deep? Could they loosen the stones?

She opened the curtains of her huge gold bed. (The king always slept alone these days. He said it was the wars. Had he taken some mistress?) Already the chamber was alive with light—the chambermaid always threw the windows wide open at six o'clock. Orderly details make orderly days, Queen Louisa believed. Also, toads like the early morning damp. Every surface, every plane or flange or lozenge of the furniture gleamed, almost sang, with light. The combs and brushes on her dressing table were so bright she had to blink.

Carefully, she slipped her toes into the cold, then her shins and knees. The floor, when she reached it, was deliciously icy. She'd catch her death of pneumonia, she realized, and hurriedly felt left and right for her slippers.

The door flew open, and the chambermaid rushed in. She was supposed to be here when the queen awakened. Queen Louisa felt a catch and thoughtfully narrowed her large and luminous (she knew) eyes. What had the chambermaid been up to? she wondered. The girl looked flushed. She was fourteen, no older. She looked—the queen touched her bosom in alarm—she looked pregnant!

At Queen Louisa's moan, the child rushed to her and seized her hands.

"Are you ill, your majesty?" On her cheeks, two bright roses. Her eyes were gray.

"*I'm* well enough," the queen said very cautiously.

158

Her mind raced over whom it might be. Not the page, certainly. He was fat as a pig and reeked of old cider. She did hope not one of those trumpet players! It couldn't be one of the knights, of course, because of the wars—unless perhaps one of the wounded ones. Her mind fixed with horrible and vaguely pleasurable fascination on the thought of the chambermaid creeping to the infirmary, slipping into bed with some great gored creature with a six-month beard. She secretly whispered a prayer to protect her from salacious thoughts.

"I just stepped out for a minute, your majesty," the chambermaid said.

Queen Louisa was sick with worry now. Perhaps it was no one from the castle at all. Perhaps the girl's father, some peasant from the village.

"Help me with my dressing-gown," the queen said weakly.

"Of course, your majesty!" She bowed very low and went pale for an instant. A sign of pregnancy if ever there was one! But the queen said nothing. Mad she might be—so everyone maintained, though they did not seem so all right themselves, in her opinion—but she was not a person who poked into other people's business. A little cry escaped her. The lady-in-waiting who'd been fighting with her husband should be here now too. Was she off with the great dog, the chambermaid's father? The girl was studying her, alarmed by the cry. Queen Louisa smiled gently, and the girl was reassured. Queen Louisa extended her arms for the golden sleeves.

"Is his majesty at breakfast?" Queen Louisa asked. It was important to keep one's servants at ease, keep their minds occupied.

"He left in the middle of the night, my lady. The wars, you know." The child's voice sounded so apologetic you'd have thought the wars were all her fault.

John Gardner

"Well, no matter, my dear," Queen Louisa said. "I'm sure we'll manage."

"I do *hope* so, your majesty!"

Queen Louisa froze. There was no mistaking the distress in the voice of her chambermaid. It was something beyond any personal distress. (Mad Queen Louisa had a sense about these things.) She moved toward her gold and ivory mirror, lacing up the front of her dressing gown. Very casually, she said, "Is something wrong, my dear?"

Suddenly, touched off by the tender concern in her majesty's voice, the chambermaid burst into tears. "Oh, my lady, my lady, how dare I reveal it?"

Queen Louisa frowned, profoundly worried, then hurriedly smiled, for fear she might shake the child's foundations, and lightly patted the chambermaid's hand. "Tell me everything," she said, "and Queen Louisa will fix it."

The child required no further encouragement. Clinging to her majesty's hand, she said, "A witch has appeared on the mountain and put all the hermits to flight. The peasants are so frightened they can hardly speak for shuddering. What are we to do? Oh, your majesty, your majesty! The king and his knights are a hundred miles away!"

Queen Louisa sighed but refused to tremble. She put her arm gently around the poor girl and sadly gazed into the mirror. Her great heavy-lidded eyes gazed back at her, and her wide, sad toad's mouth. The golden dressing-gown clung tightly to her thick, rough, swamp-green torso, though the sleeves were loose and a little too long. "Never mind," she said. "Queen Louisa will fix it." And she would. No question. All the same, it was inconsiderate and irrational of the king to leave his kingdom in the hands of a queen who was insane. Fleetingly, she wondered who his mistress might be. *Not* her own lady-in-waiting, surely! But the moment the thought occurred to her, she was certain she was right. (These hunches of hers were infallible.) —But if so, then his majesty was the chambermaid's fat peasant father, who was sleeping with the lady-in-waiting because of her troubles with her husband; and the peasant's child, that is, the king's, her little chambermaid, could be only—her own lost daughter! Queen Louisa smiled, feeling wildly happy, but said nothing for the moment, biding her time. She felt warm all over, and strangely majestic. She was soon to be a grandmother.

2

"The Court is now in session," Queen Louisa said.

The judges looked befuddled and a trifle annoyed, which she could well understand. But the facts were simple, and nothing makes a trial run more smoothly than simple facts. It was not, of course, the business of royalty to explain itself to mere judges of the realm. ("Never complain, never explain" was Queen Louisa's motto.) And the facts were these: that the king and his knights were all far away, except for the knights in the infirmary, and there was no one at home to deal with the troubles but the Royal Court. Therefore Queen Louisa had assembled the Court.

The chief justice looked over the tops of his spectacles, holding his wig away with the backs of the fingers of his hands, partly for the sake of seeing better, partly for the sake of hearing. He looked from the empty defendant's chair to the empty benches where the various lawyers and their witnesses should be. It was a tense moment, and the chambermaid glanced in alarm at the queen. The lower justices, one on each side of the chief justice, pretended to study their copious notes and copy them over more legibly, though the queen suspected they had nothing written down in the first place. Queen Louisa could easily forgive them, however. Indeed, she'd have done the same herself. Surely they'd never encountered a case quite like this before.

Timidly, but with a hint of irritation, the chief justice said, "Where is the defendant?"

The lower justices smiled as they always smiled at every question he asked, as if saying to themselves, "Very shrewdly put!" Their smiles emboldened him to ask it again, even letting out a little smile himself: *"Your majesty, where is the defendant?"*

Queen Louisa smiled too, though she pitied them, really: dependent as children, hopelessly shackled in rules and procedures, wholly unprepared for the rich and strange. In their long white wigs they looked like sheep. In fact, when she saw how they held their pencils—poked between their pointed hooves—she became half-convinced that they *were* sheep. With the greatest possible dignity—to set a good example for the chambermaid, since a kingdom where the honor of courts is forgotten is a kingdom in trouble, and also because sheep are people, too, whose feelings can be hurt—but mainly because she had a vague suspicion that only by speaking with the greatest possible dignity could she prevent her words from seeming ridiculous, even to a sheep—Queen Louisa said: "You ask me where the defendant is. *That,* my lord justices"—she paused dramatically—"I leave to the wisdom of this Court."

They looked at each other, and the chief of the justices paled a little and glanced at the clock. Again he peered down at the empty benches where the defendant, witnesses, and lawyers should be. He cleaned his spectacles. "Your majesty," he said at last, like a creature completely baffled . . . but he let his words trail off.

Queen Louisa said nothing, merely patted the chambermaid's knee to show that all was well. The child, of course, never having been in a court before, had no idea how long these things took. She too kept glancing anxiously at the clock, wringing her hands, and pulling at her kerchief till it was so twisted around one could hardly see her face.

Meekly, the justices began to make guesses. "Is the defendant somewhere else?" asked the one on the left.

Queen Louisa pursed her lips and thought. "You're warm," she said at last. She exchanged winks with the chambermaid.

"Somewhere outside the castle?" asked the one on the right.

"Warmer!" said the queen, and squeezed her hands together.

"He's having his coffee!" the chief justice cried.

"Cold," snapped the queen.

"Poor devil!" they moaned. They had no real understanding of trials, she saw, or else they weren't really trying.

"In my opinion," the chambermaid whispered, "this Court's getting *nowhere*."

"Trials are like that, my dear," said Queen Louisa. "But if you insist, I'll give their honors a hint."

"Would you?" begged the girl.

Queen Louisa rose and extended her long-sleeved arms for silence. "My lord justices," she said, "let me give you a hint."

They accepted eagerly, all three of them waiting with their pencils poised.

"Our business, I think you'll agree," said the queen, "is justice."

The justices furtively glanced at each other, as self-conscious and timid as newts. For no clear reason, she was suddenly filled with a profound sadness. Still the justices waited, hoping for something more and scratching their foreheads with their chewed-down eraser ends.

("Justice," the chief justice kept mumbling, picking at his lip. He wrote down: "Just Ice?")

Queen Louisa continued, watching them carefully for a sign they'd got it: "You've perhaps heard that our hermits have been frightened from the mountain by an alleged witch." She paused, startled, rather pleased that she'd thought to say *alleged*. It was the first real clue. The witch was perhaps in fact *not* a witch, in which case, of course, the whole trial . . . She glanced suspiciously at the chambermaid, then remembered, in confusion, that the child was her daughter. The child glanced suspiciously back at her. But still the judges' faces were blank. Queen Louisa sighed and worried that she might be spoiling everything by revealing too much. She continued, however: "Since the king and his knights are all away, it seems to me our bounden duty to investigate this matter. I therefore suggest that we ride to the mountain and investigate."

"Hear, hear!" the judges cried wildly, all three of them at once, and glanced at each other.

That must have been the answer (though Queen Louisa had to admit she'd gotten lost somewhere), because the poor little chambermaid was trembling all over and clapping her hands and weeping.

3

There was some difficulty with the queen's horse. In the end, they all rode in the royal carriage. The chambermaid huddled in the shadow of the queen, contributing nothing to the conversation, no doubt partly because, sitting with the queen, she was wedged in tight.

"I was born of simple, honest stock," the queen narrated. The chambermaid looked up at her eagerly, from the seat beside her. Outside, the landscape was glittering white. On the castle wall, now far in the distance, the gored knights from the infirmary were all waving colored banners and shouting. The three old sheep sat leaning far forward, for Queen Louisa was speaking very softly, harkening back. All three had their thin hooves folded on their knees and their bowlers in their laps, for the ceiling of the carriage was strangely low. She was reminded, and spoke of, the ceiling of the cottage at the edge of the forest where her parents lived. (She sat with her knees pulled tightly together, despite cramp and discomfort, but even so she could give no more room to the chambermaid. As she spoke, Queen Louisa kept her hands carefully in front of her great green wattles, merely as a kindness to the others. Personally, she rather enjoyed her appearance. "A queen with a *difference*," she liked to say, winking coyly.)

"It was a marriage no one believed would work. Mother was Irish, and Father was a dragon. Except for a very few dear friends, they were cut off by both communities. But the cruelty of people who had supposedly loved them served only to intensify their love and deep respect for one another. I was the youngest of the children, of whom there were sometimes seven and sometimes four, depending."

"Depending on what?" the chief justice broke in, not at all urgently—in fact tears were streaming from his large, pink eyes.

"Depending on our parents," Queen Louisa explained, and realized now for perhaps the first time how profoundly true that was. "We were poor but extremely proud, you see.—Of course it was difficult for Father to get work." She remembered with a pang how he'd sit by the fireplace pretending to read the evening paper, though in fact, as everyone in the family knew, it was a

John Gardner

paper from last year. A tear ran down the side of Queen Louisa's nose. "It was difficult," she said once more—merely to find her place again—"for Father to get work."

"It would be, yes," said the sheep on the left, "being married to a Catholic."

Queen Louisa brightened. "But poor as we were, we had each other!"

"Perhaps that's why sometimes there were only four," the chief justice said.

She had a curious feeling, which she couldn't in the least explain to herself, that the conversation was losing direction. She decided to leap forward. "When I was nine, there was a fire in the old wooden church in the nearby village. Naturally, Father was blamed for it." She paused, frowning, though she was secretly flattered. "Excuse me," she said to the chief justice, "are you writing all this down?"

He looked up, startled, still weeping profusely, then immediately blushed. He held the paper toward her, on which he'd been writing, in large block letters, with the greatest imaginable concentration. The paper said: JUSTICE   ST. JUICE   CUTE JEST [crossed off]   SUITE   SITE   TIE   IS   US   USE

Queen Louisa mused, the chambermaid peeking around past her elbow. "Ist!" Queen Louisa said suddenly in German.

"Tu es," cried the chambermaid in French.

"Je suis," cried the sheep on the left.

They merely looked at him.

Queen Louisa sighed. "Well," she said, "they took Father away. I remember his parting words to us. He was a poet at heart, I've always felt. It was a wintry morning very like this one." She gazed sadly out the window. "He gazed sadly out the window, a policeman standing at each side of him—he had only his old

166

singed overcoat on, and I remember the tears were cours-
ing down his cheeks—and he said:

> " 'My loves, do not blame the authorities for this.
>   Who can swear
>   that his own apprehension of reality is valid?
>   There are certain insects—
>   I forget which ones—that have no apparatus for
>   determining
>   that other insects of their own same kind exist.
>   Such is
>   our lot. Have faith! Love even those who bring
>   sorrow to you!' "

"Hexameters—loosely," the chief justice said.
She looked at him with new respect.

There, unfortunately, she was forced to discon-
tinue her narrative. They'd arrived at their destination.

4

The monastery gates were open wide. Queen Louisa
discovered, descending from the carriage and keeping
the chambermaid's hand in hers to give the poor child
courage, that in the monastery yard there was no one
at all, not even a footprint in the snow to suggest that
possibly someone had been there, or at least someone's
shoe. She tiptoed softly to the monastery door, leading
the child, and the three old sheep came audiculously
behind her, huddled close together and holding their
bowlers on with both hand, as people would do in a
windstorm. There was, of course, not a breath of wind,
but logic was not their strong point (she thought fondly)

and, also, the bowlers were new. The inside of the monastery was also empty. She tried the back door.

"I'm frightened," said the chambermaid.

"Call me Mother, if you like," Queen Louisa said.

The chambermaid looked at her, then looked away, sucked in her lower lip, and seemed to think about it.

Queen Louisa laughed gently. "You young people!" she said.

In the snowy back garden they encountered a truly amazing sight.

The garden's stone walls were encased in ice, as was every tree and shrub and leftover flower stalk. But in the center of the garden there was a glorious rosebush in triumphant bloom, such bloom as would hardly be natural on even the warmest summer day. And beside the bush there was a horrible ugly old witchlike person who was trying to cut down the rosebush with an axe. With every swipe she took, the trunk of the bush grew wider and stronger, and the roses bloomed more brightly. At the feet of the ugly witchlike person, an old red hound lay whimpering and whining.

Queen Louisa stared in astonishment, believing for an instant that her whole life had been a terrible mistake. But somehow or other she collected her wits and called out in a stern and commanding voice, "Stop!" —for she was capable of such things, if driven too far.

At once both the witchlike person and the dog looked up at her. For an instant the witchlike person was thrown, but only for an instant. "Never!" she cried, her lean lips trembling and her eyes so ferociously green with evil that Queen Louisa was fearful that the chambermaid might faint. Immediately the witchlike person began swinging the axe like someone in a drunken rage, and the old dog whimpered and whined in such awful and unspeakable misery that even the Royal Court was moved to tears. The rosebush, of course, grew stronger by leaps and bounds.

"Stop her! Do something!" the chambermaid hissed, clinging to Queen Louisa with trembling hands.

But Queen Louisa thoughtfully narrowed her eyes, pursed her lips, and calmed the chambermaid by patting her hand. "Be quiet, Muriel," she said very softly. "I don't think we've quite understood this situation."

"Muriel?" said the chambermaid.

"My dear," said Queen Louisa in a stern but not unfriendly voice, signifying by a look that she was addressing the person swinging the axe, "every stroke you strike makes the rosebush stronger."

"Good point!" said the judges, frantically searching through their trouser pockets for their notebooks.

"Get away! Be gone!" said the witchlike person.

Queen Louisa smiled. She said, "Dog, come here."

With an awful groan, the old red hound got up and came timidly toward her. It settled at her feet and closed its eyes like a creature enormously embarrassed.

"Muriel," Queen Louisa said out of the side of her mouth, "meet your ridiculous father."

The chambermaid looked at the dog, touching her chin with three fingers. "How do you do," she said at last.

The witchlike person was perspiring now. Her black robe clung to her armpits and back, and her nose and chin (which were as blue and as pointed as icicles) dripped. She stopped swinging and leaned on her axe, panting, "I'm not beaten," she whispered.

Immediately, as if at a signal, a hundred wolves in the robes of pious monks came bounding over the garden wall and crouched, growling, with their ghastly fangs bared, in a semicircle around Queen Louisa and her friends.

The witchlike person laughed. "You see, my ancient enemy," she cried, "your whole life has been a terrible mistake! The forces of evil do exist! Ha ha!" Words cannot describe the unearthly horror of that final "Ha ha!" She raised the axe in one hand and brandished it. "We're cosmic accidents!" cried the witchlike person. "Life is gratuitous, it has no meaning till we make one up by our intensity. That is why these gentle monks have joined me in seeking to wreak havoc on the kingdom. Not for personal gain. Ha ha! Ha ha! But to end the boredom! To end all those mornings of waking up vaguely irritable! Ha ha!" She sidled toward the queen. "I have seduced your husband. What do you think of that? I have filled him with the feeling that life *is* meaningful, if only because it can be thrown away. I have—"

Suddenly Queen Louisa heard, behind her in the formerly empty monastery, a thrilling crashing and clanking of armor. The witchlike person went pale with fear. "Strike now!" she exclaimed to the wolves. "Strike now, and quickly, before it's too late!"

But the wolves stood trembling and wringing their paws, too terrified to move an inch. And before you could say Jack Robinson, the door behind Queen Louisa opened and a thousand gory wounded knights came out, pushing into every available space in the garden, saying "Excuse me" as they passed Queen Louisa and her friends, and they raised their swords to execute the wolves.

"Stop!" cried Queen Louisa.

Everybody stopped.

Queen Louisa walked with great dignity and calm to the miraculous rosebush, her webbed hands gracefully crossed across her wattles.

"You've all misunderstood everything," she said. "Or else I have. But no matter, since I'm the queen." She could have explained, if she wanted to, how sorry she felt for the wicked of this world, who couldn't even cut a rosebush down. Though she'd admit, in all fairness, that perhaps the rosebush *was* cut down, since she was insane and could never know anything for sure, and perhaps the whole story was taking place in a hotel in Philadelphia.

"Watch!" said Queen Louisa. She closed her large and luminous eyes and concentrated. A gasp went through the monastery garden, for behold, Queen Louisa had changed from an enormous toad to a magnificently beautiful redheaded woman with a pale, freckled nose. Her white, white arms were so delicately dimpled at the elbows that neither knight nor wolf could refrain from licking his lips with desire. "Mother!" cried the chambermaid. "My beloved!" cried the king—changed that same instant from the dog he was before. The witchlike person was reduced in a flash to the lady-in-waiting. She sat weeping and groaning at her monstrous betrayal of everybody, and especially her husband. The leader of the wolves said, "Let us pray." The rosebush, being of no further use, withered to an ice-clad stick.

Queen Louisa extended her soft white arm to the chambermaid. "My sweet," she said, "it's natural that youth should be rebellious. I was rebellious myself. But I want you to know that if you want to come home, your father and I agree, you're welcome."

Neither demanding nor expecting that the others would follow her, lovely Queen Louisa turned, with a gentle bow, and went back into the monastery and through it to the yard and on to the carriage. She got in and, with a thoughtful frown, turned back into a toad. Immediately the three sheep got in, and after them Queen Louisa's daughter, Muriel, and then His Majesty the King and Her Majesty's lady-in-waiting. The wounded knights lined up behind the carriage to follow it home. With two extra people beside them now, the three sheep were so crowded they could hardly breathe. Yet they smiled like madmen in their joy at the king's proxsimity.

Queen Louisa said—the child looked up at her with

admiration like a gasp—"Don't blame yourself, my sweet. It's true, of course, that your dramatic leaving gave your father ideas. The poor old fool was in his forties then, and, I'm sorry to say, all people in their thirties and early forties have this awful lust—this ridiculous hunger for experience, so to speak. And the pretty way you mocked him, of course, and flirted with him—"

"*I* did all this?" the chambermaid said.

Queen Louisa smiled sadly at the look of dismay and bafflement in little Muriel's eyes. Then, with the carriage gently swaying and the snow falling softly from the pitchdark sky, Mad Queen Louisa told her beautiful newfound daughter the story of her life.

The boy beside the coachman said: "Isn't this **a** marvelous tale to be in?"

The coachman, who was silver-haired and wise, gave his nephew a wink. "You barely made it, laddie!"

ORDER OF INSECTS

William H. Gass

We certainly had no complaints about the house after all we had been through in the other place, but we hadn't lived there very long before I began to notice every morning the bodies of a large black bug spotted about the downstairs carpet; haphazardly, as earth worms must die on the street after a rain; looking when I first saw them like rolls of dark wool or pieces of mud from the children's shoes, or sometimes, if the drapes were pulled, so like ink stains or deep burns they terrified me, for I had been intimidated by that thick rug very early and the first week had walked over it wishing my bare feet would swallow my shoes. The shells were usually broken. Legs and other parts I couldn't then identify would be scattered near like flakes of rust. Occasionally I would find them on their backs, their quilted undersides showing orange, while beside them were smudges of dark-brown powder that had to be vacuumed carefully. We believed our cat had killed them. She was frequently sick during the night then—a rare thing for her—and we could think of no other reason. Overturned like that they looked pathetic even dead.

I could not imagine where the bugs had come from. I am terribly meticulous myself. The house was clean, the cupboards tight and orderly, and we never saw one alive. The other place had been infested with those flat brown fuzzy roaches, all wires and speed, and we'd seen *them* all right, frightened by the kitchen light, sifting through the baseboards and the floor's cracks; and in the pantry I had nearly closed my fingers on one before it fled, tossing its shadow across the starch like an image of the startle in my hand.

Dead, overturned, their three pairs of legs would be delicately drawn up and folded shyly over their stomachs. When they walked I suppose their forelegs were thrust out and then bent to draw the body up. I still wonder if they jumped. More than once I've seen our cat hook one of her claws under a shell and toss it in the air, crouching while the insect fell, feigning leaps—but there was daylight; the bug was dead; she was not really interested any more; and she would walk immediately away. That image takes the place of jumping. Even if I actually saw those two back pairs of legs unhinge, as they would have to if one leaped, I think I'd find the result unreal and mechanical, a poor try measured by that sudden, high, head-over-heels flight from our cat's paw. I could look it up, I guess, but it's no study for a woman . . . bugs.

At first I reacted as I should, bending over, wondering what in the world; yet even before I recognized them I'd withdrawn my hand, shuddering. Fierce, ugly, armored things: they used their shadows to seem large. The machine sucked them up while I looked the other way. I remember the sudden thrill of horror I had hearing one rattle up the wand. I was relieved that they were dead, of course, for I could never have killed one, and if they had been popped, alive, into the dust bag of the cleaner, I believe I would have had nightmares again as I did the time my husband fought the red ants in our kitchen. All night I lay awake thinking of the ants alive in the belly of the machine, and when toward morning I finally slept I found myself in the dreadful elastic tunnel of the suction tube where ahead of me I heard them: a hundred bodies rustling in the dirt.

I never think of their species as alive but as comprised entirely by the dead ones on our carpet, all the new dead manufactured by the action of some mysterious spoor—perhaps that dust they sometimes lie in—carried in the air, solidified by night and shaped, from body into body, spontaneously, as maggots were before the age of science. I have a single book about insects, a little dated handbook in French which a good friend gave me as a joke—because of my garden, the quaintness of the plates, the fun of reading about worms in such an elegant tongue—and my bug has his picture there climbing the stem of an orchid. Beneath the picture is his name: *Periplaneta orientalis L. Ces répugnants insectes ne sont que trop communs dans les cuisines des vieilles habitations des villes, dans les magasins, entrepôts, boulangeries, brasseries, restaurants, dans la cale des navires, etc.,* the text begins. Nevertheless they are a new experience for me and I think that I am grateful for it now.

The picture didn't need to show me there were two, adult and nymph, for by that time I'd seen the bodies of both kinds. Nymph. My god the names we use. The one was dark, squat, ugly, sly. The other, slimmer, had hard sheath-like wings drawn over its back like another shell, and you could see delicate interwoven lines spun like fossil gauze across them. The nymph was a rich golden color deepening in its interstices to mahogany. Both had legs that looked under a glass like the canes of a rose, and the nymph's were sufficiently transparent in a good light you thought you saw its nerves merge and run like a jagged crack to each ultimate claw.

Tipped, their legs have fallen shut, and the more I look at them the less I believe my eyes. Corruption, in these bugs, is splendid. I've a collection now I keep in typewriter-ribbon tins, and though, in time, their bodies dry and the interior flesh decays, their features hold, as I suppose they held in life, an Egyptian determination, for their protective plates are strong and death must break bones to get in. Now that the heavy soul is gone, the case is light.

I suspect if we were as familiar with our bones as with our skin, we'd never bury dead but shrine them in their rooms, arranged as we might like to find them on a visit; and our enemies, if we could steal their bodies from the battle sites, would be museumed as they died, the steel still eloquent in their sides, their metal hats askew, the protective toes of their shoes unworn, and friend and enemy would be so wondrously historical that in a hundred years we'd find the jaws still hung for the same speech and all the parts we spent our life with tilted as they always were—rib cage, collar, skull— still repetitious, still defiant, angel light, still worthy of memorial and affection. After all, what does it mean to say that when our cat has bitten through the shell and put confusion in the pulp, the life goes out of them? Alas for us, I want to cry, our bones are secret, showing last, so we must love what perishes: the muscles and the waters and the fats.

Two prongs extend like daggers from the rear. I suppose I'll never know their function. That kind of knowledge doesn't take my interest. At first I had to screw my eyes down, and as I consider it now, the whole change, the recent alteration in my life, was the consequence of finally coming near to something. It was a self-mortifying act, I recall, a penalty I laid upon myself

for the evil-tempered words I'd shouted at my children
in the middle of the night. I felt instinctively the insects
were infectious and their own disease, so when I knelt I
held a handkerchief over the lower half of my face . . .
saw only the horror . . . turned, sick, masking my eyes
. . . yet the worst of angers held me through the day:
vague, searching, guilty, and ashamed.

After that I came near often; saw, for the first time,
the gold nymph's difference; put between the mandibles
a tinted nail I'd let grow long; observed the movement
of the jaws, the stalks of the antennae, the skull-shaped
skull, the lines banding the abdomen, and found an intensity in the posture of the shell, even when tipped, like
that in the gaze of Gauguin's natives' eyes. The dark
plates glisten. They are wonderfully shaped; even the
buttons of the compound eyes show a geometrical pre-
cision which prevents my earlier horror. It isn't possible
to feel disgust toward such an order. Nevertheless, I reminded myself, a roach . . . and you a woman.

I no longer own my own imagination. I suppose
they came up the drains or out of the registers. It may
have been the rug they wanted. Crickets, too, I understand, will feed on wool. I used to rest by my husband
. . . stiffly . . . waiting for silence to settle in the house,
his sleep to come, and then the drama of their passage
would take hold of me, possess me so completely that
when I finally slept I merely passed from one dream to
another without the slightest loss of vividness or continuity. Never alive, they came with punctures; their
bodies formed from little whorls of copperish dust which
in the downstairs darknesss I couldn't possibly have
seen; and they were dead and upside down when they
materialized, for it was in that moment that our cat,
herself darkly invisible, leaped and brought her paws
together on the true soul of the roach; a soul so static
and intense, so immortally arranged, I felt, while I lay
shell-like in our bed, turned inside out, driving my mind

away, it was the same as the dark soul of the world itself
—and it was this beautiful and terrifying feeling that
took possession of me finally, stiffened me like a rod beside my husband, played caesar to my dreams.

The weather drove them up, I think . . . moisture in
the tubes of the house. The first I came on looked put
together in Japan; broken, one leg bent under like a
metal cinch; unwound. It rang inside the hollow of the
wand like metal too; brightly, like a stream of pins. The
clatter made me shiver. Well I always see what I fear.
Anything my eyes have is transformed into a threaten-
ing object: mud, or stains, or burns, or if not these, then
toys in unmendable metal pieces. Not fears to be afraid
of. The ordinary fears of daily life. Healthy fears.
Womanly, wifely, motherly ones: the children may point
at the wretch with the hunch and speak in a voice he
will hear; the cat has fleas again, they will get in the
sofa; one's face looks smeared, it's because of the heat;
is the burner on under the beans? the washing machine's
obscure disease may reoccur, it rumbles on rinse and rat-
tles on wash; my god it's already eleven o'clock; which
one of you has lost a galosh? So it was amid the worries
of our ordinary life I bent, innocent and improperly
armed, over the bug that had come undone. Let me
think back on the shock. . . . My hand would have fled
from a burn with the same speed; anyone's death or injury would have weakened me as well; and I could have
gone cold for a number of reasons, because I felt in motion in me my own murderous disease, for instance; but
none could have produced the revulsion that dim recognition did, a reaction of my whole nature that flew
ahead of understanding and made me withdraw like a
spider.

I said I was innocent. Well I was not. Innocent. My
god the names we use. What do we live with that's alive
we haven't tamed—people like me?—even our house-
plants breathe by our permission. All along I had the

fear of what it was—something ugly and poisonous, deadly and terrible—the simple insect, worse and wilder than fire—and I should rather put my arms in the heart of a flame than in the darkness of a moist and webby hole. But the eye never ceases to change. When I examine my collection now it isn't any longer roaches I observe but gracious order, wholeness, and divinity. . . . My handkerchief, that time, was useless. . . . O my husband, they are a terrible disease.

The dark soul of the world . . . a phrase I should laugh at. The roach shell sickened me. And my jaw has broken open. I lie still, listening, but there is nothing to hear. Our cat is quiet. They pass through life to immortality between her paws.

Am I grateful now my terror has another object? From time to time I think so, but I feel as though I'd been entrusted with a kind of eastern mystery, sacred to a dreadful god, and I am full of the sense of my unworthiness and the clay of my vessel. So strange. It is the sewing machine that has the fearful claw. I live in a scatter of blocks and children's voices. The chores are my clock, and time is every other moment interrupted. I had always thought that love knew nothing of order and that life itself was turmoil and confusion. Let us leap, let us shout! I have leaped, and to my shame, I have wrestled. But this bug that I hold in my hand and know to be dead is beautiful, and there is a fierce joy in its composition that beggars every other, for its joy is the joy of stone, and it lives in its tomb like a lion.

I don't know which is more surprising: to find such order in a roach, or such ideas in a woman.

I could not shake my point of view, infected as it was, and I took up their study with a manly passion. I sought out spiders and gave them sanctuary; played host to worms of every kind; was generous to katydids and lacewings, aphids, ants and various grubs; pampered several sorts of beetle; looked after crickets; sheltered bees;

aimed my husband's chemicals away from the grasshoppers, mosquitoes, moths, and flies. I have devoted hours to watching caterpillars feed. You can see the leaves they've eaten passing through them; their bodies thin and swell until the useless pulp is squeezed in perfect rounds from their rectal end; for caterpillars are a simple section of intestine, a decorated stalk of yearning muscle, and their whole being is enlisted in the effort of digestion. *Le tube digestif des Insectes est situé dans le grand axe de la cavité générale du corps . . . de la bouche vers l'anus . . . Le pharynx . . . L'œsophage . . . Le jabot . . . Le ventricule chylifique . . . Le rectum et l'iléon . . .* Yet when they crawl their curves conform to graceful laws.

My children ought to be delighted with me as my husband is, I am so diligent, it seems, on their behalf, but they have taken fright and do not care to pry or to collect. My hobby's given me a pair of dreadful eyes, and sometimes I fancy they start from my head; yet I see, perhaps, no differently than Galileo saw when he found in the pendulum its fixed intent. Nonetheless my body resists such knowledge. It wearies of its edge. And I cannot forget, even while I watch our moonvine blossoms opening, the simple principle of the bug. It is a squat black cockroach after all, such a bug as frightens housewives, and it's only come to chew on rented wool and find its death absurdly in the teeth of the renter's cat.

Strange. Absurd. I am the wife of the house. This point of view I tremble in is the point of view of a god, and I feel certain, somehow, that could I give myself entirely to it, were I not continuing a woman, I could disarm my life, find peace and order everywhere; and I lie by my husband and I touch his arm and consider the temptation. But I am a woman. I am not worthy. Then I want to cry O husband, husband, I am ill, for I have seen what I have seen. What should he do at that, poor man, starting up in the night from his sleep to such non-

Order of Insects

sense, but comfort me blindly and murmur dream, small snail, only dream, bad dream, as I do the children. I could go away like the wise cicada who abandons its shell to move to other mischief. I could leave and let my bones play cards and spank the children. . . . Peace. How can I think of such ludicrous things—beauty and peace, the dark soul of the world—for I am the wife of the house, concerned for the rug, tidy and punctual, surrounded by blocks.

ONE'S SHIP

Barton Midwood

I am up to my calves in the sea, the very beginnings of the sea which stretches before me out to the edge of the sky. My ship, my tiny ship moored in the shallows, rocks back and forth anxiously, like a schoolboy. The waves lap at its side, the cool waters. Ah, let us go, let us set forth, my ship!

But I am detained. All the women have gathered on the beachhead. We must deal with them, my ship and I. All want to make passage with us. They are shrieking, moaning, imploring. Each woman presents a plaintive convincing case. Each, it is clear from their arguments, deserves beyond the shadow of a doubt to accompany me. They love me, they cry. Of course! I am irresistible. My rudder is golden, my sails ample, I have shapely legs. On the beach, with the wind blowing in my thin hair, I make an appealing picture. I am the captain of a noble craft, of everything in fact in sight. I am the only man for miles around. I am needed, that's clear. But how should I take them all, these lovely creatures?

One's Ship

There is room for but one companion and frankly I am loath to take anyone beside myself. I am selfish, utterly. The wind blows in my hair. I turn to them and raise my arms for silence. I shall speak. A hush falls. All eyes grow round and soft and fix me tenderly. The tears flow. It is touching. The back of my shirt bellies like a sail.

"Ladies," I say, "I should like to speak to you individually. Form a line!"

They fight for first place. They pull one another's hair. They make an undignified spectacle. At last, however, they are in single file, a long line that runs back from the shore, across the beach, out to the road, and . . . to the ends of the earth for all I know. Nevertheless, I shall give them audience, each one. I must be fair!

I bid the first come forward.

"Yvonne!" I cry. "Come here, my dear. I love you passionately. Let me touch you."

I caress her thighs, she throws her arms around my neck, and we kiss so unconscionably long and hard that we fall to the ground and roll in the sand. We have no regard. One forgets oneself. There is nothing to be done.

"Have no fear," I whisper as we stand up and brush the sand from our mouths. "You are the one. I shall take you with me."

She kisses me lightly on the forehead, holding my face in her hands and standing just on her toes. Then she retires to a shady spot beneath a palm and waits, contentedly. From her purse she takes an orange and sucks it. She stares at me over it from lowered loving brows.

"Next!"

Elsa steps forward. She runs at me, leaps into the air, locking her legs around my waist, wraps her arms around my neck, those slender tan arms with the light down, and kisses me precisely on the lips.

"You are the one," I whisper. "Have no fear."

She too retires to a palm and sucks an orange. They have all brought oranges. It must be the season.

Shy and blushing comes Natalie. She looks at the ground. She falls in a faint at my feet. I lift her in my arms and lave her forehead with handfuls of the sea. She comes to.

"Be happy," she says in a swoon. "I am so embarrassed. All these people . . . oh, oh, forgive us. I love you so. You are not in debt to me. I shall always love you. You must take whom you please."

And then she falls to crying, her lips wet with her tears on my neck.

"Natalie," I say, "you are not like the others. I shall take you with me. Have no fear."

Ecstatically she too retires to a palm. She eats an apple however. She is different.

So it goes. Three, four, five days pass in this way—talking, embracing, promising, eating apples and oranges. I have spoken to one and a half billion women —yes! I have counted assiduously. I have promised each one that I shall take her with me. It is difficult to say no. How does one say no when one is intoxicated with saying yes? Saying yes is my whiskey. It burns so pleasantly. And after the first few, the rest go down so easily! Yes, yes, yes! It is only no that tastes bitter in my mouth. And what do I care for bitterness? What do I care for . . .

I know. You will say, "He is a fool. He does not know how to handle his affairs. He does not appreciate fully the efficacy of saying no. He is a sensualist and cares for nothing but the moment. He has not a practical vision. He will cause nothing but anguish in this world with his infernal yes."

And so be it! Say it! I know all that! And I care not!

They sit there now, my pretty little one and a half billion; I face them with my hands on my hips. What now? I could make a dash for the ship but they would be on me, crawling over the deck, before I could hoist the mainsail. They would destroy the ship in a moment. I know something about crowds.

I turn my back to them. Bobbing up and down in the sea are the lovely mermaids with the long flowing hair—light green hair, with streaks of blonde that shimmer in the sun. Breasts high and firm, bellies silky, these creatures are not half fish as the mythologies say. Under the surface of the waters, from the waist down, they are womanly, with sleek strong legs. The poets have cunningly perpetrated that half fish business on the public in order to discourage exploitation.

"Ladies," I announce, suddenly, whirling around. "I must test the ship. I must take a brief spin about the harbor. I shall return shortly. And then the chosen one will join me . . ."

This pronouncement seems to disconcert them. There is a sullen suspicious murmur of disapproval. I walk very cautiously to the ship. I make no sudden movement that might alarm them. I walk slowly, slowly, cautiously, as a man who walks past a mad dog. I attempt to make myself invisible. I hold my breath.

The mainsail is up. I push off, I glide . . . glide upon the waters. I am safe, free! I glide, glide! I laugh! I wave my handkerchief in farewell! I am safe! Out of touch! The mermaids beckon me with their arms, their heads tilted slightly upward. They burst into a chorus of song—an ethereal song, fathomless and sea-struck. I cannot whistle that tune, but I hear it in my dreams—every note I know. I have heard it, every note, before. Why then can I not whistle it? I am not a bad whistler. In fact, I am rather musical. I know, like the palm of my hand, the music at the bottom of things.

There is a rustling sound below—footsteps coming up the ladder from the hold. A woman climbs on deck. She has a child cradled in her arms and a fierce expression in her eyes. Of course. One hopes beyond hope.

There is no escape. One knew it all along. The mermaids make piteous lament! Their song is swallowed in the roar of the sea. There is a storm coming out of the west. There is always a storm coming out of the west; one accepts that. One never examines one's ship carefully enough. One escapes the beach, one escapes half the world, but never looks thoroughly enough into the nooks and crannies of one's own ship. One is a shithead. One hates oneself. One is not one. One is multitudinous.

"Well!" says one. "What the hell are you doing here on one's ship? And who's the brat? Never mind! Take the raft! Paddle yourselves back to shore! One is displeased! Do you hear? Displeased!"

Without a word she loosens the chains from the raft and kicks it into the sea.

"The raft!" I cry. "What have you done?"

She says nothing. Her eyes accuse me. One is made to feel guilty by those eyes. And then the brat sets to howling. A vicious discourteous little monster. And then the storm is coming out of the west . . . one has set off; one is on one's voyage.

I sit on the deck, hang my hands limply over the edge . . . the mermaids kiss my fingertips. I go on but I know not where I go. A return to the beach is out of the question. I entertain thoughts of pushing the stowaways overboard, but they are tenacious. And then, perhaps, yes, perhaps I need them for ballast. I comfort myself with these thoughts. I contrive reasons for needing them. That is how one's mind works. One has them, one cannot rid oneself easily of them—at least not without committing a heinous crime—so one contrives reasons for needing them. One always needs what one has. If ever one allows oneself to think one does not need what one has, then one is . . .

SAYING GOOD-BYE TO THE PRESIDENT

Robley Wilson, Jr.

We are strolling in the Rose Garden at dusk. The sky is clouded, taking on the first glow of lights from the Washington night, the traffic sounds muted by the rustling of a warm wind in the White House trees. The President walks with his hands clasped behind his back, his head bent slightly, scuffing at bits of gravel with the toes of his shoes. Behind us, at a little distance, two Secret Service men follow, talking discreetly, keeping their eyes on us.

I am the one who finally speaks, breaking a silence that has surrounded us like smoke since dinner.

"I never thought it would end this way," I say.

"No," he says. "Neither did I."

"I'll miss you."

He grins—a flicker of his mouth so slight as to be almost an inward grin. "We had good times," he says.

We turn off the path and move across a damp lawn. The agents trail us at their interval, seeming careful not to step where we have stepped, avoiding the dark places

Robley Wilson, Jr.

in the grass that mark where we have pressed the dew against the earth.

"I suppose you're all packed," I say.

"Almost," he says. "A few pictures. . . ." His voice falls; he finishes the sentence with a movement of his shoulders.

"I guess we'll both get over it."

"Things have a way of settling themselves."

"Will you think of me?"

"Can you imagine me forgetting?"

"Then I can live with this," I tell him.

He puts his right hand on my shoulder. "Try not to dwell on it," he says.

"All right," I tell him.

He signals to the agents. I turn away and begin walking rapidly in the direction of the traffic noise. I have given my oath I will not show tears.

We are at Key Biscayne, in a room whose two windows look across a deserted beach to the ocean. The President is standing, shoeless and shirtless, at one of the windows. It is daybreak; the sun streams around him and turns the room gold. He waves absently to a Secret Service man seated at the base of a palm tree, and with his other hand rubs at the grey hairs on his chest.

"They'll miss you," I say to him.

He sighs. "I suppose they will."

"They loved you the way a family would."

"They did—for a while, at least. I'll always have that."

"You've settled everything?"

"Oh, yes," he says. "All packed, ready to go."

He moves from the window and picks up a white shirt from the chair beside the bed. He draws it on carefully, the motions of his dressing like those of an old man.

"Can I help with the cuff links?" I asked him.

Saying Good-Bye to the President

"No, no," he says. "I can manage."

I stub out my cigarette in the glass ashtray. "Then I think we'd better get on with it." I stand up.

"Just let me put on my shoes," he says.

While he sits on the edge of the bed, slipping on the shoes, I button and adjust my jacket. I say: "It's going to be a scorcher"—not because I care, but because I am embarrassed and wish to say something.

The President nods, stands, scoops up his coat. At the door of the room I put my hand out to him. His mouth hardens.

"I think we can do without those, can't we?" he says.

"Yes, sir," I say, and follow him out through the bedlam of photographers to the waiting van.

We are aboard the *Sequoia*. It is a starless night; a light breeze is blowing over the mouth of the Potomac and there is no sound save the low murmur of a foghorn. The President is kneeling at the rail of the yacht. He wears a wet suit, goggles pushed up from his brow. He is checking the pressure of his air tanks. When he talks, it is in a voice scarcely louder than a whisper, and the words come fast upon one another. The *Sequoia* rocks gently in the rising tide.

"You've got it all straight?" the President says.

"Yes, sir. Trust me, sir."

"All right," he hoists the tanks onto his back. I help him adjust the fastenings. He takes the air piece into his mouth, checks the tanks one last time.

"Good luck," I tell him.

"Thanks. Remember—not a word to anyone."

"Right."

"You won't hear from me for two weeks, but don't worry. Everything's arranged. In thirteen days, mail the package to Cuernavaca; in twenty-seven days, mail the large envelope to Caracas." He pulls down the goggles. "After that, you'll get instructions every two weeks."

"Yes, sir."

He shakes my hand. "I'm counting on you," he says.
The next moment he has slipped over the side of the
yacht—a dim wake phosphorescent from the ship's
lights. Then a crewman appears at the rail beside me.

"What's up?" says the crewman. "I thought I heard
a splash."

"You did," I tell him. "The President just fell
overboard."

The crewman lights a cigarette. "No kidding?" he
says. He offers me a Kool. We smoke in silence.

We are at Camp David, in a large clearing not far
from the main compound. The balloon is not yet in-
flated; it is laid flat on the grass, nearly a hundred feet
long, striped blue and white. The staff is milling about.
The President is in earnest conversation with the Secretary of State. Two men in overalls are fussing with the
burners, while a third man is loading the gondola.

I am standing just close enough to overhear the
President.

"You've booked passage?" the President is saying.

"I have," the Secretary answers.

"Capital," says the President. "Now you'll probably
lose sight of me somewhere along the north shore. You
know what to do."

The Secretary nods.

I drift to the edge of the field. The balloon is being
filled, the great bag beginning to tug at its shrouds, men
arranged in an oval seeing to it that the balloon expands
evenly. In another twenty minutes the balloon is full,
bulging in the afternoon sunlight like a spinnaker, its
ground crew ranged around the gondola. The President
climbs in, listens to instructions from a thin man in
overalls who points to the burner controls. The man
backs away. The balloon begins to rise.

The President waves to the onlookers, blows kisses

to his family, leans out over the ballast bags and calls
out to the crowd.

"Don't worry," he says. "Keep your ears open. Keep
your eyes peeled. Keep your nose clean."

He is looking directly at me as these instructions
trail off and are no longer audible. I watch until the
balloon is only a speck in the northeast sky. Then I return to my car. I am not certain if the President was
talking to the Secretary or to me—nor am I at all clear
about the meaning of the words.

We are outside the city of P., racing down a narrow
road lined with scrawny trees. I am driving a black Mer-
cedes to a secret rendezvous, the radio blaring curious
music, the tires kicking up stones that bang against the
car's underpan. I am driving very fast, smoking a Turkish cigarette. It is close to noon. The President, a gag
over his mouth, his arms and legs trussed with clothes-
line, is in the trunk of the car.

Once inside the city I drive slowly over cobbled
streets, streets teeming with men and women in native
dress. I reach a marketplace. In the square some people
are shooting a film; I count three cameras. Several men,
wearing the foreign garments but looking like Americans, are sitting at the edge of the market with beer
bottles in their hands. I stop at a curb, not far from an
alley too narrow to enter except on foot, and step out
of the car. A real foreigner approaches me; he is tall,
bearded, has a battered black cap pulled down to his
eyes. He bows. I return the bow.

I say: *The moon is new*.

He smiles. *But the stars know the cares of eternity*,
he says.

I say: *All light weakens with time*.

He says: *Try to stay out of camera range*. He enters
the alley and waits for me. I follow.

"I have the order," I say.

"I have the money," he tells me, and holds up a cloth pouch. "It is in deutsche marks."

"That's thoughtful."

"He is alive?"

"Yes," I say.

"He is strong?"

"The ordeal of travel may have weakened him."

"Where is he?"

"In the trunk, the boot of the car."

He gives me the pouch of money. "Wait five minutes," says the foreigner. "Then return to your auto, drive out of the city, and do not look back." He leaves the alley.

I wait. After five minutes have passed, I go back to the car. I look into the trunk; it is empty. I get into the car, start the engine, drive off. The cameras are grinding.

We are on the San Clemente shore at sunset.

"There never *were* such sunsets," the President says. "I'll miss them terribly."

"And they'll miss you," I say.

"I wonder," he says after a moment's musing. "Things have a way of settling themselves."

"They do, sir."

"Of course I've packed up all my belongings."

"Yes, sir."

"And sent postcards to everyone I could think of."

"Yes. I remember mailing them, sir."

The President rubs his eyes. When he turns his back to the sun, two Secret Service men duck down behind the shrubbery. The President looks natty; he is wearing a Park Service uniform, the Sam Browne belt freshly saddle-soaped, the wide-brimmed hat tipped jauntily forward. Down at the main gate a car horn sounds.

"Well," the President says, "that's my ride."

He salutes briskly and jogs down the graveled drive

toward the gate. I will never see him again. A year from now I will hear that he is transferred to Yellowstone. Two years from now I will find a postcard pushed through my mail slot. It reads:

I am the world's happiest man.

We are at an airport in the Midwest. It is a crisp morning in October, a smell of snow in the air, a panorama of flat brown fields sprawling as far as the eye can see. The President's plane has just come to a stop on the terminal apron; the Secret Service is filing down from the rear exit. The forward door of Air Force One pops out and slides open. The President appears. He acknowledges us from the top of the stairway.

The terminal area is mobbed. Counts range as high as thirty thousand, and the people are—as they say— from all walks of life. The press are waving cameras, housewives wave handkerchief, political factionists wave signs. When the President descends, he is met by local dignitaries who take his hand and must be persuaded— a protocol officer whispering in their ears—to let go. A military band is playing astonishing melodies. Cheers erupt on every side. Black limousines are nearly submerged under the winter coats of the crowd.

I am at his right hand as the President begins his movement from the aircraft to the limousine waiting to whisk him into the city. "Hello," the President is saying as he struggles forward. "Good morning. You're very kind. I'm delighted to be here."

To me he says: "Help me. Get me into the car, for God's sake."

I step ahead. With my elbows wide I break a path for him. The crush is incredible; every now and again I am stopped, almost thrown back.

"Excuse us," I say. Then: "Make way here. Look out. Get the hell back, will you? Move aside. *Move.*"

The crowd thickens. It is like a coagulation; our

pace is excruciatingly slow. Finally, yards short of the car, I am stopped in my tracks.

"What is it?" says the President.

Before I can answer, the crowd has separated me from the President. They are upon him. When I squirm around he is hidden from me by the swarm of men and women. The agents assigned to him are helpless; like me, they have been forced to the outside of the circle. All of us are fighting to get back in. Now I see the crowd's hands lifting items aloft—the President's coat, his necktie, his shirt; then one shoe and the other, socks, cotton underwear. *Save me!* It is the voice of the President.

"Make way," I scream. "Make way!"

I can hear the President crying out for help, and once, just for an instant, I catch sight of his face, eyes wild, mouth twisted on some new word he cannot utter.

METAFICTION

RESTRICTION

LIFE-STORY

John Barth

1

Without discarding what he'd already written he began his story afresh in a somewhat different manner. Whereas his earlier version had opened in a straightforward documentary fashion and then degenerated or at least modulated intentionally into irrealism and dissonance he decided this time to tell his tale from start to finish in a conservative, "realistic," unself-conscious way. He being by vocation an author of novels and stories it was perhaps inevitable that one afternoon the possibility would occur to the writer of these lines that his own life might be a fiction, in which he was the leading or an accessory character. He happened at the time * to be in his study attempting to draft the opening pages of a new short story; its general idea had preoccupied him for

* 9:00 A.M., Monday, June 20, 1966.

some months along with other general ideas, but certain elements of the conceit, without which he could scarcely proceed, remained unclear. More specifically: narrative plots may be imagined as consisting of a "ground-situation" (Scheherazade desires not to die) focused and dramatized by a "vehicle-situation" (Scheherazade beguiles the King with endless stories), the several incidents of which have their final value in terms of their bearing upon the "ground-situation." In our author's case it was the "vehicle" that had vouchsafed itself, first as a germinal proposition in his commonplace book—D comes to suspect that the world is a novel, himself a fictional personage—subsequently as an articulated conceit explored over several pages of the workbook in which he elaborated more systematically his casual inspirations: since D is writing a fictional account of this conviction he has indisputably a fictional existence in his account, replicating what he suspects to be his own situation. Moreover E, hero of D's account, is said to be writing a similar account, and so the replication is in both ontological directions, et cetera. But the "ground-situation"—some state of affairs on D's part which would give dramatic resonance to his attempts to prove himself factual, assuming he made such attempts—obstinately withheld itself from his imagination. As is commonly the case the question reduced to one of stakes: what were to be the consequences of D's—and finally E's —disproving or verifying his suspicion, and why should a reader be interested?

What a dreary way to begin a story he said to himself upon reviewing his long introduction. Not only is there no "ground-situation," but the prose style is heavy and somewhat old-fashioned, like an English translation of Thomas Mann, and the so-called "vehicle" itself is at least questionable: self-conscious, vertiginously arch, fashionably solipsistic, unoriginal—in fact a convention of twentieth-century literature. Another story about a writer writing a story! Another regressus in infinitum! Who doesn't prefer art that at least overtly imitates something other than its own processes? That doesn't continually proclaim "Don't forget I'm an artifice!"? That takes for granted its mimetic nature instead of asserting it in order (not so slyly after all) to deny it, or vice-versa? Though his critics sympathetic and otherwise described his own work as avant-garde, in his heart of hearts he disliked literature of an experimental, self-despising, or overtly metaphysical character, like Samuel Beckett's, Marian Cutler's, Jorge Borges's. The logical fantasies of Lewis Carroll pleased him less than straight-forward tales of adventure, subtly sentimental romances, even densely circumstantial realisms like Tolstoy's. His favorite contemporary authors were John Updike, Georges Simenon, Nicole Riboud. He had no use for the theater of absurdity, for "black humor," for allegory in any form, for apocalyptic preachments meretriciously tricked out in dramatic garb.

Neither had his wife and adolescent daughters, who for that matter preferred life to literature and read fiction when at all for entertainment. Their kind of story (his too, finally) would begin if not once upon a time at least with arresting circumstance, bold character, trenchant action. C flung away the whining manuscript and pushed impatiently through the french doors leading to the terrace from his oak-wainscoted study. Pausing at the stone balustrade to light his briar he remarked through a lavender cascade of wisteria that lithe-limbed Gloria, Gloria of timorous eye and militant breast, had once again chosen his boat-wharf as her basking-place.

By Jove he exclaimed to himself. It's particularly disquieting to suspect not only that one is a fictional character but that the fiction one's in—the fiction one is —is quite the sort one least prefers. His wife entered the study with coffee and an apple-pastry, set them at his elbow on his work table, returned to the living room.

John Barth

Ed' pelut' kondo nedode; nyoing nyang. One manifestation of schizophrenia as everyone knows is the movement from reality toward fantasy, a progress which not infrequently takes the form of distorted and fragmented representation, abstract formalism, an increasing preoccupation, even obsession, with pattern and design for their own sakes—especially patterns of a baroque, enormously detailed character—to the (virtual) exclusion of representative "content." There are other manifestations. Ironically, in the case of graphic and plastic artists for example the work produced in the advanced stages of their affliction may be more powerful and interesting than the realistic productions of their earlier "sanity." Whether the artists themselves are gratified by this possibility is not reported.

B called upon a literary acquaintance, B_____, summering with Mrs. B and children on the Eastern Shore of Maryland. "You say you lack a ground-situation. Has it occurred to you that that circumstance may be your ground-situation? What occurs to me is that if it is it isn't. And conversely. The case being thus, what's really wanting after all is a well-articulated vehicle, a foreground or upstage situation to dramatize the narrator's or author's grundlage. His what. To write merely C comes to suspect that the world is a novel, himself a fictional personage is but to introduce the vehicle; the next step must be to initiate its uphill motion by establishing and complicating some conflict. I would advise in addition the eschewal of overt and self-conscious discussion of the narrative process. I would advise in addition the eschewal of overt and self-conscious discussion of the narrative process. The via negativa and its positive counterpart are it is to be remembered poles after all of the same cell. Returning to his study.

If I'm going to be a fictional character G declared to himself I want to be in a rousing good yarn as they say, not some piece of avant-garde preciousness. I want passion and bravura action in my plot, heroes I can admire, heroines I can love, memorable speeches, colorful accessory characters, poetical language. It doesn't matter to me how naively linear the anecdote is; never mind modernity! How reactionary J appears to be. How will such nonsense sound thirty-six years from now? * As if. If he can only get K through his story I reflected grimly; if he can only retain his self-possession to the end of this sentence; not go mad; not destroy himself and/or others. Then what I wondered grimly. Another sentence fast, another story. Scheherazade my only love! All those nights you kept your secret from the King my rival, that after your defloration he was unnecessary, you'd have killed yourself in any case when your invention failed.

Why could he not begin his story afresh X wondered, for example with the words why could he not begin his story afresh et cetera? Y's wife came into the study as he was about to throw out the baby with the bathwater. "Not for an instant to throw out the baby while every instant discarding the bathwater is perhaps a chief task of civilized people at this hour of the world.* I used to tell B_____ that without success. What makes you so sure it's not a film he's in or a theater-piece?

Because U responded while he certainly felt rather often that he was merely acting his own role or roles he had no idea who the actor was, whereas even the most Stanislavsky-methodist would presumably if questioned closely recollect his offstage identity even onstage in mid-act. Moreover a great pair of T's "drama," most of his life in fact, was non-visual, consisting entirely in introspection, which the visual dramatic media couldn't manage easily. He had for example mentioned to no one his growing conviction that he was a fictional

* 10:00 A.M., Monday, June 20, 1966.
* 11:00 A.M., Monday, June 20, 1966.

character, and since he was not given to audible soliloquizing a "spectator" would take him for a cheerful, conventional fellow, little suspecting that et cetera. It was of course imaginable that much goes on in the mind of King Oedipus in addition to his spoken sentiments; any number of interior dramas might be being played out in the actors' or characters' minds, dramas of which the audience is as unaware as are V's wife and friends of his growing conviction that he's a fictional character. But everything suggested that the medium of his life was prose fiction—moreover a fiction narrated from either the first-person or the third-person-omniscient point of view.

Why is it L wondered with mild disgust that both K and M for example choose to write such stuff when life is so sweet and painful and full of such a variety of people, places, situations, and activities other than self-conscious and after all rather blank introspection? Why is it N wondered et cetera that both M and O et cetera when the world is in such parlous explosive case? Why et cetera et cetera et cetera when the word, which was in the beginning, is now evidently nearing the end of its road? Am I being strung out in this ad libitum fashion I wondered merely to keep my author from the pistol? What sort of story is it whose drama lies always in the next frame out? If Sinbad sinks it's Scheherazade who drowns; whose neck one wonders is on her line?

2

Discarding what he'd already written as he could wish to discard the mumbling pages of his life he began his story afresh, resolved this time to eschew overt and self-conscious discussion of his narrative process and to recount instead in the straight-forwardest manner possible the several complications of his character's conviction that he was a character in a work of fiction, arranging them into dramatically ascending stages if he could for his readers' sake and leading them (the stages) to an exciting climax and dénouement if he could.

He rather suspected that the medium and genre in which he worked—the only ones for which he felt any vocation—were moribund if not already dead. The idea pleased him. One of the successfullest men he knew was a blacksmith of the old school who et cetera. He meditated upon the grandest sailing-vessel ever built, the *France II,* constructed in Bordeaux in 1911 not only when but because the age of sail had passed. Other phenomena that consoled and inspired him were the great flying-boat *Hercules,* the zeppelin *Hindenburg,* the *Tsar Pushka* cannon, the then-record Dow-Jones industrial average of 381.17 attained on September 3, 1929.

He rather suspected that the society in which he persisted—the only one with which he felt any degree of identification—was moribund if not et cetera. He knew beyond any doubt that the body which he inhabited—the only one et cetera—was et cetera. The idea et cetera. He had for thirty-years lacking a few hours been one of our dustmote's three billion tenants give or take five hundred million, and happening to be as well a white male citizen of the United States of America he had thirty-six years plus a few hours more to cope with one way or another unless the actuarial tables were mistaken, not bloody likely, or his term was unexpectedly reduced.

Had he written for his readers' sake? The phrase implied a thitherto-unappreciated metaphysical dimension. Suspense. If his life was a fictional narrative it consisted of three terms—teller, tale, told—each dependent on the other two but not in the same ways. His author could as well tell some other character's tale or some other tale of the same character as the one being told as he himself could in his own character as author; his "reader" could as easily read some other story, would be well advised to; but his own "life" depended absolutely on a particular author's original persistence, thereafter upon some reader's. From this consideration any number of things followed, some less tiresome than others. No use appealing to his author, of whom he'd come to dislike even to think. The idea of his playing with his characters' and his own self-consciousness! He himself tended in that direction and despised the tendency. The idea of his or her smiling smugly to himself as the "words" flowed from his "pen" in which his the protagonist's unhappy inner life was exposed! Ah he had mistaken the nature of his narrative; he had thought it very long, longer than Proust's, longer than any German's, longer than *The Thousand Nights and a Night* in ten quarto volumes. Moreover he'd thought it the most prolix and pedestrian *tranche-de-vie* realism, unredeemed by even the limited virtues of colorful squalor, solid specification, an engaging variety of scenes and characters—in a word a bore, of the sort he himself not only would not write but would not read either. Now he understood that his author might as probably resemble himself and the protagonist of his own story-in-progress. Like himself, like his character aforementioned, his author not impossibly deplored the obsolescence of humanism, the passing of *savoir-vivre*, et cetera; admired the outmoded values of fidelity, courage, tact, restraint, amiability, self-discipline, et cetera; preferred fictions in which were to be found stirring actions, characters to love as well as ditto to despise, speeches and deeds to affect us strongly, et cetera. He too might wish to make some final effort to put by his fictional character and achieve factuality or at least to figure in if not be hero of a more attractive fiction, but be caught like the writer of these lines in some more or less desperate tour de force. For him to attempt to come to an understanding with such an author were as futile as for one of his own creations to et cetera.

But the reader! Even if his author were his only reader as was he himself of his work-in-progress as of the sentence-in-progress and his protagonist of his, et cetera, his character as reader was not the same as his character as author, a fact which might be turned to account. What suspense.

As he prepared to explore this possibility one of his mistresses whereof he had none entered his brown study unannounced. "The passion of love," she announced, "which I regard as no less essential to a satisfying life than those values itemized above and which I infer from my presence here that you too esteem highly, does not in fact play in your life a role of sufficient importance to sustain my presence here. It plays in fact little role at all outside your imaginative and/or ary life. I tell you this not in a criticizing spirit, for I judge you to be as capable of the sentiment aforementioned as any other imagin[ative], deep-feeling man in good physical health more or less precisely in the middle of the road of our life. What hampers, even cripples you in this regard is your final preference, which I refrain from analyzing, for the sedater, more responsible pleasures of monogamous fidelity and the serener affections of domesticity, notwithstanding the fact that your enjoyment of these is correspondingly inhibited though not altogether spoiled by an essentially romantical, unstable, irresponsible, death-wishing fancy. V. S. Pritchett, English critic and author, will put the matter succinctly in a soon-to-be-written essay on Flaubert, whose work he'll say depicts the course of ardent longings and violent desires that rise from the horrible, the sensual, and the sadistic. They turn into the virginal and mystical, only to become numb by satiety. At this point pathological boredom leads to a final desire for death and nothingness—the Romantic syndrome. If, not to be unfair, we qualify somewhat the terms horrible and sadistic and understand satiety to include a large measure of vicariousness, this description undeniably applies to one aspect of yourself and your work; and while your ditto has other, even contrary aspects, the net fact is that you have elected familial responsibilities and rewards—indeed, straight-laced middle-classness in general—over the higher expenses of spirit and wastes of shame attendant upon a less regular, more glamorous style of life. So to elect is surely admirable for the layman, even essential if the social fabric, without which there can be no culture, is to be preserved. For the artist, however, and in particular the writer, whose traditional material has been the passions of men and women, the choice is fatal. You having made it I bid you goodnight probably forever."

Even as she left he reached for the sleeping pills cached conveniently in his writing desk and was restrained from their administration only by his being in the process of completing a sentence, which he cravenly strung out at some sacrifice of rhetorical effect upon realizing that he was et cetera. Moreover he added hastily he had not described the intruder for his readers' vicarious satiety: a lovely woman she was, whom he did not after all describe for his readers' et cetera inasmuch as her appearance and character were inconstant. Her interruption of his work inspired a few sentences about the extent to which his fiction inevitably made public his private life, though the trespasses in this particular were as nothing beside those of most of his profession. That is to say, while he did not draw his characters and situations directly from life nor permit his author-protagonist to do so, any moderately attentive reader of his oeuvre, his what, could infer for example that its author feared for example schizophrenia, impotence creative and sexual, suicide—in short living and dying. His fictions were preoccupied with these fears among their other, more serious preoccupations. Hot dog. As of the sentence-in-progress he was not in fact unmanageably schizophrenic, impotent in either respect, or dead by his own hand, but there was always the next sentence to worry about. But there was always the next sentence to worry about. In sum he concluded hastily such limited self-exposure did not constitute a misdemeanor, representing or mis as it did so small an aspect of his total self, negligible a portion of his total life—even which totalities were they made in public would be found remarkable only for their being so unremarkable. Well shall he continue.

Bearing in mind that he had not developed what he'd mentioned earlier about turning to advantage his situation vis-à-vis his "reader" (in fact he deliberately now postponed his return to that subject, sensing that it might well constitute the climax of his story) he elaborated one or two ancillary questions, perfectly aware that he was trying, even exhausting, whatever patience might remain to whatever readers might remain to whoever elaborated yet another ancillary question. Was the novel of his life for example a *roman à clef.* ? Of that genre he was as contemptuous as of the others aforementioned; but while in the introductory adverbial clause it seemed obvious to him that he didn't "stand for" anyone else, any more than he was an actor playing the role of himself, by the time he reached the main clause he had to admit that the question was unanswerable, since the "real" man to whom he'd correspond in a *roman à clef* would not be also in the *roman à clef* and the characters in such works were not themselves aware of their irritating correspondences.

Similarly unanswerable were such questions as when "his" story (so he regarded it for convenience and consolement though for all he knew he might be not the central character; it might be his wife's story, one of his daughters's, his imaginary mistress's, the man-who-once-cleaned-his-chimney's) began. Not impossibly at his birth or even generations earlier: a *Bildungsroman,* an

John Barth

Erziehungsroman, a *roman fleuve.* ! More likely at the moment he became convinced of his fictional nature: that's where he'd have begun it, as he'd begun the piece currently under his pen. If so it followed that the years of his childhood and younger manhood weren't "real," he'd suspected as much, in the first-order sense, but a mere "background" consisting of a few well-placed expository insinuations, perhaps misleading, or inferences, perhaps unwarranted, from strategic hints in his present reflections. God so to speak spare his readers from heavy-footed forced expositions of the sort that begin in the countryside near_____ in May of the year_____it occurred to the novelist_____ that his own life might be a_____, in which he was the leading or an accessory character. He happened at the time to be in the oak-wainscoted study of the old family summer residence; through a lavender cascade of hysteria he observed that his wife had once again chosen to be the subject of this clause, itself the direct object of his observation. A lovely woman she was, whom he did not describe in keeping with his policy against drawing characters from life as who should draw a condemnee to the gallows. Begging his pardon. Flinging his tiresome tale away he pushed impatiently through the french windows leading from his study to a sheer drop from the then-record high into a nearly fatal depression.

He clung onto his narrative depressed by the disproportion of its ratiocination to its dramatization, reflection to action. One had heard *Hamlet* criticized as a collection of soliloquies for which the implausible plot was a mere excuse; witnessed Italian operas whose dramatic portions were no more than interstitial relief and arbitrary continuity between the arias. If it was true that he didn't take his "real" life seriously enough even when it had him by the throat, the fact didn't lead him to consider whether the fact was a cause or a consequence of his tale's tedium or both.

Concluding these reflections he concluded these reflections: that there was at this advancèd page still apparently no ground-situation suggested that his story was dramatically meaningless. If one regarded the absence of a ground-situation, more accurately the protagonist's anguish at that absence and his vain endeavors to supply the defect, as itself a sort of ground-situation, did his life-story thereby take on a kind of meaning? A "dramatic" sort he supposed, though of so sophistical a character as more likely to annoy than to engage

3

The reader! You, dogged, uninsultable, print-oriented bastard, it's you I'm addressing, who else, from inside this monstrous fiction. You've read me this far, then? Even this far? For what discreditable motive? How is it you don't go to a movie, watch TV, stare at a wall, play tennis with a friend, make amorous advances to the person who comes to your mind when I speak of amorous advances? Can nothing surfeit, saturate you, turn you off? Where's your shame?

Having let go this barrage of rhetorical or at least unanswered questions and observing himself nevertheless in midst of yet another sentence he concluded and caused the "hero" of his story to conclude that one or more of three things must be true: 1) his author was his sole and indefatigable reader; 2) he was in a sense his own author, telling his story to himself, in which case in which case; and/or 3) his reader was not only tireless and shameless but sadistic, masochistic if he was himself.

For why do you suppose—you! you!—he's gone on so, so relentlessly refusing to entertain you as he might

John Barth

have at a less desperate than this hour of the world *
with felicitious language, exciting situation, unforget-
table character and image? Why has he as it were ruth-
lessly set about not to win you over but to turn you
away? Because your own author bless and damn you his
life is in your hands! He writes and reads himself; don't
you think he knows who gives his creatures their lives
and deaths? Do they exist except as he or others read
their words? Age except we turn their pages? And can
he die until you have no more of him? Time was obviously when his author could have turned the trick;
his pen had once to left-to-right it through these words
as does your kindless eye and might have ceased at any
one. This. This. And did not as you see but went on like
an Oriental torturemaster to the end.

But you needn't! He exclaimed to you. In vain. Had
he petitioned you instead to read slowly in the happy
parts, what happy parts, swiftly in the painful no doubt
you'd have done the contrary or cut him off entirely.
But as he longs to die and can't without your help you
force him on, force him on. Will you deny you've read
this sentence? This? To get away with murder doesn't
appeal to you, is that it? As if your hands weren't inky
with other dyings! As if he'd know you'd killed him!
Come on. He dares you.

In vain. You haven't: the burden of his knowledge.
That he continues means that he continues, a fortiori
you too. Suicide's impossible: he can't kill himself without your help. Those petitions aforementioned, even
his silly plea for death—don't you think he understands
their sophistry, having authored their like for the
wretches he's authored? Read him fast or slow, inter-
mittently, continuously, repeatedly, backward, not at
all, he won't know it; he only guesses someone's reading or composing his sentences, such as this one, be-

* 11:00 P.M., Monday, June 20, 1966.

cause he's reading or composing sentences such as this
one; the net effect is that there's a net effect, of continuity and an apparently consistent flow of time,
though his pages do seem to pass more swiftly as they
near his end.

To what conclusion will he come? He'd been about
to append to his own tale inasmuch as the old analogy
between Author and God, novel and world, can no
longer be employed unless deliberately as a false analogy, certain things follow: 1) fiction must acknowledge its fictitiousness and metaphoric invalidity or 2)
choose to ignore the question or deny its relevance or
3) establish some other, acceptable relation between itself, its author, its reader. Just as he finished doing so
however his real wife and imaginary mistresses entered
his study; "It's a little past midnight" she announced
with a smile; "do you know what that means?"

Though she'd come into his story unannounced at
a critical moment he did not describe her, for even as
he recollected that he'd seen his first light just thirty-six
years before the night incumbent he saw his last: that
he could not after all be a character in a work of fiction
inasmuch as such a fiction would be of an entirely different character from what he thought of as fiction. Fiction consisted of such monuments of the imagination as
Cutler's *Morganfield*, Riboud's *Tales Within Tales*, his
own creations; fact of such as for example read those
fictions. More, he could demonstrate by syllogism that
the story of his life was a work of fact: though assaults
upon the boundary between life and art, reality and
dream, were undeniably a staple of his own and his century's literature as they'd been of Shakespeare's and Cer-
vantes's, yet it was a fact that in the corpus of fiction as
far as he knew no fictional character had become convinced as had he that he was a character in a work of
fiction. This being the case and he having in fact become thus convinced it followed that his conviction was

false. "Happy birthday," said his wife et cetera, kissing him et cetera to obstruct his view of the end of the sentence he was nearing the end of, playfully refusing to be nay-said so that in fact he did at last as did his fictional character end his ending story endless by interruption, cap his pen.

SENTENCE

Donald Barthelme

Or a long sentence moving at a certain pace down
the page aiming for the bottom—if not the bottom of
this page then of some other page—where it can rest,
or stop for a moment to think about the questions raised
by its own (temporary) existence, which ends when the
page is turned, or the sentence falls out of the mind that
holds it (temporarily) in some kind of an embrace, not
necessarily an ardent one, but more perhaps the kind
of embrace enjoyed (or endured) by a wife who has just
waked up and is on her way to the bathroom in the
morning to wash her hair, and is bumped into by her
husband, who has been lounging at the breakfast table
reading the newspaper, and didn't see her coming out
of the bedroom, but, when he bumps into her, or is
bumped into by her, raises his hands to embrace her
lightly, transiently, because he knows that if he gives
her a real embrace so early in the morning, before she
has properly shaken the dreams out of her head, and
got her duds on, she won't respond, and may even be-

come slightly angry, and say something wounding, and
so the husband invests in this embrace not so much
physical or emotional pressure as he might, because he
doesn't want to waste anything—with this sort of feeling,
then, the sentence passes through the mind more or
less, and there is another way of describing the situation too, which is to say that the sentence crawls
through the mind like something someone says to you
while you're listening very hard to the FM radio, some
rock group there, with its thrilling sound, and so, with
your attention or the major part of it at least already
awarded, there is not much mind room you can give to
the remark, especially considering that you have probably just quarreled with that person, the maker of the
remark, over the radio being too loud, or something
like that, and the view you take, of the remark, is that
you'd really rather not hear it, but if you have to hear
it, you want to listen to it for the smallest possible
length of time, and during a commercial, because immediately after the commercial they're going to play
a new rock song by your favorite group, a cut that
has never been aired before, and you want to hear it
and respond to it in a new way, a way that accords with
whatever you're feeling at the moment, or might feel, if
the threat of new experience could be (temporarily)
overbalanced by the promise of possible positive bene-
fits, or what the mind construes as such, remembering
that these are often, really, disguised defeats (not that
such defeats are not, at times, good for your character,
teaching you that it is not by success alone that one sur-
mounts life, but that setbacks, too, contribute to that
roughening of the personality that, by providing a tex-
tured surface to place against that of life, enables you
to leave slight traces, or smudges, on the face of human
history—your mark) and after all, benefit-seeking always has something of the smell of raw vanity about it,
as if you wished to decorate your own brow with laurel,

or wear your medals to a cookout, when the invitation
had said nothing about them, and although the ego is
always hungry (we are told) it is well to remember that
ongoing success is nearly as meaningless as ongoing lack
of success, which can make you sick, and that it is good
to leave a few crumbs on the table for the rest of your
brethren, not to sweep it all into the little beaded purse
of your soul but to allow others, too, part of the grati-
fication, and if you share in this way you will find the
clouds smiling on you, and the postman bringing you
letters, and bicycles available when you want to rent
them, and many other signs, however guarded and limited, of the community's (temporary) approval of you,
or at least of its willingness to let you believe (temporarily) that it finds you not so lacking in commendable
virtues as it had previously allowed you to think, from
its scorn of your merits, as it might be put, or anyway
its consistent refusal to recognize your basic humanness
and its secret blackball of the project of your remaining alive, made in executive session by its ruling bodies,
which, as everyone knows, carry out concealed pro-
grams of reward and punishment, under the rose, caus-
ing faint alterations of the status quo, behind your back,
at various points along the periphery of community
life, together with other enterprises not dissimilar in
tone, such as producing films that have special qualities,
or attributes, such as a film where the second half of it
is a holy mystery, and girls and women are not per-
mitted to see it, or writing novels in which the final
chapter is a plastic bag filled with water, which you can
touch, but not drink: in this way, or ways, the underground mental life of the collectivity is botched, or
denied, or turned into something else never imagined
by the planners, who, returning from the latest seminar
in crisis management and being asked what they have
learned, say they have learned how to throw up their
hands; the sentence meanwhile, although not insensible

of these considerations, has a festering conscience of its
own, which persuades it to follow its star, and to move
with all deliberate speed from one place to another,
without losing any of the "riders" it may have picked
up just being there, on the page, and turning this way
and that, to see what is over there, under that oddly-
shaped tree, or over there, reflected in the rain barrel of
the imagination, even though it is true that in our
young manhood we were taught that short, punchy sentences were best (but what did he mean? doesn't
"punchy" mean punch-drunk? I think he probably intended to say "short, *punching* sentences," meaning sentences that lashed out at you, bloodying your brain if
possible, and looking up the word just now I came
across the nearby "punkah," which is a large fan suspended from the ceiling in India, operated by an attendant pulling a rope—that is what I want for my
sentence, to keep it cool!) we are mature enough now
to stand the shock of learning that much of what we
were taught in our youth was wrong, or improperly understood by those who were teaching it, or perhaps
shaded a bit, the shading resulting from the personal
needs of the teachers, who as human beings had a tendency to introduce some of their heart's blood into
their work, and sometimes this may not have been of the
first water, this heart's blood, and even if they thought
they were moving the "knowledge" out, as the Board
of Education had mandated, they could have noticed
that their sentences weren't having the knockdown
power of the new weapons whose bullets tumble end-
over-end (but it is true that we didn't have these weapons at that time) and they might have taken into account the fundamental dubiousness of their project
(but all the intelligently conceived projects have been
eaten up already, like the moon and the stars) leaving
us, in our best clothes, with only things to do like con-
ducting vigorous wars of attrition against our wives,

who have now thoroughly come awake, and slipped into their striped bells, and pulled sweaters over their torsi, and adamantly refused to wear any bras under the sweaters, carefully explaining the political significance of this refusal to anyone who will listen, or look, but not touch, because that has nothing to do with it, so they say; leaving us, as it were, with only things to do like floating sheets of Reynolds Wrap around the room, trying to find out how many we can keep in the air at the same time, which at least gives us a sense of participation, as though we were the Buddha, looking down at the mystery of your smile, which needs to be investigated, and I think I'll do that right now, while there's still enough light, if you'll sit down over there, in the best chair, and take off all your clothes, and put your feet in that electric toe caddy (which prevents pneumonia) and slip into this permanent press white hospital gown, to cover your nakedness—why, if you do all that, we'll be ready to begin! after I wash my hands, because you pick up an amazing amount of exuviae in this city, just by walking around in the open air, and nodding to acquaintances, and speaking to friends, and copulating with lovers, in the ordinary course (and death to our enemies! by the by)—but I'm getting a little uptight, just about washing my hands, because I can't find the soap, which somebody has used and not put back in the soap dish, all of which is extremely irritating, if you have a beautiful patient sitting in the examining room, naked inside her gown, and peering at her moles in the mirror, with her immense brown eyes following your every movement (when they are not watching the moles, expecting them, as in a Disney nature film, to exfoliate) and her immense brown head wondering what you're going to do to her, the pierced places in the head letting that question leak out, while the therapist decides just to wash his hands in plain water, and hang the soap! and does so, and then looks

Donald Barthelme

around for a towel, but all the towels have been collected by the towel service, and are not there, so he wipes his hands on his pants, in the back (so as to avoid suspicious stains on the front) thinking: what must she think of me? and, all this is very unprofessional and at-sea looking! trying to visualize the contretemps from her point of view, if she has one (but how can she? she is not in the washroom) and then stopping, because it is finally his own point of view that he cares about and not hers, and with this firmly in mind, and a light, confident step, such as you might find in the works of Bulwer-Lytton, he enters the space she occupies so prettily and, taking her by the hand, proceeds to tear off the stiff white hospital gown (but no, we cannot have that kind of pornographic *merde* in this majestic and high-minded sentence, which will probably end up in the Library of Congress) (that was just something that took place inside his consciousness, as he looked at her, and since we know that consciousness is always consciousness *of* something, she is not entirely without responsibility in the matter) so, then, taking her by the hand, he falls into the stupendous white purée of her abyss, no, I mean rather that he asks her how long it has been since her last visit, and she says a fortnight, and he shudders, and tells her that with a condition like hers (she is an immensely popular soldier, and her troops win all their battles by pretending to be forests, the enemy discovering, at the last moment, that those trees they have eaten their lunch under have eyes and swords) (which reminds me of the performance, in 1845, of Robert-Houdin, called *The Fantastic Orange Tree*, wherein Robert-Houdin borrowed a lady's handkerchief, rubbed it between his hands and passed it into the center of an egg, after which he passed the egg into the center of a lemon, after which he passed the lemon into the center of an orange, then pressed the orange between his hands, making it smaller and smaller, until only a powder remained, whereupon he asked for a small potted orange tree and sprinkled the powder thereupon, upon which the tree burst into blossom, the blossoms turning into oranges, the oranges turning into butterflies, and the butterflies turning into beautiful young ladies, who then married members of the audience), a condition so damaging to real-time social intercourse of any kind, the best thing she can do is give up, and lay down her arms, and he will lie down in them, and together they will permit themselves a bit of the old slap and tickle, she wearing only her Mr. Christopher medal, on its silver chain, and he (for such is the latitude granted the professional classes) worrying about the sentence, about its thin wires of dramatic tension, which have been omitted, about whether we should write down some natural events occurring in the sky (birds, lightning bolts), and about a possible coup d'etat within the sentence, whereby its chief verb would be— but at this moment a messenger rushes into the sentence, bleeding from a hat of thorns he's wearing, and cries out: "You don't know what you're doing! Stop making this sentence, and begin instead to make Moholy-Nagy cocktails, for those are what we really need, on the frontiers of bad behavior!" and then he falls to the floor, and a trap door opens under him, and he falls through that, into a damp pit where a blue narwhal waits, its horn poised (but maybe the weight of the messenger, falling from such a height, will break off the horn)—thus, considering everything carefully, in the sweet light of the ceremonial axes, in the run-mad skimble-skamble of information sickness, we must make a decision as to whether we should proceed, or go back, in the latter case enjoying the pathos of eradication, in the former case reading an erotic advertisement which begins, *How to Make Your Mouth a Blowtorch of Excitement* (but wouldn't that overtax our mouthwashes?) attempting, during the pause, while our burned mouths are being smeared with fat, to imagine a better sentence, worthier, more meaningful, like those in the Declaration of Independence, or a bank statement showing that you have seven thousand kroner more than you thought you had—a statement summing up the unreasonable demands that you make on life, and one that also asks the question, if you can imagine these demands, why are they not routinely met, tall fool? but of course it is not that query that this infected sentence has set out to answer (and hello! to our girl friend, Rosetta Stone, who has stuck by us through thin and thin) but some other query that we shall some day discover the nature of, and here comes Ludwig, the expert on sentence construction we have borrowed from the Bauhaus, who will—"Guten Tag, Ludwig!"—probably find a way to cure the sentence's sprawl, by using the improved ways of thinking developed in Weimar—"I am sorry to inform you that the Bauhaus no longer exists, that all of the great masters who formerly thought there are either dead or retired, and that I myself have been reduced to constructing books on how to pass the examination for police sergeant"—and Ludwig falls through the Tugendhat House into the history of man-made objects; a disappointment, to be sure, but it reminds us that the sentence itself is a man-made object, not the one we wanted of course, but still a construction of man, a structure to be treasured for its weakness, as opposed to the strength of stones

THE MOON
IN ITS FLIGHT

Gilbert Sorrentino

This was in 1948. A group of young people sitting on the darkened porch of a New Jersey summer cottage in a lake resort community. The host some Bernie wearing an Upsala College sweat shirt. The late June night so soft one can, in retrospect, forgive America for everything. There were perhaps eight or nine people there, two of them the people that this story sketches.

Bernie was talking about Sonny Stitt's alto on "That's Earl, Brother." As good as Bird, he said. Arnie said, bullshit: he was a very hip young man from Washington Heights, wore mirrored sunglasses. A bop drummer in his senior year at the High School of Performing Arts. Our young man, nineteen at this time, listened only to Rebecca, a girl of fifteen, remarkable in her New Look clothes. A long full skirt, black, snug tailored shirt of blue and white stripes with a high white collar and black velvet string tie, black kid Capezios. It is no wonder that lesbians like women.

At some point during the evening he walked

Rebecca home. She lived on Lake Shore Drive, a wide road that skirted the beach and ran parallel to the small river that flowed into Lake Minnehaha. Lake Ramapo? Lake Tomahawk. Lake O-shi-wa-noh? Lake Sunburst. Leaning against her father's powder-blue Buick convertible, lost, in the indigo night, the creamy stars, sound of crickets, they kissed. They fell in love.

One of the songs that summer was "For Heaven's Sake." Another, "It's Magic." Who remembers the clarity of Claude Thornhill and Sarah Vaughan, their exquisite irrelevance? They are gone where the useless chrome doughnuts on the Buick's hood have gone. That Valhalla of Amos 'n' Andy and guinea fruit peddlers with golden earrings. "Pleasa No Squeeza Da Banana." In 1948, the whole world semed beautiful to young people of a certain milieu, or let me say, possible. Yes, it seemed a possible world. This idea persisted until 1950, at which time it died, along with many of the young people who had held it. In Korea, the Chinese played "Scrapple from the Apple" over loudspeakers pointed at the American lines. That savage and virile alto blue-clear on the sub-zero night. This is, of course, old news.

Rebecca was fair. She was fair. Lovely Jewish girl from the remote and exotic Bronx. To him, that vast borough seemed a Cythera—that it could house such fantastic creatures as she! He wanted to be Jewish. He was, instead, a Roman Catholic, awash in sin and redemption. What loathing he had for the Irish girls who went to eleven o'clock Mass, legions of blushing pink and lavender spring coats, flat white straw hats, the crinkly veils over their open faces. Church clothes, under which their inviolate crotches sweetly nestled in soft hair.

She had white and perfect teeth. Wide mouth. Creamy stars, pale nights. Dusty black roads out past the beach. The sunlight on the raft, moonlight on the lake. Sprinkle of freckles on her shoulders. Aromatic breeze.

Of course this was a summer romance, but bear with me and see with what banal literary irony it all turns out—or does not turn out at all. The country bowled and spoke of Truman's grit and spunk. How softly we had slid off the edge of civilization.

The liquid moonlight filling the small parking area outside the gates to the beach. Bass flopping softly in dark waters. What was the scent of the perfume she wore? The sound of a car radio in the cool nights, collective American memory. Her browned body, delicate hair bleached golden on her thighs. In the beach pavilion they danced and drank Cokes. Mel Tormé and the Mell-Tones. Dizzy Gillespie. "Too Soon To Know." In the mornings, the sun so crystal and lucent it seemed the very exhalation of the sky, he would swim alone to the raft and lie there, the beach empty, music from the pavilion attendant's radio coming to him in splinters. At such times he would thrill himself by pretending that he had not yet met Rebecca and that he would see her that afternoon for the first time.

The first time he touched her breasts he cried in his shame and delight. Can all this really have taken place in America? The trees rustled for him, as the rain did rain. One day, in New York, he bought her a silver friendship ring, tiny perfect hearts in bas-relief running around it so that the point of one heart nestled in the cleft of another. Innocent symbol that tortured his blood. She stood before him in the pale light in white bra and panties, her shorts and blouse hung on the hurricane fence of the abandoned and weed-grown tennis court and he held her, stroking her flanks and buttocks and kissing her shoulders. The smell of her

Gilbert Sorrentino

flesh, vague sweat and perfume. Of course he was insane. She caressed him so far as she understood how
through his faded denim shorts. Thus did they flay
themselves, burning. What were they to do? Where
were they to go? The very thought of the condom in
his pocket made his heart career in despair. Nothing
was like anything said it was after all. He adored her.

She was entering her second year at Evander Childs
that coming fall. He hated this school he had never
seen, and hated all her fellow students. He longed to
be Jewish, dark and mysterious and devoid of sin. He
stroked her hair and fingered her nipples, masturbated
fiercely on the dark roads after he had seen her home.
Why didn't he at least *live* in the Bronx?

Any fool can see that with the slightest twist one
way or another all of this is fit material for a sophisticated comic's routine. David Steinberg, say. One can
hear his precise voice recording these picayune disasters
as jokes. Yet all that moonlight was real. He kissed her
luminous fingernails and died over and over again. The
maimings of love are endlessly funny, as are the tiny
figures of talking animals being blown to pieces in car-
toons.

It was this same youth who, three years later, rav-
ished the whores of Mexican border towns in a kind of
drunken hilarity, falling down in the dusty streets of
Nuevo Laredo, Villa Acuña, and Piedras Negras, the
pungency of the overpowering perfume wedded to his
rumpled khakis, his flowered shirt, his scuffed and beer-
spattered low quarters scraping across the thresholds of
the Blue Room, Ofelia's, The 1-2-3 Club, Felicia's, the
Cadillac, Tres Hermanas. It would be a great pleasure
for me to allow him to meet her there, in a yellow chif-
fon cocktail dress and spike heels, lost in prostitution.

One night, a huge smiling Indian whore bathed his

224

member in gin as a testament to the strict hygiene she claimed to practice and he absurdly thought of Rebecca, that he had never seen her naked, nor she him, as he was now in the Hollywood pink light of the whore's room, Jesus hanging in his perpetual torture from the wall above the little bed. The woman was gentle, the light glinting off her gold incisor and the tiny cross at her throat. You good fuck, Jack, she smiled in her lying whore way. He felt her flesh again warm in that long-dead New Jersey sunlight. Turn that into a joke.

They were at the amusement park at Lake Hopatcong with two other couples. A hot and breathless night toward the end of August, the patriotic smell of hot dogs and french fries in the still air. Thin and cranky music from the carrousel easing through the sparsely planted trees down toward the shore. She was pale and sweating, sick, and he took her back to the car and they smoked. They walked to the edge of the black lake stretching out before them, the red and blue neon on the far shore clear in the hot dark.

He wiped her forehead and stroked her shoulders, worshiping her pain. He went to get a Coke and brought it back to her, but she only sipped at it, then said O God! and bent over to throw up. He held her waist while she vomited, loving the waste and odor of her. She lay down on the ground and he lay next to her, stroking her breasts until the nipples were erect under her cotton blouse. My period, she said. God, it just ruins me at the beginning. You bleeding, vomiting, incredible thing, he thought. You should have stayed in, he said. The moonlight of her teeth. I didn't want to miss a night with you, she said. It's August. Stars, my friend, great flashing stars fell on Alabama.

They stood in the dark in the driving rain underneath her umbrella. Where could it have been? Nokomis

Road? Bliss Lane? Kissing with that trapped yet wholly innocent frenzy peculiar to American youth of that era. Her family was going back to the city early the next morning and his family would be leaving toward the end of the week. They kissed, they kissed. The angels sang. Where could they go, out of this driving rain?

Isn't there anyone, any magazine writer or avant-garde filmmaker, any lover of life or dedicated optimist out there who will move them toward a cottage, already closed for the season, in whose split log exterior they will find an unlocked door? Inside there will be a bed, whiskey, an electric heater. Or better, a fireplace. White lamps, soft lights. Sweet music. A radio on which they will get Cooky's Caravan or Symphony Sid. Billy Eckstine will sing "My Deep Blue Dream." Who can bring them to each other and allow him to enter her? Tears of gratitude and release, the sublime and elegantly shadowed configuration their tanned legs will make lying together. This was in America, in 1948. Not even fake art or the wearisome tricks of movies can assist them.

She tottered, holding the umbrella crookedly while he went to his knees and clasped her, the rain soaking him through, put his head under her skirt and kissed her belly, licked at her crazily through her underclothes.

All you modern lovers, freed by Mick Jagger and the orgasm, give them, for Christ's sake, for an hour, the use of your really terrific little apartment. They won't smoke your marijuana nor disturb your Indiana graphics. They won't borrow your Fanon or Cleaver or Barthelme or Vonnegut. They'll make the bed before they leave. They whisper good night and dance in the dark.

She was crying and stroking his hair. Ah God, the leaves of brown came tumbling down, remember? He watched her go into the house and saw the door close.

226

The Moon in its Flight

Some of his life washed away in the rain dripping from his chin.

A girl named Sheila whose father owned a fleet of taxis gave a reunion party in her parents' apartment in Forest Hills. Where else would it be? I will insist on purchased elegance or nothing. None of your warm and cluttered apartments in this story, cats on the stacks of books, and so on. It was the first time he had ever seen a sunken living room and it fixed his idea of the good life forever after. Rebecca was talking to Marv and Robin, who were to be married in a month. They were Jewish, incredibly and wondrously Jewish, their parents smiled upon them and loaned them money and cars. He skulked in his loud Brooklyn clothes.

I'll put her virgin flesh into a black linen suit, a single strand of pearls around her throat. Did I say that she had honey-colored hair? Believe me when I say he wanted to kiss her shoes.

Everybody was drinking Cutty Sark. This gives you an idea, not of who they were, but of what they thought they were. They worked desperately at it being August, but under the sharkskin and nylons those sunny limbs were hidden. Sheila put on "In the Still of the Night" and all six couples got up to dance. When he held her he thought he would weep.

He didn't want to hear about Evander Childs or Gun Hill Road or the 92nd Street Y. He didn't want to know what the pre-med student she was dating said. Whose hand had touched her secret thighs. It was almost unbearable since this phantom knew them in a specifically erotic way that he did not. He had touched them decorated with garters and stockings. Different thighs. She had been to the Copa, to the Royal Roost, to Lewisohn Stadium to hear the Gershwin concert. She talked about *The New Yorker* and *Vogue*, e.e. cum-

mings. She flew before him, floating in her black patent
I. Miller heels.

Sitting together on the bed in Sheila's parents'
room, she told him that she still loved him, she would
always love him, but it was so hard not to go out with
a lot of other boys, she had to keep her parents happy.
They were concerned about him. They didn't really
know him. He wasn't Jewish. All right. All right. But
did she have to let Shelley? Did she have to go to the
Museum of Modern Art? The Met? Where were these
places? What is the University of Miami? Who is
Brooklyn Law? What sort of god borrows a Chrysler and
goes to the Latin Quarter? What is a supper club? What
does Benedictine cost? Her epic acts, his Flagg Brothers
shoes.

There was one boy who had almost made her. She
had allowed him to take off her blouse and skirt, nothing else! at a CCNY sophomore party. She was a little
high and he—messed—all over her slip. It was wicked
and she was ashamed. Battering his heart in her candor.
Well, I almost slipped too, he lied, and was terrified
that she seemed relieved. He got up and closed the door,
then lay down on the bed with her and took off her
jacket and brassiere. She zipped open his trousers. Long
enough! Sheila said, knocking on the door, then opening it to see him with his head on her breasts. Oh, oh,
she said, and closed the door. Of course, it was all
ruined. We got rid of a lot of these repressed people in
the next decade, and now we are all happy and free.

At three o'clock, he kissed her good night on Yellowstone Boulevard in a thin drizzle. Call me, he said,
and I'll call you. I'll see you soon, she said, getting into
Marv's car. I love you. She went into her glossy Jewish
life, toward mambos and the Blue Angel.

Let me come and sleep with you. Let me lie in
your bed and look at you in your beautiful pajamas. I'll

do anything you say. I'll honor thy beautiful father and mother. I'll hide in the closet and be no trouble. I'll work as a stock boy in your father's beautiful sweater factory. It's not my fault I'm not Marvin or Shelley. I don't even know where CCNY is! Who is Conrad Aiken? What is Bronx Science? Who is Berlioz? What is a Stravinsky? How do you play Mah-Jongg? What is schmooz, schlepp, Purim, Moo Goo Gai Pan? Help me.

When he got off the train in Brooklyn an hour later, he saw his friends through the window of the all-night diner, pouring coffee into the great pit of their beer drunks. He despised them as he despised himself and the neighborhood. He fought against the thought of her so that he would not have to place her subtle finesse in these streets of vulgar hells, benedictions, and incense.

On Christmas Eve, he left the office party at two, even though one of the file girls, her Catholicism temporarily displaced by Four Roses and ginger, stuck her tongue into his mouth in the stock room.

Rebecca was outside, waiting on the corner of 46th and Broadway, and they clasped hands, oh briefly, briefly. They walked aimlessly around in the gray bitter cold, standing for a while at the Rockefeller Center rink, watching the people who owned Manhattan. When it got too cold, they walked some more, ending up at the Automat across the street from Bryant Park. When she slipped her coat off her breasts moved under the crocheted sweater she wore. They had coffee and doughnuts, surrounded by office party drunks sobering up for the trip home.

Then it went this way: We can go to Maryland and get married, she said. You know I was sixteen a month ago. I want to marry you, I can't stand it. He was excited and frightened, and got an erection. How could he bear this image? Her breasts, her familiar perfume, enor-

mous figures of movie queens resplendent in silk and
lace in the snug bedrooms of Vermont inns—shutters
banging, the rain pouring down, all entangled, married!
How do we get to *Maryland?* he said.

Against the table top her hand, its long and delicate fingers, the perfect moons, Carolina moons, of her
nails. I'll give her every marvel: push gently the scent
of magnolia and jasmine between her legs and permit
her to piss champagne.

Against the table top her hand, glowing crescent
moons over lakes of Prussian blue in evergreen twi-
lights. Her eyes gray, flecked with bronze. In her fingers a golden chain and on the chain a car key. My
father's car, she said. We can take it and be there tonight. We can be married Christmas then, he said, but
you're Jewish. He saw a drunk going out onto Sixth
Avenue carrying their lives along in a paper bag. I
mean it, she said. I can't stand it, I love you. I love
you, he said, but I can't drive. He smiled. I *mean* it,
she said. She put the key in his hand. The car is in
midtown here, over by Ninth Avenue. I really *can't*
drive, he said. He could shoot pool and drink boiler-
makers, keep score at baseball games and handicap
horses, but he couldn't drive.

The key in his hand, fascinating wrinkle of sweater
at her waist. Of course, life is a conspiracy of defeat, a
sophisticated joke, endless, endless. I'll get some money
and we'll go the holiday week, he said, we'll take a train,
O.K.? O.K., she said. She smiled and asked for another
coffee, taking the key and dropping it into her bag. It
was a joke after all. They walked to the subway and he
said I'll give you a call right after Christmas. Gray bitter
sky. What he remembered was her gray cashmere coat
swirling around her calves as she turned at the foot of
the stairs to smile at him, making the gesture of dialing
a phone and pointing at him and then at herself.

Give these children a Silver Phantom and a chauffeur. A black chauffeur, to complete the America that owned them.

Now I come to the literary part of this story, and the reader may prefer to let it go and watch her profile against the slick tiles of the IRT stairwell, since she has gone out of the reality of narrative, however splintered. This postscript offers something different, something finely artificial and discrete, one of the designer sweaters her father makes now, white and stylish as a sailor's summer bells. I grant you it will be unbelievable.

I put the young man into 1958. He has served in the army, and once told the Automat story to a group of friends as proof of his sexual prowess. They believed him: what else was there for them to believe? This shabby use of a fragile occurrence was occasioned by the smell of honeysuckle and magnolia in the tobacco country outside Winston-Salem. It brought her to him so that he was possessed. He felt the magic key in his hand again. To master this overpowering wave of nostalgia he cheapened it. Certainly the reader will recall such shoddy incidents in his own life.

After his discharge he married some girl and had three children by her. He allowed her her divers interests and she tolerated his few stupid infidelities. He had a good job in advertising and they lived in Kew Gardens in a brick semi-detached house. Let me give them a sunken living room to give this the appearance of realism. His mother died in 1958 and left the lake house to him. Since he had not been there for ten years he decided to sell it, against his wife's wishes. The community was growing and the property was worth twice the original price.

This is a ruse to get him up there one soft spring day in May. He drives up in a year-old Pontiac. The realtor's office, the papers, etc. Certainly, a shimmer of nostalgia about it all, although he felt a total stranger.

He left the car on the main road, deciding to walk down
to the lake, partly visible through the new-leaved trees.
All right, now here we go. A Cadillac station wagon
passed and then stopped about fifteen yards ahead of
him and she got out. She was wearing white shorts and
sneakers and a blue sweat shirt. Her hair was the same,
shorter perhaps, tied with a ribbon of navy velour.

It's too impossible to invent conversation for them.
He got in her car. Her perfume was not the same. They
drove to her parents' house for a cup of coffee—for old
times' sake. How else would they get themselves together and alone? She had come up to open the house
for the season. Her husband was a college traveler for a
publishing house and was on the road, her son and
daughter were staying at their grandparents' for the day.
Popular songs, the lyrics half-remembered. You will do
well if you think of the ambience of the whole scene as
akin to one in detective novels where the private investi-
gator goes to the murdered man's summer house. This is
always in off-season because it is magical then, one sees
oneself as a being somehow existing outside time, the
year-round residents are drawings in flat space.

When they walked into the chilly house she reached
past him to latch the door and he touched her hand on
the lock, then her forearm, her shoulder. Take your
clothes off, he said, gently. Oh gently. Please. Take your
clothes off? He opened the button of her shorts. You see
that they now have the retreat I begged for them a
decade ago. If one has faith all things will come. Her
flesh was cool.

In the bedroom, she turned down the spread and
fluffed the pillows, then sat and undressed. As she un-
laced her sneakers, he put the last of his clothes on a
chair. She got up, her breasts quivering slightly, and he
saw faint stretch marks running into the shadowy sym-
metry of her pubic hair. She plugged in a small electric
heater, bending before him, and he put his hands under

her buttocks and held her there. She sighed and trembled and straightened up, turning toward him. Let me have a mist of tears in her eyes, of acrid joy and shame, of despair. She lay on the bed and opened her thighs and they made love without elaboration.

In the evening, he followed her car back into the city. They had promised to meet again the following week. Of course it wouldn't be sordid. What, then, would it be? He had perhaps wept bitterly that afternoon as she kissed his knees. She would call him, he would call her. They could find a place to go. Was she happy? Really happy? God knows, he wasn't *happy!* In the city they stopped for a drink in a Village bar and sat facing each other in the booth, their knees touching, holding hands. They carefully avoided speaking of the past, they made no jokes. He felt his heart rattling around in his chest in large jagged pieces. It was rotten for everybody, it was rotten but they would see each other, they were somehow owed it. They would find a place with clean sheets, a radio, whiskey, they would just—continue. Why not?

These destructive and bittersweet accidents do not happen every day. He put her number in his address book, but he wouldn't call her. Perhaps she would call him, and if she did, well, they'd see, they'd see. But he would *not* call her. He wasn't that crazy. On the way out to Queens he felt himself in her again and the car swerved erratically. When he got home he was exhausted.

You are perfectly justified in scoffing at the outrageous transparency of it if I tell you that his wife said that he was so pale that he looked as if he had seen a ghost, but that is, indeed, what she said. Art cannot rescue anybody from anything.

WHAT'S YOUR STORY

Ronald Sukenick

The moon is out and full. The sky is that near blue of bright clear nights, so bright that one can see only a few of the brightest stars. On the horizon the sharp, barren mountains, then the desert, like a sea. Here the barren ground, the vulnerable figure protected by its sleep, and that peculiarly self-contained lion. One assumes he—or is it she—is asleep, though from the look of the face he might be dead, the skin blackened by the desert sun. This perhaps would explain the quiescence of the lion. Natural repugnance for dead meat strike carrion. Leather bones rotten meat. Dead one would say, from the odd angle of the feet protruding from the robe strike striped robe that could be by Noland or Morris Louis, from the exposed teeth, the eyes open perhaps very slightly. Or is he about to awake, the eyes opening strike the eyes on the point of opening, to confront the lion with his stick and his mandolin, or is it lute, by his side. Next to the lute, we'll call it a lute, a brown jug, of water let's hope, then a thick band of white, then brown, white, brownish-white, muddied water, snow, rotting ice, a boat making its way through ice floes, a person in the bow pushes aside a floating cake of ice with a stick and his foot, others pole the boat, in the stern one man handles the rudder, in the center a man standing one foot on the gunwale, hand on knee, cocked hat, sword, big nose, behind him a flag, American, partly furled. One would say it's cold out there. This scene repeated again again again, a fleet of facsimiles, it heads for a slightly projecting, off-white vertical, a recess, another narrower vertical of the same color, snow on the ground, part of a stone wall—large rocks trimmed with snow—a tree trunk rising from the ground straight, a brown tangle of bushes, a snowy field, at the left a road recedes, curves, and disappears further to the left, cutting through bare trees, brown bushes, green pines, misty distance, background of grey sky through bare boughs strike background of grey sky through lattice of bare boughs. High, a jet growls once, twice, fades. Drip of melting snow from eaves. A gunshot echoes through the distance. I look to the left through a window at right angles to the first: black boughs, a road, snowy field, low wall of piled rocks, woods, horizon of soft contoured hills, grey light of wintry afternoon. The bright morning light floods the fields, lights up the woods, shapes the hills. The field beyond the road is brown and green with patches of snow. The air is blue, the breeze a blue breath, the trees sway at the bottom of a sea of blue. Heavy grey clouds lower over the brown, barren flatland. Pit in concentric pit lay sunken in the center of a huge concavity, mud-yellow, rimmed by a rutted road. Greasy black smoke against dirty grey sky. Gulls like swarms of flies hover, drift, swoop in a huge, slow vortex, screaming like Harpies. A shaft of late afternoon sun strike a shaft of yellowish late afternoon sun glints off broken bits of tin, shattered glass, then disappears. The fires redden the deepening shadows. One cannot see much in

the cobbled court, the limestone blocks of the building,
windows like a Renaissance palazzo. The smoky, lucent,
humid winter air, pearl-grey, seeps down to the bottom
of the court. From where I sit at my escritoire, and from
there only, I can see out the courtyard through an arch,
through an arch through an arch through an arch, beyond a slim, distant, tapered column, a dark massive monumental arch suspended in the haze. There is so much
movement down in the street it is as if one were watching
strike as if one were looking into a motley collection of
fish in an overcrowded tank, frightened by an occult
cause, rather than at men women children dogs cats
babycarriages carts cars trucks buses. The noise is so
constant it is part of the landscape, like the tenements
across the avenue. Here there is no weather. Large flakes
of soot fall visibly from the sky. The atmosphere consists
of carbon, sulphur, oxides that displace the air and seep
through the windows. From the courtyard unbelievably
loud a brokenhearted lover wails a high fidelity lament
in an incomprehensible dialect of Spanish. The hills are
absent beyond the visible circumference of misty woods
within which the fields, green-brown, patches strike occasional remnants of last night's flurries, the road to
where it curves. The mist glows with its own inner light,
very *intime*, tracing the nearer trees in heavy chiaroscuro, the more distant trees rise like ghosts from a
graveyard. The woods lack depth. Light filters between
the trunks from somewhere offstage. A clump of pines
looms heavy, without color. Mist muffles bare boughs,
hangs from the tips of branches in shimmering drops.
The stillness is part of the landscape, like the stone
wall at the far end of the field that is there, but invisible. Now and then the house creaks the obscure complaints of its two hundred years. George Washington
crosses the Delaware on the walls. Under the moon the
lion watches, the figure sleeps, or wakes up, or rots. I sit
at my desk and gaze into the mysterious woods. The

desk, square, classical proportions. One thinks of the richer Colonial houses, or better, English of the Augustan period. Its lamp, wood, glass, suggesting wick and whale oil, its shaded bulb an incongruity. We're getting to know one another, this desk and I, we're learning to get along. Already we're getting to be friends. There's a flat, clear, open quality about it, a lucidity, a balance, an obvious and unquestionable respectability. No there's nothing suspect about this desk, nothing secret or ambiguous, nothing baroque, nothing intense, nothing intricate. Nothing like desks where I've holed up and held out. Safe at last. The fields are bright, the desk is lit by a shaft of light coming through the woods, George Washington crosses the Delaware on the walls. Wild grey clouds scud low beneath the black sky, gulls flock and hover about this point or that, so many they seem more like swarms of flies. Fires flare along the sides of the pit, sending up thick black smoke that disappears into the black of the sky. The desk is a large black rectangle with drawers running down one side. The glossy desk-top reflects the light of the gooseneck lamp in one corner. In the center of the large black rectangle, the smaller white strike the white rectangle of an open notebook. The open page said: ever clearly known it and tested it. It was as though unperceiving. I had awakened from the American dream of tomorrow to the flat truth of today. Black ink, my handwriting.

Why don't you get rid of that desk asked Joan. Relevant to nothing, as usual. Her large, dark eyes, with their distended irises, shone with the black luster of my desk-top as she stared at me with her characteristic vacant expression.

Why? I asked.

I don't know.

Look I have to work now. I had stolen the desk and I was fond of it.

I suppose you want me to leave she said.

Ronald Sukenick

What would you like to do.

She shrugged and started putting her clothes back on. She was a terrific piece of ass, a slim fertility goddess, dazed with too much fucking and too many abortions. Later, after I put her into a story, after a lot of aimless traveling, a sexual tourist, she wound up marrying an Iraqi sheik, and went to live in a harem in Baghdad. She was a passive lay but she liked it, and she never complained about anything. I felt a little bad about letting her leave like that, right after making love, but I knew she was sleeping with two other guys, both older and with a lot more bread than me, a student, and both of whom wanted to marry her. So what the hell. You wouldn't have thought so, but I loved Joan, with the kind of desperation you have when you love something that you want to get away from. I kept comparing her to Josephine, who I knew from around McDougal Street, another extreme case, but a kind I had a lot more respect for. Joan liked money, she liked glamor, she liked secrets, she liked to make her hole the subject of exciting high intrigue. Josephine didn't give a damn. She fucked who she wanted, when she wanted, how she wanted, and she didn't bother to make a secret of it. She never knew where her next penny was coming from. If she really liked a man she had his baby. She had two already and she took them wherever she went. She tossed over all the moral garbage we use for ballast, and she acted as if nothing could hurt her. Dead now. These were the crazy people I knew then, all extreme cases, all failures every one of them, driven way out by the grey fifties. I liked failures. I aimed at being one myself some day. I was living in Cambridge, a graduate student, surrounded by Harvard, Radcliffe, M.I.T. I lived across from the dump. It was more picturesque, in its way, than Harvard Square. I had one old friend there, a painter, even poorer than myself. I had traveled across country with him in an old Ford before we'd gone to college, Route 66, El Paso, Old Glory, Arizona to the Coast. You could see him getting crazier every day, psychoanalysis didn't help. He'd quit a high-paying job as a commercial artist, and did nothing but lay around his cheap apartment drinking and watching television. He never went out. Finally one day in a drunken stupor, he jumped out a third story window, landed on his head, got up, and took a cab to the hospital. If they'd had taller buildings in Boston he would have been killed. After that he pulled out of it, went to New York and eventually became a famous painter. Even now he walks around with a bent neck from that business. No one got out of that time unscathed. There wasn't much to that Cambridge apartment besides the desk and bed. Very ascetic. Between that and the dump across the street, which smelled to high heaven all the time of putrefaction or the rotten-egg smell of burning garbage —the real smell of Cambridge I always used to think— I wasn't set up to entertain. But it was there that I began to get visits from certain peculiar individuals, odd characters, who came without invitation and left, sometimes, before I would have liked them to leave. There was April Foxbite, who I knew from the Coast, for example, glowing, California vulgarian. There was Jack Gold, consummate square. I knew him through Josephine of all people, what did she see in him—the same thing I did? He had an old, oak, traditional, compartmented, pigeonholed, rolltop desk, that at one time I thought I wanted more than any kind of desk that had ever stood on the face of the earth. One day I noticed a shiny black Cadillac pulling up outside. That in itself was a major event across from the dump. There was a knock on the door. It was Ruby Geranium.

Eh goombah.

A short thick figure, white fedora, dark glasses, heavy padded black cashmere overcoat, black double-breasted suit, white-on-white shirt, white silk tie with a

portrait of an old woman in a black shawl painted on it.
You here? I said.

Just in from the Coast. A little business in the
North End.

His knuckles were loaded with gold and silver, barbaric gems. He looked around, nodding, sneering.

So this is where you hole up. Who you hiding from?
I'm glad you like it.

You're not smart Ronnie. Looka this crap. He
slapped his knuckles against a bridge table I used to eat
on. It collapsed. Look at this look at this. He punched
two left jabs at the plasterboard wall. He left two hollow, cracked depressions.

Where'd you get this desk he said. He tipped it up
with two fingers under a corner as if to see what it was
made of. My notebook and pen went sliding onto the
floor. Gee sorry he said. He let it drop with a bang.

I stole it I told him.

You don't say. You stole it. That's not nice Ronnie.
You shouldn't do things like that. That's small time.
You don't take risks for peanuts. That's bush-league
stuff. You're not smart. But you got the right instincts.
Whata you get outa living on peanuts Ronnie? Come on,
why you holed up? Who ya hiding from? He put his
foot on my notebook strike he stepped on my notebook
and pulled it toward him across the floor.

Take it easy with that I said.

Relax. I'm just tryin to set you straight Ronnie.
Between pals, you know what I mean. "It was as
though," he read slowly, "un-" what? What's that mean?
What is this crap?

It's a story.

A story he exclaimed. What about, Mother Goose?
You make me mad Ronnie. He took a step toward me.
He clenched his fist to show me his rings. Don't waste
my time. I come with a deal for you between pals and
you tell me you're writing Mother Goose?

What's Your Story

It's a story I said.

What story.

Suppose I put you in it. Then it would be about you.

Oh, about me. You're writing a story about me. That's nice. Why didn't you say so? I like that.

Yeah, good.

I'll tell you what he said. How about puttin my tie in it? He held out his tie. See that, that's a picture of my mother. Painted right on. Put that in the story.

Well I don't know if there's room in this story I said.

Whatyamean no room.

I'll put it in another one I said.

Okay that's better. Say who's that dame you got comin in and outa here all the time? The one who sometimes she comes at night and leaves in the morning.

That's Joan, a girlfriend.

I mean is she a nice girl? You know what I mean?

Yeah she's a nice girl.

I mean do you make her you know what I mean fuck you you know what I mean? A nice girl like that?

Come on, it's none of your business.

Like I'm just tryin to set you straight Ronnie you know what I mean? Between pals. You shouldn't do a thing like that to a nice girl like that Ronnie. You want dames I can get you all the dames you want. But I mean a nice girl you know what I mean? That's what I call moral turpentine. What are you some kinda beatnik?

What's the deal Ruby?

The deal is I wanna cut you in. I wanna put you on the main line. I wanna get you outa hiding. It's simple. You don't know how to do things Ronnie. I just show you how to do things. Anything you want. You wanna write, radio, TV, ads, you wanna work in college even, whatever it is. Don't worry about it we got friends all over. You're smart Ronnie. You'll become a big man in

Ronald Sukenick

no time. I'll show you how to do it, it's all the same.
You don't even have to do anything for us. We wouldn't
be so crude. We just want you to be a big man. We have
only your interests at heart. We just want you to be a
big success.

And then?

And then we just come and see you sometimes.
That's all. Like old friends. We just come and see you
sometimes. In case we need a favor. You know what I
mean?

I'll think about it.

Yeah. Think about it. No rush. Do your thing.
We'll be waiting. You'll come around. Because there's
no place else. And when you come, you'll come all the
way. You know what I mean? It's like in my line. You
can't afford to be yellow. You're either on top or on bottom, that's the way it works. And pretty soon you get
tired of the bottom. Just tryin to set ya straight Ronnie.
Between friends. Wise up. Know what I mean?

A few days after Ruby Geranium's visit, there was
another unexpected knock at the door.

Who is it?

Police.

Who?

Open up. Police.

I opened the door and found a tall bulky figure in
a brown fedora with the brim pulled down and an overcoat with the collar turned up so that I couldn't see his
face.

All right Ronnie came a boozy baritone. Relax.
Just routine.

Sergeant GunCannon. Is that you?

Looks like we finally caught up with you, hey Ronnie? He pushed past me into the room.

I ignored his remark. GunCannon always talked
like that. How long you been in from the Coast? I asked
him.

What's Your Story

I got a little business in the North End he said. All right Ronnie, why'd you do it?

Come on Sergeant, I didn't do anything.

Yes you have Ronnie. Everyone's done something. You're no different from anybody else.

Well is there anything special you had in mind Sergeant?

Just checking he said.

Same old Sergeant GunCannon I said. Put er there. He had both hands shoved deep into his overcoat pockets. He withdrew his right and thrust it at me. In it was a revolver, almost completely concealed by Gun-Cannon's huge hand. That was the only thing that really scared me about Sergeant GunCannon. He had huge hands.

Ever seen this before Ronnie? He let the gun lie on its side in the palm of his hand. It had a pearl handle with a portrait of an old woman in a black shawl. It looked familiar, I didn't know why.

Never saw it before Sergeant. What's up?

He dropped the gun back into his pocket. Nothing he said. Just a few routine questions.

What's going on GunCannon? Are you still working in the movies? Is this a movie?

You've heard of Interpol? he said.

Yeah.

He nodded.

Why are you hiding out in this crummy place he asked me sharply.

I'm not hiding I said.

He looked at me with narrow eyes. Come on, this is a hideout, don't kid me. I know a hideout when I see one.

I live here because I have no money Sergeant.

That's a way of hiding Ronnie. You could make some money if you wanted. Who you hiding from?

Ronald Sukenick

I'm just trying to stay by myself and mind my own business.

You can't do that Ronnie. You got to pay your debt to society. Every man owes a debt to society.

Not me Sergeant. Not this society.

You're a loafer Ronnie. You're a parasite on the face of society. You got a debt to pay and one way or another you're gonna pay it. It's on the books. Why don't you go out and get a job. You might as well make a buck for yourself while you're at it. It's compensation. No one likes to work Ronnie. None of us likes what they make us do to earn a living. You think I enjoy going around making it hot for guys like you? I like you Ronnie. You're a nice fella. Only some of the things that you're into are pretty disgusting. You been keeping women here. You can't expect to get away with something like that.

No I haven't Sergeant.

Yes you have. You been keeping women here, you've been making them undress and lie down on your bed, and you've been fucking them. All night.

Prove it.

He shoved his hand deep into his pocket and pulled out an old dried-up used condom. Explain that he said.

It's not mine.

We got laboratory tests.

I deny it.

Then you been masturbating. You can't masturbate in Boston Ronnie. There's laws against it. That's a very serious offense. That's vice. We can always get you on a vice charge Ronnie. We can get anyone on a vice charge. Fucking and masturbating. I know people are corrupt Ronnie, but Jesus, you really beat the band.

Look Sergeant all I'm trying to do is get away from it all and be by myself. I don't like what I see so I try to get away from it. That's why I'm poor that's why I live here. Okay?

Yeah it certainly is a ratty setup, even for a graduate student. You know I been up to see the Dean, Ronnie. I took a look at your records. It seems like you don't even do your work very much. You're no graduate student you just wanna stay out of the army don't kid me. What's your draft board again, forty? Where'd you get that desk?

Somebody gave it to me.

You're guilty as hell Ronnie. On every count. I could book you right now. You can't fool an old cop like me. Vice, draft dodging, petty larceny, consorting with known criminals. Where's Ruby Geranium?

Whatyamean?

Don't play dumb, where is he? Come on Ronnie I'm getting tired of this. He took his huge hands out of his pockets and started cracking his knuckles.

I never heard of the guy I said.

We know he came to see you. What did he want, where did he go?

I never saw him I never heard of him.

He flexed his knuckles, opening and closing his huge hands, then shoved them back into his pockets.

Okay Ronnie. We'll let it go for now. But I'll be seeing you. I'll be seeing you. No matter where you are, Interpol will be there too. And meantime let me give you a piece of advice between old friends. You got to make up your mind whose side you're on. It don't matter which, but you got to pick a side. Everybody got to play the game. Because if you don't, that's when you get into trouble. Bad trouble. Understand?

The desk gleamed dully under its gooseneck lamp, with a suggestion of depths, interiors, as one mused over it, elbows resting on its glossy black. The small room, the cheap furniture, the dump across the street, seemed muffled, muted, the desk absorbed everything into its blackness till there was nothing left outside, while within it gathered a potent concentration. The snow

had been falling still fell strike the snow had been falling still falls. Outside, the fields, the road are a white
blank, a mirror that turns you back to yourself. The
brown veneer of the square, classical desk is so highly
polished you can see your reflection in it. I open my
escritoire and sit down as one might sit down at a har-
monium. Under the lucent grey of the sky an invisible
rain darkens the grey of the limestone building, the
grey of the cobbled court. I look through the court, its
arch, the arch, the court, the arch, beyond which an
opacity of mist. Toward the gardens, the tapered needle,
the boulevard, the monumental arch I know are there,
but invisible. Harmony, order. There I walked each
day through arches gardens courtyards to the Bibli-
othèque. It was like living in an abstraction, a theorem,
an equation in which the unknown term was myself.
Only I was haunted by fellow expatriates, phantasmal
tourists, Americans who wouldn't leave me alone. Morris from the Bronx, bony sharp-faced green complexion.
He was here with Selma. His first trip to Europe, a be-
lated honeymoon, and the first and as far as I could see
the only thing that strikes him is the potential of the
import-export business. He always had a valise full of
things like Swiss watches German cameras Italian type-
writers Spanish mantillas English pipes Ukrainian ba-
bushkas Moroccan boxes Persian rugs Russian icons
Greek antiquities Amsterdam diamonds French per-
fumes Havana cigars Chinese jade and spices from all
the Asias. He was always trying to sell me something. It
didn't matter that I had no money, or that I wouldn't
buy anything if I had. He knew that. It was just a tic.
He related to the world in terms of merchandise.

You got to buy a pair of these gloves Ronnie.
You're crazy if you don't. You can't get real French
gloves at a price like this. I'm selling below cost, a sacrifice. A bargain, a fire sale, everything must go. I'm selling out. Look at this watch, are you kidding? At a price

like that you should buy two of them. You're crazy Ronnie, you have to buy something. You mean to tell me you come to Europe, an American, and you don't even buy anything? With a discount for dollars? No import taxes? Come on Ronnie, don't say no at least, say maybe. For Selma's sake. Let me show you some of this German merchandise. I gotta sell you something Ronnie.

Morris, you have to sell it but I don't have to buy it. Listen to what I'm telling you. If you don't buy anything you don't have to sell anything. That's one of the first things I figured out for myself.

Look Ronnie, you see this scarf. Pure silk. I'm not going to sell it to you. I'm gonna give it to you. Here, it's a present, take it.

I don't want it.

And all you have to do is buy this mantilla for your girlfriend. The mantilla I'm giving you at a loss.

Then there was Walter, who was a real expatriate, that is, he'd inherited money. There was something casual aimless disembodied wraith-like about Walter. He was always urging me to stay in Europe.

What do you want to go back for? There's no place for you in the States. You know that.

There's no place for me here either Walter.

Of course not. You wanted to escape, and this is an escape. You have to face that. And once you make up your mind to escape, there's nothing to do but keep escaping. You have to keep moving, that's the answer.

What's the question?

Walter would always stir up the worst ghost of all, my doppelgänger from the States, myself as graduate student, penance and purgatory, a purgatory which meant nothing, since I didn't believe in paradise.

Eh goombah.

One day Ruby Geranium turned up at my door.

Just come up from Palermo he said. Thought I'd take a little vacation. He lumbered over to the escritoire and sat down in the red-plush chair that went with it, sweeping aside my papers. He looked around the room.

So, what are ya, on the lam, uh.

I'm not on the lam Ruby.

Don't tell me you're not on the lam. What else you doing in Paris. He glared at me, chin thrust out. Then he laughed. Come on let's be straight Ronnie, it saves time. I know you're on the lam. I'm on the lam too. Why don't we team up?

What are you talking about?

How you doing for cash Ronnie. You don't have to tell me, not so good. He thrust his hand into his pants pocket and grunting, pulled out a huge naked roll of bills. He licked his thumb, pulled off the top one, and without looking at it tossed it on the escritoire. It was a hundred dollars. Live it up he said. It's gonna be a long time before you have enough money to get to Paris again, a guy like you.

What's that for? I asked him.

Doncha wanna travel a little while you're in Europe Ronnie? He picked up my notebook by a corner, dangled it in front of my face for a minute, and let it drop on the floor. You don wanna waste all your time on this crap do ya? Live it up a little.

Take it easy with that I said.

Ever been to Italy Ronnie. Ah it's a beautiful country. I just come back from there. You think Paris is good. I want you to get a look at places like Roma, Napoli, Palermo. Travel is educational. I wanna help support your travels. I want you to see my hometown where I was born, Catania. I want you to take a nice, easy trip, down through Italy, and when you get to Catania, I want you to drop in and see my mama. I want you to tell her her boy is feelin good. And I want you to pick up one of her salamis for me. Nobody makes salami like mama. And when you get it I want you to take a plane back here to Paris with it before it spoils. As a favor between old friends. I pay expenses. And more. A lot more. For time lost from—he put his foot on my notebook—this crap.

Not interested Ruby.

Not interested. All right you're not interested. Maybe you be interested in one of our other businesses. What'd you think we are we're business men, just like anyone else. There's no law in business. When you can't do something with a lawyer you do it with a gun. That's free enterprise. And when you get what you want incorporate and contribute to charities. That's the way it works. You know Ronnie we're really on the same side of the fence. Outsiders. The underworld. Underdogs. Join the underground, get into some big money for once. You start making a good living, you find a nice girl, you get married, raise bambini, that's the way to do. Who's that big German dame you shack up with?

Who says I'm shacking up?

Kem on I know a shackup when I see one. Pair a tits on her she's worth a lot of dough your Kraut chick, you know that? The Arabs got the hots for German dames. What a you care about another Nazi, it's a chance to get even. You slip a pill in her beer, next thing you know she wakes up in a harem in Yemen with her legs spread. Pair a tits on her. Come on Ronnie, we can work something out. What a you wanna go back to the States in that same old hole? Ain't you sick a that bush-league stuff? You got money in your pocket, you want something, you buy it. You run your life the way you want. It just takes a little guts, that's all.

Voici le temps des assassins, I thought. I was sick of my incapacity. I thought of Sade Rimbaud Verlaine Lautréamont Jarry Cendrars Artaud Genet.

What about that shack? There's no rush. Wait until you get tired of her.

She's just a kid I said.

Good. The younger the better. Kids are worth more.

You think about it Ronnie. Pair a tits on her. We can work something out. And keep that bill. That's a present. Between old friends.

Ruby left. I sat down at my escritoire and looked out through the court. Harmony, order. The obelisk, stolen from Egypt, the Arc a monument to sheer power, the Etoile itself a grand plan for clearing multiple trajectories for the emperor's canon in case the population should rise. That's order. Too bad about Irmenfrida. I was going to miss her. And besides it was a kind of ratty thing to do to a girl if you really thought about it. Still who knows some girls like that kind of stuff. It's exotic, there's a lot of adventure to it, it involves travel. Irmenfrida loved to travel, like all Germans she was a tourist at heart. And besides she didn't want to go home any more than I did and like me she knew she couldn't stay in Paris where we existed, as I said in a story at the time, like two abstractions whose intersection created their own reality. She had an incipient rape complex anyway, all women do. And she was a big girl she could take a lot of fucking. She'd probably get to like it. I could give her the right orientation, take her to see Rudolph Valentino in *The Sheik,* buy her a copy of *The Story of O.* In any case it would be a good way of terminating our relationship, which couldn't last forever after all. The final solution. For her. But what about me? It wasn't long before Sergeant GunCannon turned up.

Ronnie, this time you're really in trouble. We know every move Ruby makes. We know he's been here. He's walking around with a roll of marked bills. And the minute we catch up with one of those bills, Ruby is finished. We know you made a deal with him. I could pull you in right now on suspicion. A little routine questioning. He cracked his knuckles. But I'm not going to. Because I'm glad you made a deal with Geranium. And you know why I'm glad? Because now we got you where we want you. And you know where we want you? We want you to keep moving. We're gonna keep you moving from Palermo to Yemen to New York to the North End to El Paso, clear back to Old Glory, Arizona, all the way across the country to the Coast. Every city or little hick town where Ruby Geranium's got a contact to make, you're gonna make it, and then you're gonna move on. You're gonna play ball with Ruby Geranium, Ronnie. And every now and then I'm gonna pay you a little visit. Just like old friends. Have fun Ronnie. Be seeing you.

Paris was an abstraction, a theorem, an equation in which I was the unknown term. In the algebra of my fate it had nothing to do with Sergeant GunCannon or Ruby Geranium. It was exempt from my consciousness, and that was why I liked it. The escritoire was Directoire. Paris was a museum, a playground. I was on the lam. Get your kicks. Keep moving. Outside it's twenty degrees. The night is black despite the snow on the ground. The limit of my vision by the light going through the window is the snow-capped rocks of the low wall marking the nearer field. It looks like one of those New England walls from behind which minutemen fought. George Washington crosses the Delaware on the walls. It's amusing how the Colonial decor strike it's amusing how the decor of this Colonial house gives me an illusion of safety. The Sleeping Gypsy, my contribution, sleeps, or rots, the lion waits, and I wonder what happens when and if he wakes up. A remark someone made about me the other day: When you walk into a place—I was walking with him into a place—everybody turns and looks, so that I find myself deciding whose side I'm going to be on when the lynch mob comes. They know you don't play the game. What game? Now we go to my apartment on the Lower East Side of Manhattan, where I wound up in '60, and that I still call home. Now this is where we get to the point, this is where the real story takes place. What story? I was sitting at my desk one day, my wife was out, my girlfriend strike my wife was out. The desk itself is interesting, two rounded curves sweeping out from the back and scooping in at front so you had the sense of the desk wrapping around you, enveloping you as you sat at it, very baroque, curved rows of drawers on either side with many intricate little fascinating compartments in them. And yet it wasn't a frivolous desk, but heavy, massive, solid, and with a surface of labyrinthine grained veneer that I had refinished myself. As I say I was sitting at my desk, the noise came up through the courtyard, clamored along Avenue B. The weather wasn't worth looking at or thinking about, smog followed by soot. But Ruby Geranium had been on my mind again. I thought I finally knew what to do about Ruby Geranium. So I developed the following dialogue with Sergeant Gun-Cannon.

Sergeant, I want to make a deal with you about Ruby Geranium.

We don't make deals Ronnie. What is it?

The other day Ruby came around asking a lot of questions about you. He knows I know you, he knows you're after him. Now I'm sick of this, I want to get both of you off my neck. I just want to be left alone. So here's what I'm going to do. I'm going to put you in touch with Ruby. I'm going to arrange a little meeting. I'm going to tell him that you're open to influence.

Now wait a minute Ronnie.

Don't worry Sergeant, I thought of everything. I go up to GunCannon talking quickly under my breath. You wait till he offers you a bribe, then you clap the cuffs on him. I'm the witness. Smart, huh?

Not so fast Ronnie. I gotta think about this.

Too late Sergeant, Ruby Geranium is waiting in the next room. I thought of everything. I open the door.

Come on in Ruby. Much to my surprise, Ruby walks right up to GunCannon and shakes his hand.

Eh goombah.

How's the boy Ruby. Hey says GunCannon, your friend here wants me to turn you in for trying to bribe an officer.

Ah forget this jerk says Ruby. He don't know how it works. He holds his five jewel-loaded fingers in front of his chin and gestures at me. Hey, jerk, why doncha learn how it works? he says, grinning. Then he closes his fingers into a fist, and he stops grinning. GunCannon cracks his knuckles. Why don't we teach him how it works says Ruby. Let's play cops and robbers. I bribe you, you arrest me. He reaches into his pocket and grunting pulls out a huge roll of bills. He licks his thumb, counts off five, and looks up at GunCannon. GunCannon looks off into space. He doesn't see anything. All right a little extra today says Ruby. In honor of our friend the jerk. He counts off another three bills, pulls them off the roll, and folds them up. GunCannon doesn't see anything. He turns around and gazes out the window, but his huge hand is stuck out behind him, palm open. Ruby drops the folded bills into the hand. They disappear. All right says Ruby. Arrest me.

Arrest you says GunCannon. For what?

For trying to bribe an officer.

Ah come on Ruby. You can't bribe no officers. Officers are too honest to be bribed. You know that.

Ah gee come on Sergeant, arrest me.

Okay Geranium. You're under arrest.

You'll never get me alive says Ruby. He pulls his hand out of his pocket and shapes his thumb and forefinger into a gun. But GunCannon, too quick for him, already has his forefinger aimed and his thumb cocked. Bang bang you're dead says GunCannon.

Ya got me says Ruby. Hah hah hah he rumbles.

Hah hah hah echoes GunCannon. He laughs like a car trying to start on a cold morning.

How about that says Ruby. Don't that look like the real thing.

Sure it's the real thing says GunCannon. I know how it works. Don't forget, I used to be in the movies.

Okay I'm tired of this I said. I still have that marked bill you strike I still have that bill you gave me in Paris. That marked bill, remember Ruby? Geranium and GunCannon looked at one another. I told you I think of everything I said.

You're not going to sing says Geranium.

Come on Ronnie says GunCanon. Why ruin a good thing? We'll cut you in.

Sure says Geranium. We're all in the same boat.

We just follow orders says GunCannon.

We just do what the big boys tell us says Geranium.

We take our money and keep quiet says GunCannon. Like anyone else.

Why do ya wanna go and spoil everything says Geranium.

They'll let us die says GunCannon. If you're not useful they let you die.

They'll kill us says Geranium. You get in the way they kill ya.

Beat it I told them, just like that. Beat it. The story's over. The game is up.

GunCannon cracked his knuckles. Geranium held up his barbaric jeweled fist. We'll be back said GunCannon. And they disappeared.

The droplets rain from the eaves. The shadow of a cloud dims the snow dazzle. George Washington crosses the Delaware on the walls. I sit at my desk, making this up, and keep an eye on the road, waiting for a car to come cruising around the curve, a shiny black Cadillac, an anomyous four-door sedan. A gunshot echoes through the distance. They'll be back. Against that day prepare.

You sit at your desk, you look down at the slum. You begin to understand how it works. Or you drown in it.

People are on your side or they're not. You make contacts, compare notes. It helps you to breathe. Let's not suffocate in our own experience.

They'll be back, are already here, always with me. A gunshot echoes through the distance. The gypsy wakes, if he's still alive, faces the lion, and picks up his lute.

Start with immediate situation. One scene after another, disparate, opaque, absolutely concrete. Later, a fable, a gloss, begins to develop, abstractions appear. End with illuminating formulation. Simple, direct utterance.

A gunshot echoes through the distance.

They'll be back, are already here, always with us.

"The communication of our experience to others is the elemental act of civilization."

They're coming for you.

What's your story?

PARODY & PUT-ON

THE LOOP
GAROO KID

Ishmael Reed

Folks. This here is the story of the Loop Garoo Kid. A cowboy so bad he made a working posse of spells phone in sick. A bullwhacker so unfeeling he left the print of winged mice on hides of crawling women. A desperado so onery he made the Pope cry and the most powerful of cattlemen shed his head to the Executioner's swine.

A terrible cuss of a thousand shivs he was who wasted whole herds, made the fruit black and wormy, dried up the water holes and caused people's eyes to grow from tiny black dots into slapjacks wherever his feet fell.

Now, he wasn't always bad, trump over hearts diamonds and clubs. Once a wild joker he cut the fool before bemused Egyptians, dressed like Mortimer Snerd and spilled french fries on his lap at Las Vegas' top of the strip.

Booted out of his father's house after a quarrel, whores snapped at his heels and trick dogs did the fandango on his belly. Men called him brother only to cop his coin and tell malicious stories about his cleft foot.

Born with a caul over his face and ghost lobes on his ears, he was a mean night tripper who moved from town to town quoting Thomas Jefferson and allowing bandits to build a flophouse around his genius.

A funny blue hippo who painted himself with water flowers only to be drummed out of each tribe dressed down publicly, his medals ripped off.

●

Finally he joined a small circus and happily performed with his fellow 86-D—a Juggler a dancing Bear a fast talking Barker and Zozo Labrique, charter member of the American Hoo-Doo Church.

Their fame spread throughout the frontier and bouquets of flowers greeted them in every town until they moved into that city which seemed a section of Hell chipped off and shipped upstairs, Yellow Back Radio, where even the sun was afraid to show its bottom.

●

Some of the wheels of the caravan were stuck in thick red mud formed by a heavy afternoon downpour. The oxen had to be repeatedly whipped. They had become irritable from the rain which splashed against their faces. In the valley below black dust rose in foreboding clouds from herds of wild horses that roamed there. Loop Garoo was driving the horse hitched to Zozo Labrique's covered wagon.

Those were some dangerous stunts you did in the last town, boy, bucking those killer broncos like that. A few more turns up with that bull and you would have been really used up. Why you try so hard?

She sent me a letter in the last town, Zozo. She wants me to come to her. The old man spends his time grooming his fur and posing for non-academic painters. He's more wrapped up in himself than ever before and the other one, he's really gone dipso this time. Invites winos up there who pass the bottle and make advances on her. Call her sweet stuff and honey bun—she's really in hard times. She's a constant guest in my dreams Zozo, her face appears the way she looked the night she went uptown on me.

Serves her right Loop, the way she treated you. And that trash she collected around her. They were all butch. As soon as she left, zoom they were gone. And that angel in drag like a john, he gave her the news and showed her her notices—right off it went to her head. When she humiliated you—that emboldened the others to do like-wise. Mustache Sal deserted you and Mighty Dike teamed up with that jive fur trapper who's always hand-ing you subpoenas. You know how they are, Loop, you're the original pimp, the royal stud—soon as a bot-tom trick finds your weakness your whole stable will up and split.

I let her open my nose Zozo. I should have known that if she wasn't loyal to him with as big a reputation as he had—I couldn't expect her to revere me. What a line that guy had. A mitt man from his soul. And her kissing his feet just because those three drunken re-porters were there to record it. Ever read their copy on that event Zozo? It's as if they were all witnessing some-thing entirely different. The very next night she was in my bunk gnashing her teeth and uttering obscenities as I climbed into her skull.

She got to your breathing all right Loop. Even the love potions you asked me to mix didn't work, the fol-low-me-powder. Her connaissance was as strong as mine.

Zozo Labrique lit a corncob pipe. She wore a full skirt and a bandana on her head. Her face was black wrinkled and hard. The sun suddenly appeared, caus-ing the gold hoops on her ears to sparkle.

Ishmael Reed

Jake the Barker rode up alongside the wagon.

Well Loop, Zozo, won't be long now. Maybe thirty minutes before we pull into Yellow Back Radio. We're booked by some guy named Happy Times, who we're to meet at the Hotel.

Jake rode down the mountain's path to advise the rest of the troupe.

This was a pretty good season Loop, what are you going to do with your roll?

O I don't know Zozo, maybe I'll hire some bounty hunters to put a claim on my lost territory.

O Loop quit your joking.

What are you going to do Zozo?

Think the old bag will head back to New Orleans, mecca of Black America. First Doc John kicked out then me—she got her cronies in City Hall to close down my operation. We had to go underground. Things started to disappear from my humfo—even Henry my snake and mummies appeared in the curtains. She warned my clients that if they visited me she'd cross them. Everybody got shook and stayed away. Finally she layed a trick on me so strong that it almost wasted old Zozo, Loop. That Marie is a mess. Seems now though my old arch enemy is about to die. Rumor has it that the daughter is going to take over but I know nothing will come of that fast gal. Nobody but Marie has the type of connaissance to make men get down on their knees and howl like dogs and women to throw back their heads and cackle. Well . . . maybe your old lady, Loop, what's the hussy's name?

Diane, Black Diane, Zozo, you know her name.

Sometimes it's hard to tell, Loop, the bitch has so many aliases.

Before their wagon rounded the mountain curve they heard a gasp go up on the other side. A dead man was hanging upside down from a tree. He had been shot.

262

The Loop Garoo Kid

He wore a frilled ruffled collar knee britches a fancy shirt and turned up shoes. A cone shaped hat with a carnation on its rim had fallen to the ground.

The two climbed down from the wagon and walked to where Jake the Barker and the Juggler were staring at the hanging man. The dancing Bear watched from his cage, his paws gripping the bars, his head swinging from side to side with curiosity. Handbills which had dropped from the man's pockets littered the ground about the scene.

> *Plug In Your Head*
> *Look Here Citizens!!*
> *Coming to Yellow Back Radio*
> *Jake the Barker's lecture room*
> *New Orleans Hoodooine Zozo Labrique*
> *Amazing Loop Garoo lariat tricks*
> *Dancing Bear and Juggler too*
> *Free   Beer*

Above the man's head on the hoodoo rock fat nasty buzzards were arriving. Jake removed his hat and was surrounded by members of the bewildered troupe.

Nearest town Video Junction is about fifty miles away. There's not enough grub in the chuck wagon to supply us for a journey of that length. Besides the horses and oxen have to be bedded down. I wouldn't want any of you to take risks. If this means danger up ahead maybe we should disband here, split the take and put everybody on his own.

We've come this far Jake, may as well go on into Yellow Back Radio, the Juggler said.

Count me in too, Loop said, we've braved alkali, coyotes, wolves, rattlesnakes, catamounts, hunters. Nothing I'm sure could be as fierce down in that town —why it even looks peaceful from here.

I'll go along with the rest, Zozo said. But I have a

funny feeling that everything isn't all right down there.

After burying the advance man on a slope they rode farther down the mountain until finally, from a vantage point, they could see the rest of Yellow Back Radio.

The wooden buildings stood in the shadows. The Jail House, the Hat and Boot store the Hardware store the Hotel and Big Lizzy's Rabid Black Cougar Saloon.

Sinister hogs with iron jaws were fenced in behind the scaffold standing in the square. They were the swine of the notorious Hangman, who was such a connoisseur of his trade he kept up with all the latest techniques of murder.

A new device stood on the platform. Imported from France, it was said to be as rational as their recent revolution. The hogs ate the remains of those unfortunate enough to climb the platform. Human heads were particularly delectable to these strange beasts.

The troupe drove through the deserted main street of the town. Suddenly they were surrounded by children dressed in the attire of the Plains Indians. It appeared as if cows had been shucked and their skins passed to the children's nakedness for their shoes and clothes were made of the animals' hides.

Reach for the sky, whiskey drinkers, a little spokesman warned. One hundred flintlocks were aimed at them.

Hey it's a circus, one of the children cried, and some dropped their rifles and began to dance.

A circus? one of the boys who made the warning asked. How do we know this isn't a trap sprung by the cheating old of Yellow Back Radio?

Jake the Barker, holding up his hands, looked around to the other members of the troupe. Amused, Loop, Zozo and the Juggler complied with the little gunmen's request.

What's going on here? Jake asked. We're the circus

264

that travels around this territory each season. We're supposed to end the tour in your town. We're invited by Mister Happy Times. We're to meet him at the Hotel. Where are the adults? The Marshal, the Doctor, the Preacher, or someone in charge?

Some of the children snickered, but became silent when their spokesman called them into a huddle. After some haggling, he stepped towards the lead wagon upon which Jake the Barker rode.

We chased them out of town. We were tired of them ordering us around. They worked us day and night in the mines, made us herd animals harvest the crops and for three hours a day we went to school to hear teachers praise the old. Made us learn facts by rote. Lies really bent upon making us behave. We decided to create our own fiction.

One day we found these pearl-shaped pills in a cave of a mountain. They're what people ages ago called devil's pills. We put them in the streams so that when the grown-ups went to fill their buckets they swallowed some. It confused them more than they were so we moved on them and chased them out of town. Good riddance. They listened to this old Woman on the talk show who filled their heads with rot. She was against joy and life the decrepit bag of sticks, and she put them into the same mood. They always demanded we march and fight heathens.

Where are the old people now? Jake asked.

They're camped out at Drag Gibson's spread. We think they're preparing to launch some kind of invasion but we're ready for them. Drag just sent his herd up the Chisholm to market yesterday but there are enough cowpokes left behind to give us a good fight. Our Indian informant out at Drag's spread tells us the townspeople haven't given in to Drag's conditions yet. He wants them to sign over all of their property in exchange for lending his men to drive us out.

Then he will not only rule his spread which is as large as Venezuela but the whole town as well. He's the richest man in the valley, with prosperous herds, abundant resources and an ego as wide as the Grand Canyon.

This nonsense would never happen in the Seven Cities of Cibola, Jake the Barker said.

The Seven Cities of Cibola? the children asked, moving in closer to Jake's wagon.

Inanimate things, computers do the work, feed the fowl, and programmed cows give cartons of milkshakes in 26 flavors.

Yippppeeeeee, the children yelled. Where is it?

It's as far as you can see from where you're standing now. I'm going to search for it as soon as the show is over here but since there is no sponsor to greet us we may as well disband now, Jake said, looking about at the other members of the troupe.

Why don't you entertain us? the children asked.

It's a plot. We decided that we wouldn't trust anybody greying about the temples anymore!

O don't be paranoid, silly, another child replied to the tiny skeptic. Always trying to be the leader just like those old people we ran into the hills. These aren't ordinary old people they're children like us—look at their costumes and their faces.

Let's have the circus, a cry went up.

Well I don't know—you see we have no leaders holy men or gurus either so I'd have to ask the rest of the troupe.

Loop, Zozo and the Juggler said yes by nodding their heads. The Bear jumped up and down in his chains.

Delighted, the children escorted the small circus group to the outskirts of Yellow Back Radio where they pitched the tents, bedded down the weary horses and oxen and made preparations for the show.

•

Three horsemen—the Banker, the Marshal and the Doctor—decided to pay a little visit to Drag Gibson's ranch. They had to wait because Drag was at his usual hobby, embracing his property.

A green mustang had been led out of its stall. It served as a symbol for his streams of fish, his herds, his fruit so large they weighed down the mountains, black gold and diamonds which lay in untapped fields, and his barnyard overflowing with robust and erotic fowl.

Holding their Stetsons in their hands the delegation looked on as Drag prepared to kiss his holdings. The ranch hands dragged the animal from his compartment towards the front of the Big Black House where Drag bent over and french kissed the animal between his teeth, licking the slaver from around the horse's gums.

This was one lonely horse. The male horses avoided him because they thought him stuck-up and the females because they thought that since green he was a queer horse. See, he had turned green from old nightmares.

After the ceremony the unfortunate critter was led back to his stall, a hoof covering his eye.

Drag removed a tube from his pocket and applied it to his lips. He then led the men to a table set up in front of the House. Four bottles of whiskey were placed on the table by Drag's faithful Chinese servant, who picked a stray louse from Drag's fur coat only to put it down the cattleman's back. Drag smiled and twitched a bit, slapping his back until his hand found the bullseye. Killing the pest, he and the servant exchanged grins.

Bewildered, the men glanced at each other.

What brings you here? I told you to come only if

you were ready for business. Sign the town and your property over to me so that my quest for power will be satisfied. If you do that I'll have my men go in there and wipe them menaces out.

We decided to give in, Drag. Why, we're losing money each day the children hold the town and we have to be around our wives all the time and they call us stupid jerks, buster lamebrain and unpolite things like that. It's a bargain, Drag. What do we do now?

Now you're talking business Doc. Sign this stiffycate which gives me what I asked for and I'll have them scamps out of your hair in no time.

Drag brought forth an official looking document from inside his robe, to which the Banker, Marshal and Doctor affixed their signatures.

It's a good thing we got the people to see it your way, the Banker said, wiping the sweat on his forehead with a crimson handkerchief. Some reinforcements were arriving today. They were in some wagons that was painted real weird and we hanged and shot one who was dressed like a clown. We thought they might be heathens from up North, you dig?

You mulish goofies, that was the circus I ordered to divert the kids so's we could ambush them. Any damned fool knows kids like circuses.

Drag we're confused and nervous. Just today four boxes of drexol were stolen from our already dwindling supply of goods. That's why we didn't think when we killed that man. The old people are wandering around the camp bumping into each other they're so tightened up. All day people are saying hey stupid idiot watch where you're going. It's a mad house.

And the Preacher Rev. Boyd, he's in the dumps in a strong and serious way this time. You know how hard he tried with the kids and the town's heathen, how he'd smoke hookahs with them brats and get stoned with Chief Showcase the only surviving injun and that volume of hip pastorale poetry he's putting together, *Stomp Me O Lord*. He thought that Protestantism would survive at least another month and he's tearing up the Red-Eye and writing more of them poems trying to keep up with the times. Drag you know how out of focus things are around here. After all Drag it's your world completely now.

How can you be so confident your men can take care of them varmits Drag? It takes a trail boss a dozen or so cowboys and a wrangler to get the herd North. You can't have many cowpokes left behind. Don't get me wrong I'm not afraid for myself cause I rode with Doc Holiday and the Dalton Boys before I went peace officer—I have handled a whole slew of punks passing through the hopper in my day . . . why if I hadn't been up the creek at the Law Enforcement Conference it wouldn't have happened anyway.

You always seem to be at some convention when the town needs you Marshal, Drag said, looking into a hand mirror and with a neckerchief wiping the smudges of mascara that showed above his batting lashes.

Drag, the women folk, well you know how women are, what strange creatures they be during menopause. They're against us wiping out the kids. That's one of the reasons we didn't cast lots quicker to give you the hand over of Yellow Back Radio, so that you could adjust all the knobs and turn to whatever station you wished. Anyway we tried to get Big Lizzy to talk to them but they don't recognize her as one of their own.

Pshaw, don't worry about the women Doc, Drag Gibson said, bringing his old fat and ugly frame to its feet. Start appeasing them and pretty soon they'll be trying to run the whole show like that kook back in Wichita who campaigned to cut out likker. Now quit your whining and get back to camp and see after them townsfolk. Leave the job up to me.

The dignitaries rose and tumbled down the hill.

The Banker rolled over a couple of times as Drag stood jerking his shoulders and with one finger in his ear as pellet after pellet flew over the Marshal's, Banker's and Doctor's heads. He relaxed, drank a glass of rotgut and gave the appearance of a statesman by returning to his book *The Life of Catherine the Great*. As soon as the delegation disappeared, he slammed the book shut and called his boys.

Get in here cowpokes, we're in business.

Skinny McCullough the foreman followed by some cowhands rushed onto the lawn and surrounded their boss.

Chinaboy! Chinaboy! Bring me that there package.

The Chinese servant rushed into the scene with his arms weighed down with a bundle.

O.K. men, Drag said, this is the opportunity we've been waiting for. They signed the town over to me, the chumps, haw haw.

He opened the package and placed its contents on the table.

This is a brand new revolving cylinder. It has eight chambers. A murderer's dream with a rapid firing breech-loading firearm.

The cowpokes' eyes lit up and foam began to form around their lips.

It was invented by a nice gent lecturer named Dr. Coult of New York London and Calcutta. Just bought it from Royal Flush Gooseman, the shrewd, cunning and wicked fur trapper, the one who sold them injuns those defected flintlocks allowing us to wipe them out.

The kids are down there with a circus I booked under a pseudonym. I been watching them through my long glass. Now get busy and before you know it Drag Gibson will be the big name in Yellow Back Radio then Video Junction then va-va-voom on to the East, heh heh heh.

The cowpokes from Drag Gibson's Purple Bar-B

drank some two-bits-a-throw from a common horn and armed with their shiny new weapons headed towards the outskirts of Yellow Back Radio on their nefarious mission.

●

The Dancing Bear, the Juggler, Loop and Zozo entertained the children far into the night. The Dancing Bear did acrobatic feats with great deftness, Loop his loco lariat tricks, and Zozo read the children's palms and told their fortunes.

Finally Jake the Barker gathered them near the fire to tell of the Seven Cities of Cibola, magnificent legendary American paradise where tranquilized and smiling machines gladly did all of the work so that man could be free to dream. A paradise whose streets were paved with opals from Idaho, sapphire from Montana, turquoise and silver from the great Southwest:

In the early half of the sixteenth century about 1528 an expedition which included the black slave Estevancio landed at Tampa Bay. He and his companions were lost trapped and enslaved by Indians. Other expeditions also vanished mysteriously. Legend has it that the city can only be found by those of innocent motives, the young without yellow fever in their eyes.

Stupid historians who are hired by the cattlemen to promote reason, law and order—toad men who adore facts—say that such an anarchotechnological paradise where robots feed information into inanimate steer and mechanical fowl where machines do everything from dig irrigation ditches to mine the food of the sea help old ladies across the street and nurture infants is as real as a green horse's nightmare. Shucks I've always been a fool, eros appeals more to me than logos. I'm just silly enough to strike out for it tomorrow as soon as the circus splits up.

A place without gurus monarchs leaders cops tax

collectors jails matriarchs patriarchs and all the other galoots who in cahoots have made the earth a pile of human bones under the feet of wolves.

Why don't we all go, the children shrieked.

Wait a minute, Jake said, we don't have enough supplies for the trip. It lies somewhere far to the south.

That's no task, supplies, one of the children said.

After huddling together they all started into the town, leaving the troupe behind. Finally having had a loot-in on the Hat and Boot store, the Feed store and the Bank they returned with enough supplies to make the long journey.

I guess I can't argue against that, Jake said turning to Loop, Zozo and the Juggler. Welcome to my expedition into the unknown.

The children reveled and danced around.

When they finished storing provisions into the wagons the entire party went to sleep. The next morning there would be much work to do. The troupe bedded down in their wagons and the children slept beneath warm buffalo robes.

●

Loop Garoo was dreaming of bringing down the stars with his tail when all at once he smelled smoke. He awoke to find horsemen surrounding the circle. The children began to scream and some of their clothes caught fire from torches the bandits had tossed into the area. Rapid gunfire started up and the children fell upon each other and ran about in circles as they tried to break the seizure's grip. Zozo Labrique looked out of her wagon and was shot between the eyes. She dropped to the ground next to the wagon. The pitiful moans of the children could be heard above the din of hoofbeats and gunfire as one by one they were picked off by horsemen who fired with amazing accuracy. The Juggler was firing two rifles and before catching a bul-

The Loop Garoo Kid

let in his throat was able to down two of the horsemen.

Loop crawled to the place where Zozo lay dying. Blood trickled from her nose and mouth.

Zozo let me see if I can get you inside your wagon.

Flee boy, save yourself, I'm done for, the woman murmured pressing smoething into his hand. It's a mad dog's tooth it'll bring you connaissance and don't forget the gris gris, the mojo, the wangols old Zozo taught you and when you need more power play poker with the dead.

But Zozo I'll try to get you a horse, Loop began— but with a start the woman slumped in his arms.

The grizzly bear had escaped from the cage and was mangling two horsemen. This allowed an opening in the circle which two children raced through, hanging from the sides of horses. Loop did likewise but so as to divert the men from the children rode in a different direction, towards the desert.

Bullet after bullet zitted above his head. When the burning scene of children and carny freaks was almost out of his sight he looked back. His friends the Juggler, a dancing bear, the fast talking Barker and Zozo Labrique were trapped in a deadly circle. Their figurines were beginning to melt.

A LOT OF COWBOYS

Judith Rascoe

When it began to snow all the cowboys came into town and rented motel rooms with free TV. One of the cowboys said his favorite program was "Bonanza." "It's pretty authentic."

"Aw shit, what do you know about authentic?"

"Well, I know. I'm a cowboy, ain't I?"

"Well, so am I, and I think 'Bonanza' is a bunch of bull-pucky. Now if you want authentic stuff you ought to watch 'Gunsmoke.' "

"Well, you old cuss, I will show you what's authentic." So the cowboy hit the other cowboy with his fist.

"No fighting in here, so you cut that out," said the motel manager.

"You're right," the cowboys said. They got some ice and some White Horse and some Coca-Cola. The motel manager said to his wife, "By God, you can't tell them dumb cowhands nothing. They mix good scotch with Coca-Cola."

"I knew I never wanted to marry a cowboy," his

wife said. "I knew *all* about them. They weren't the fellows for me." She was keeping her eye on a young couple who weren't married; the girl seemed to have made a wedding ring out of a gold cellophane strip from a cigarette package. Looked mean; good thing the poor fellow hadn't married her yet. That night in the bar the motel manager's wife told him he shouldn't marry her.

"Huh?" he inquired.

A number of cowboys went to see the Ford dealer. He turned on the lights in his office and brought out two fifths of bourbon. The cars stood around the showroom like cows around a campfire, reflecting little gleams from the office and little gleams from the street. You could almost hear them sighing.

"Goddamn, that Maverick is a pretty little car," a cowboy said.

"Yeah, yeah," another cowboy said. "But I tell you, I got my eye on a pickup so pretty you'd like to cry. Dark-green gold-flecked. Air conditioning. And I'd hang toolboxes on the side. And maybe—"

He had their attention.

"—and maybe I do and maybe I don't know a Mexican fellow who wants to make me hand-tooled leather seat covers."

"Aaaaooooow-*ha*. WooooooooowwEEEEE."

Also little tsk-tsk-tsk noises. Head shakes. Lip bites. Breaths indrawn.

"Pwuh," said the Ford dealer. He was a classicist. He couldn't stand to think of a hand-tooled Mexican leather seat cover. Of course he was a town fellow.

"When I was in the Army," one of the cowboys said illustratively, "I got me a tailor over in Munich, and I went in and I said—well, I drew him what I wanted, and he made me a suit, *bitte schön!* Mama, oh that were a suit! It had six slantpockets in the jacket.

Course, uh, course, I don't wear it too often, you understand."

Oh, yes, they understood!

There were those cowboys laughing like they were fit to be tied.

An old woman living above the Western Auto store stuck her head out the window and listened to the cowboys come and go. The snow was falling slowly, and down the street Stan Melchek was sitting in his car waiting for a speeder. A pair of lights appeared in the distance but it was a big tractor-trailer rig, after all, pulling slowly through town, and its taillights went past the All Nite Truck Café, and the old woman pulled her head back inside and closed the window.

One cowboy lay on one twin bed and another cowboy lay on the other. One cowboy said, "I like Tammy Wynette. I sure get a kick out of her. My favorite record is 'Stand By Your Man.' My little sister sings it just like her. You close your eyes and you don't know it ain't Tammy Wynette singing. She wants to get a guitar and learn to play and accompany her."

"I wrote a song once," the other cowboy said. "I showed it to this fellow works in Denver, and he said maybe I could publish it and maybe I couldn't."

"Oh, there's money there," the first cowboy said.

"Oh, you better believe it."

"What's on now?"

" 'Hawaii Five-O.' "

"Shee-it."

"Well?"

"We sure as hell ain't going to no drive-in tonight."

We had all these cowboys in town because of the snow, and they were mostly drinking whiskey and watching television and talking about cars. It was Saturday night, but you sure couldn't tell it from any other night because of the snow. The Basque Hall advertised a dance, but the group they were going to have didn't have chains or something and anyway called from Salt Lake and said nothing doing, so there wasn't even a dance. Some of the older fellows went to the motel bar and danced, but it was mostly Guy Lombardo, which the bartender's wife favored. Maud, the motel manager's wife, had different ideas; she sat down next to a cowboy she knew and said, "We need to light a fire under some of these old cayuses. Play some of the music the kids like."

"I don't like it," the cowboy said.

"Well, hell, no, *you* don't like it, an old fart like you. Hell, you can't dance that way with one foot in the grave."

"Now, cut it out."

"I'll wash out your mouth, Carl."

"I don't like to hear you talk like that, Maud." His eyes filled with tears. "Honest to Christ, Maud, you was the most beautiful girl I ever saw. You wore your hair the sweetest little way with two little curls in front of your ears, and you wore a green silk dress. You were the sweetest little thing."

"Now, don't start crying here."

"Well, God help me, I can't help it."

"You'll just make me cry too." She had handker-chiefs for both of them. She got another round of drinks. That mean little thing with the cellophane wedding ring was looking, and Maud bet *she'd* never known a real man like Carl. These cowboys were always getting drunk and bawling, and it made her bawl too, to tell the truth.

So, you see, everybody was either in a motel room or in the motel bar, and it was snowing pretty heavily, and then George Byron Cutler drove into town. He was something of a celebrity because his picture was up in post offices, and he was known as G. Byron Cutler and Byron George Cutler and G. B. Cutler, to give only a few of his aliases. He was wanted mostly for mail fraud, but he had also held up a post office and was armed, and considered himself dangerous. He usually wore khaki shirts and trousers, but he wore good boots. Most criminals have a peculiarity like that. Anyhow, George Byron Cutler went to the motel and asked for a room, and then stuck his head in the bar and yelled, "Where's the action?"

"Well, now, I thought you was bringing it," somebody yelled back.

"Well, I was, but she didn't have a friend."

"Well, bring her in."

It kind of fell flat. He winked at Maud.

"Is my old man at the desk?" she yelled.

"Yeah, your old man is at the desk," said a voice behind George Byron Cutler. And so Cutler went on to his room, and about an hour later two sheriff's men came by and said they were looking for him.

"Christ almighty! I got to tell Maud," her husband said. "Don't you do nothing 'til I tell Maud. She won't forgive me if we got a bandido in the motel and she's not here."

"You done us a favor," the sheriff's men said, agreeable. They accepted a Coke apiece. They left snow on the Astroturf. "That's Astroturf," Maud's husband said.

"God almighty," the sheriff's men said.

So Maud's husband went in to get Maud, and she said real loud, "You mean we got a criminal in this here motel? Oh, I don't know why this hasn't happened before. We are the only motel for fifty miles. The only motel you'd stop at, that's to say. Of course there's always Mrs. Oldon's place. You boys don't stop there, you hear?" A lot of coarse laughter greeted this remark, because the cowboys knew that Mrs. Oldon had a prostitute come through in the summer. Every summer she had a different prostitute, and these girls were known as Winnemucca Discards. It was a common joke that only sheepherders went to Mrs. Oldon. "I am feeling like a sheepherder tonight," a cowboy would say, and the reply to that was, "I'd get a sheep instead."

"What sort of criminal is this fellow?" Maud asked.

"He's a mail fraud," her husband said.

"Sounds like a pansy to me," a cowboy said.

"I want to see the police capture him anyways," Maud said. She rose to her feet, showing a lot of bosom to the assembled, and led the way to the motel lobby, and all the cowboys and even the mean girl with the cellophane wedding ring and her "husband" followed. The sheriff's men were feeling the Astroturf.

"Snowing like all hell," one of the sheriff's men said.

"Is this feller dangerous?" Maud said.

"Well he is armed and considered dangerous," one of the patrolmen said.

"He's in 211," her husband said.

"Then everybody can see," Maud said. They all looked outside and saw the two layers of rooms, and 211 was pretty well located, being close to the big light and close to the middle of the balcony. The sheriff's men told everybody their names and shook some hands and then went out while everybody watched from the lobby. They went up to 211, and you could see them knock at the door. They didn't even have their guns out.

"He can't be very dangerous if they don't even take out their guns," Maud said.

"It's a Supreme Court rule now," somebody said.

"I don't know how they catch anybody."

Then there was an awful sound like a board breaking and nobody knew what it was at first and then one of the sheriff's men started yelling and all the cowboys and everybody else started yelling. "He's been shot!

Jesus Christ, he shot him! Oh, get out of the way." The
other sheriff's man started running, and then 211 opened
the door and George Byron Cutler stood there with a
gun in his hand.

He was shouting something but nobody heard it.
Finally a cowboy lying on the Astroturf slid open the
double glass door and yelled back, "What did you say?"

"I said I just want to get out of here," yelled George
Byron Cutler. "I have killed a man, and I have nothing
to lose now."

"Did you hear what he said?" Maud asked somebody. "I would never have featured it."

"Where is that other sheriff's man? Did he shoot
him too?"

It turned out the other sheriff's man was back in
his car calling for help. And all the cowboys in the
motel rooms were calling to find out what was going
wrong. Maud got on the switchboard and told everybody, "Don't peek out. God almighty, don't peek out.
Just keep your door locked and lie low. He has a gun,
and he has killed a police officer."

George Byron Cutler walked toward the lobby with
his gun shaking. All the cowboys and women were on
top of each other on the floor or crawling away, and a
lot of people were crying. Maud said to the switchboard, "Dear Lord, he is coming in here. I got to hang
up now. Do not come here. You cannot help us."

Then George Byron Cutler tried to open the lobby
door, but it was cold and stuck. He began making faces
and pounding at it. "Wait wait wait wait." A cowboy
got up real slow and opened the door for him.

"Just stay as you are," Cutler said to everybody.
"Give me your money."

"I'll give it to you," Maud said. "But I haven't got
much cash."

He thought a long time. Then he told everybody
to throw down their credit cards. He took the whole pile

of credit cards and put them in his shirt and said, "This will take some time to work out, boys."

Later Maud said she'd thought at first he was scared but he surely showed he was a cool customer.

Then he went out again and they heard a car start and make lots of noise and roar away, and then they heard some more shots, and finally somebody went out and found the cowboys from the Ford dealer's place all standing around the street where George Byron Cutler was lying dead, shot by Stan Melchek.

"I thought at first he was a speeder, but when I stopped him he fired his gun at me."

"I guess you didn't tell him his rights," one of the cowboys said.

"Oh, shut your mouth," another cowboy said. "This fellow has been killed."

Nobody could sleep after that. Maud opened the coffee shop and heated some bear claws. She sat down with Carl and a couple of the younger fellows.

"Stan Melchek is a cowboy," she said. "He is a cowboy by nature. Those fellows shoot first and ask questions later. That's the code of the West. These big-city criminals don't realize they're out in the Wild West. Out on the frontier here."

"They don't realize," Carl said.

In a very sad voice Maud said, "Well, I guess he learned."

"You don't fool around with a cowboy. You don't fool around in this country," Carl said.

"The cowboy is a vanishing race," one of the cowboys said.

"But he's not finished yet," Maud said.

"Not by a long shot," said one of the cowboys.

AT THE NATIONAL FESTIVAL

John Batki

It was a springtime festival, the National Festival of the Arts, held at the smallest and newest college in Wisconsin awaiting accreditation amidst green forested hills near a superhighway and ancient Indian mounds.

> *Right, right, the Indians knew what they were doing, putting these mounds near the highway, so we can get a sense of both cultures.*
>
> —Anonymous

The organizers of the Festival, through desperate effort, state grants, and the luck of the draw, managed to gather an impressive disarray of talent, from all over the country, and students flocked in from everywhere to rub elbows with the famous, to experience them in the flesh, to attend seminars and bars in five solid days of Festival.

> *WELCOME TO THE FESTIVAL! YOU ARE THE FESTIVAL!*
>
> —Okot p'Bitek

At the National Festival

Karen, the Golden Girl, was the immediate and unanimous choice for Earth Mother of the Festival. Men collected around her to watch her dance on the green for two hours each morning. Afterward, she would smile with patience and understanding. It was for Karen that a crazy and beautiful poet from San Francisco invented the line, "Into the valley of Death rode the six hundred, shouting, DIG IT!"

On the very first night of the Festival, Melanie promised her virginity to a young man wearing jeans and an embroidered Ukrainian shirt. Melanie had one of the lovelier bodies at the Festival. She was nineteen and planned to travel to California later in the summer.

As for Amy, she had an excellent background in the theater: years of summer stock, and she was not even twenty yet. On the very first day, someone told her that she looked like she had just stepped out of a film by Truffaut.

Early in the Festival, Melanie found an odd-looking crooked stick to which she affixed a little bracelet, the kind you get in bubble-gum machines. She walked around, from workshop to seminar to performance, zapping everyone with her "magic wand." At first she wanted to call it a "scepter," but had trouble separating the concepts "scepter," "specter," and "sepulcher," so she just called it her "magic wand." Melanie had blue eyes.

> *A seminar at eight in the morning? You must be joking. At eight in the morning I don't even know who I am.*
>
> —Nicolas Born

Late at night on the second day Amy proved to be a very fine dancer. This was after she had gone through

283

John Batki

eight joints. Yes, she was now a much happier person than she had been earlier in the year, back in Minneapolis, where she had been on heroin for two months while living at home with her family and finishing high school. At night she would watch television, with pinpoint pupils; a strange and wonderful experience in those days.

"Love is the greatest natural high," said a poet from Harlem. "Man, you be walking down the street, and you meet a friend with this big smile on your face, and you stop and talk for a while, and you say, 'Well, I gotta be going now, I just gotta get home to my friend. . . .'"

Melanie, the daughter of affluent and indulgent parents, had dropped out of college after her first year and started her own boutique in South Orange, New Jersey. With a little help from her father to cover the initial investment, she found the business a plausible, if not too exotic, *modus vivendi*. But living at home was getting to be a drag.

The Festival was entering its third day and large numbers of men were discovering that Karen, who wore nothing but a slight and slippery shift, and who lived as a very sexy Earth Mother in their minds, was planning to go on a fishing trip to northern Michigan with her boy friend, as soon as the Festival was over. She had brought her friend all the way from Oregon, along with three bags of her own groceries; she was heavily into organic food. She was looking forward to all that fresh fish—perch, trout, bass, pike—a great way to enrich your diet.

Back on Wednesday, Melanie had made a promise to a young man wearing a Ukrainian shirt. However, by Thursday night, the night of the modern-dance performance, the night of the chanting and reading of "primitive poetry," she no longer had what she had promised. Unfortunately, she had written a letter confirming her promise, and the letter had been mailed. Now it was worse than academic, it was no longer valid, it was a letter devoid of meaning and truth. Melanie, that striking girl, was in genuine despair.

> *But that's O.K. too.*
>> —Finnish folk saying

By Friday night, Karen had been woven into the mental tapestries of thirty-nine poets, twenty-four painters and sculptors, eighteen musicians and dancers, and one translator. The warmth of her understanding left all of them appeased and at peace with nature. Her friend witnessed the proceedings with a cheerful calmness. His immense knowledge of Indian lore and history was available to all comers.

> *It is almost twelve. I think I am going to turn in now. Good night, everybody.*
>> —Philip Whalen

After two months on heroin Amy joined an Encounter group, gave up drugs, and stopped mentally undressing every attractive male. Here at the Festival, she found two men especially appealing. She told one of them, on a walk in the nearby woods, that he was the best-looking man around. She explained that although she felt extremely vulnerable, she could not sleep with him because she had two other ongoing commitments, namely, David, her friend in Minneapolis, and Neil, her new friend at school. She trembled while she said this, and there was a misty look in her eyes. "I don't know why I am quaking," she said.

At Saturday morning's open reading, Karen read a long poem of stunning frankness. She wore bluejeans with nothing but a blue workshirt hanging loose. Some men thought this was to emphasize her blondness and her full breasts, but that was their problem. She stood and read, her blue eyes looking away over her audience, an amorphous group sitting and reclining on the floor of the lounge. In her poem, she spoke about her lover. She read well. After the reading, many people came up to her, some of them with genuine admiration in their eyes.

> *This hamburger sure tasted good. Let's make sure to eat again real soon!*
> —Jay, quoting R. Crumb

Amy's father, an above-the-average tennis player, had met a Swiss fellow named Jurgen on the courts. Jurgen, an exchange student, was invited over and he cooked a delicious Swiss meal for the entire family. However, Army found it difficult to talk to Jurgen. Instead, she focused her pinpoint pupils on the TV screen.

From early Saturday afternoon on, a prominent Minnesota poet barnacled himself to Karen and her group. He talked about the Earth Mother with persistence. That night, at intermission, he brought coffee and cookies, and continued to pour out words with formidable energy. Karen's friend became mildly concerned, and maintained a loosely vigilant presence. His was the steady virility of the good husbandman, the sheer staying power of good husbandry; he was the farmer who knows the earth, waits and bides his time, plows the land and sows his seed at the right time, and who, in the end, always gathers his harvest.

> *Not in the/But in the not*

Melanie had been to numerous ethnic restaurants in New York and New Jersey. Now, on Saturday night, she thought she would enjoy the multimedia presentation on ethnic cultures, but new and insistent demands were being made on her each minute; her neighbor, high on mescaline, kept passing her notes ("Desperado that I am" and "I smirk, what else?" and "Will you LET me?"). She walked out of the auditorium before the end of the show, locked herself in her room, and slept peacefully for the first time in four days.

> *And that's O.K. too.*
> —Icelandic wisdom

Amy had her own car, but no money for gas. She smoked two packs a day, and had to bum her cigarettes. To save money, she washed her own clothes by hand. The summer job she had been promised fell through. Now she walked around the campus with a flute swung across her back. Jay said to her, "Women really kill me. Each time it's an avalanche. I am totally wiped out." And, "You look like you just stepped out of a film by Truffaut."

For the better part of a year, Karen had lived by herself on an isolated farm in the Pacific Northwest. Oh yes, there were occasional visitors, mostly on weekends, but much of the time it was just she and her fears. Her fears were not of the dark and not of other people. One night she realized it was one single fear: the fear of herself. After that, living on her own became easier. There were difficult times, such as the night she thought she would die of cocaine. She had sniffed the white powder with some friends who had to leave around midnight; they lived miles away. Hours later, she realized that something was terribly wrong. There was no one for miles around, and she had no phone at the time. She sat in her kitchen all night looking at the clock, and with the passage of each hour, she said to herself, "I am still alive."

Throughout the Festival of the Arts, Jay wore his Mexican straw sombrero with the brim turned down all

John Batki

around, in the manner of certain nineteenth-century French painters, notably Cezanne and Camille Pissaro the man who lost nearly half a lifetime's work in the Franco-Prussian War of 1870.

UNDER
THE MICROSCOPE

John Updike

It was not his kind of pond; the water tasted slightly acid. He was a Cyclops, the commonest of copepods, and this crowd seemed exotically cladoceran —stylish water-fleas with transparent carapaces, all shimmer and bubbles and twitch. His hostess, a magnificent Daph-

nia fully an eighth of an inch tall, her heart and cephalic ganglion visibly pulsing, welcomed him with a lavish gesture of her ciliate, branching antennae; for a moment he feared she would eat him. Instead she offered him a platter of living desmids. They were bright green in color and shaped like crescents, hourglasses, omens. "Who do you know here?" Her voice was a distinct constant above the din. "Everybody knows *you,* of course. They've read your books." His books, taken all together, with gener-

John Updike

ous margins, would easily have fitted on the period that ends this sentence.

 The Cyclops modestly grimaced, answered "No one," and turned to a young specimen of water-mite, probably *Hydrachna geographica*, still bearing ruddy traces of the larval stage. "Have you been here long?" he asked, meaning less the party than the pond.

"Long enough." Her answer came as swiftly as a reflex. "I go back to the surface now and then; we breathe air, you know."

"Oh I know. I envy you." He noticed she had only six legs. She was newly hatched, then. Between her eyes, arranged in two pairs, he counted a fifth, in the middle, and wondered if in her he might find his own central single optic amplified and confirmed. His antennules yearned to touch her red spots; he wanted to ask her, *What do you see?* Young as she was, partially formed, she appeared, alerted by his abrupt confession of envy, ready to respond to any question, however presuming.

But at that moment a monstrous fairy shrimp, an

inch in length and extravagantly tinted blue, green, and bronze, swam by on its back, and the water shuddered. Furious, the Cyclops asked the water-mite, "Who invites *them*? They're not even in our scale."

She shrugged permissively, showing that indeed she had been here long enough. "They're entomostracans," she said, "just like Daphnia. They amuse her."

"They're going to eat her up," the Cyclops predicted.

Though she laughed, her fifth eye gazed steadily into his wide lone one. "But isn't that what we all want? Subconsciously, of course."

"Of course."

An elegant, mel-ancholy flatworm was passing *hors d'œuvres*. The Cy-clops took some di-atoms, cracked their

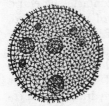

delicate shells of silica, and ate them. They tasted golden brown. Growing hungrier, he pushed through to the serving table and had a Volvox in algae dip. A shrill little rotifer, his head cilia whirling, his three-toothed mastax chattering,

leaped up before him, saying, with the mixture of put-on and pleading characteristic of this pond, "I wead all your wunnaful books, and I have a wittle bag of pomes I wote myself, and I would wove it, *wove* it if you would wead them and wecommend them to a big bad pubwisher!" At a loss for a civil answer, the Cy-

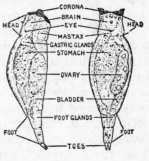

clops considered the rotifer silently, then ate him. He tasted slightly acid.

The party was thickening. A host of protozoans drifted in on a raft of sphag-num moss: a trumpet-shaped Stentor, ap-parently famous and interlocked with a lanky, bleached Spirostomum; a claque of paramœcia, swishing back and forth tickling the crustacea on the backs of their knees; an old Voticella, a plantlike animalcule as dreary, the Cyclops thought, as the batch of puffs rooted to the flap of last year's *succès*

d'estime. The kitchen was crammed with ostracods and flagellates

engaged in mutually consuming conversation, and over in a corner, beneath an African mask, a great brown hydra, the real thing, attached by its sticky foot to the

hissing steam radiator, rhythmically swung its tentacles here and there until one of them touched, in the circle of admirers, something appetizing; then the poison sacs exploded, the other tentacles contracted, and the prey was stuffed into the hydra's swollen coelenteron, which gluttony had stretched to a transparency that veiled the preceding meals like polyethylene film protecting a rack of dry-cleaned suits. Hairy with bacteria, a Simocephalus was munching a rapt nematode. The fairy shrimps, having multiplied, their crimson tails glowing with hæmoglobin, came cruising in from the empty bedrooms. The party was thinning.

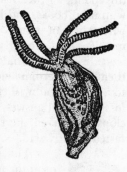

Suddenly fearful, fearing he had lost her forever, the Cyclops searched for the water-mite, and found her miserably crouching in a corner, quite drunk, her seventh and eighth legs almost sprouted. "What do you see?" he now dared ask.

"Too much," she answered swiftly. "Everything. Oh, it's horrible, horrible."

Out of mercy as much as appetite, he ate her. She felt prickly inside him. Hurriedly—the rooms were almost depleted, it was late—he sought his hostess. She was by the doorway, her antennae frazzled from waving goodbye, but still magnificent, Daphnia, her carapace a liquid shimmer of psychedelic pastel. "Don't go," she commanded, expanding, "I have a *minus*cule favor to ask. Now that my children, all thirteen billion of them, thank God, are off at school, I've taken a part-time editing job, and my first real break is this manuscript I'd be *so* grateful to have you read and comment on, whatever comes into your head, I admit it's a little long, maybe you can skim the part where Napoleon invades Russia, but it's the first *effort* by a perfectly delightful midge larva I know you'd enjoy meeting—"

"I'd adore to, but I can't," he said, explaining, "my eye. I can't afford to strain it, I have only this one . . ." He trailed off, he felt, feebly. He was beginning to feel permeable, acidic.

"You poor dear," Daphnia solemnly pronounced, and ate him.

And the next instant, a fairy shirmp, oaring by inverted, casually gathered her into the trough between his eleven pairs of undulating gill-feet and passed her toward his brazen mouth. Her scream, tinier than even the dot on this "i," was unobserved.

Joe David Bellamy is author of *The New Fiction* (1974), editor of *Apocalypse: Dominant Contemporary Forms* (1972), and a contributor to *The Vonnegut Statement* (1973). His fiction, poetry, and nonfiction have appeared in *The Atlantic Monthly, Partisan Review, Chicago Review, Paris Review, Iowa Review, New American Review,* and many other magazines. He is publisher and editor of *fiction international* and associate professor of English at St. Lawrence University in upstate New York.

VINTAGE HISTORY—AMERICAN

VINTAGE BIOGRAPHY AND AUTOBIOGRAPHY